THE
PHOENIX
FACTOR

THE
PHOENIX
FACTOR

Lessons for Success from Management Failure

David Clutterbuck
and
Sue Kernaghan

With research and contributions by
Stuart Crainer

Weidenfeld & Nicolson
LONDON

First published in Great Britain in 1990 by
George Weidenfeld & Nicolson, 91 Clapham High Street
London SW4 7TA

Copyright © Clutterbuck Associates 1990
British Library Cataloguing in Publication data
is available on request

ISBN 0 297 81123 1

Printed and bound in Great Britain by The Bath Press, Avon

Contents

Contents

Foreword

This is a book about business failure. It is about dreams that turned to nightmares. It is about proud names and edifices that collapsed in sudden catastrophe when the rotten core was unable to support the public face; or simply withered away until, like a senile politician, only the empty husk remains. It is, in a few cases, about partial recovery – a phoenix from the ashes.

What's the fascination or value of such apparently dismal stories? Firstly, for many practising managers, there is reassurance in the knowledge that other people can make a hash of it, too. The pages of business magazines and management books are not filled with tales of mishap, mayhem and mismanagement. Rather, they focus on success, on strategies that worked, on the achievement of today's wonder growth stock or trendy management theory. We have been (and continue to be) as guilty of this as any management writers – perhaps more so. This book is a recognition of the fact that the real world of business isn't one of rampant and all-embracing success – it is an apologia, if you will. Where there are winners, there are more often than not also losers. Moreover, even the winners only do things right some of the time – just more often than their competitors. And success is ephemeral. Like physical beauty, it soon passes through crow's-feet to wrinkles and arthritis. Several years ago I co-authored with Walter Goldsmith a book that examined what made Britain's most successful companies excellent. Within three years, one-third of those companies had run into serious difficulties.

The business of winning is hard work. So, too, is the business of losing and it is remarkable how hard some of the managers in the case studies that follow have worked (albeit thinking they were doing just the opposite) to lead their companies to the brink of catastrophe. It is here that the second reason for writing this book arises – there is often far more to be learned from the lessons of failure than from the lessons of success.

Foreword

In the following chapters we have tried to concentrate less on the mechanics of corporate decay than upon the behaviours, attitudes and perceptions of those who took part in each drama. It is from these that the most beneficial lessons can be learnt. For the mechanics are simply symptoms; the behaviours, attitudes and perceptions are both symptoms and causes.

Whether this book will help companies already in serious decline, is debatable. The evidence suggests that managers steadily driving their companies to failure have little time or inclination to think about the wisdom of what they are doing.

Rather, we address the lessons here to those directors and managers – concerned that they never have the time they need to evaluate whether they are doing the right thing; conscious of the mistakes they know they have made and worried about the ones they can't identify – who run today's run-of-the-mill businesses. We also address it to the managers of today's highly successful businesses, for whom the spectre of maturity and decline can only be vanquished by constant vigilance.

David Clutterbuck
Sue Kernaghan

Introduction

THE BUSINESS KILLERS

Two days before his airline collapsed, Freddie Laker commented:

> 'The future of the company is now very good. In fact, we are in a better position than we have ever been.'

> 'I cannot agree with the description of this as a high-risk venture.'
> – John De Lorean to government minister Roy Mason.

All companies decline; some just do it faster and more dramatically than others. But what brings about the destruction of the dream? There isn't a simple answer, of course. Every case is different. Yet in a sense virtually every case is the same. With the exception of those very few that can be put down to misfortune – and they are very few – the only cause of decline and/or collapse is failure by the management team to handle rightly one or more of the complex mixture of its responsibilities.

To put it another way, every failure is a failure of management focus; a misjudgement of what was truly important and a failure (or refusal) to see until too late that it threatened the business. Lack of expertise is not an adequate excuse, because part of the effective manager's job is to recognize when he is out of his depth and to buy in the resources he needs to compensate for his inadequacies. For example, the excuse, so often heard by receivers, that an entrepreneur is not an accountant or book-keeper is merely an admission of failure to recognize the importance of sound financial information and control.

In the following pages, we will therefore take two approaches to the issue of corporate decline and collapse. In the first, we will examine the attitudes that lead to disaster. In doing so we shall draw upon

I

a variety of examples from around the world; upon the observations of those who pick up the pieces and those who pick up the bill for failure; and upon a unique survey of receivers and investors.

Our second approach is via case studies of British companies that have achieved technical or actual insolvency. The cases we have chosen reflect a broad spectrum of the multitude available: recent and classic; manufacturing and service; large and small; start-up and household name. Wherever possible we have interviewed members of the management team, and frequently management teams, who presided over the downfall of each company. From their experience and from the observations of other participants – notably the receivers, investors and, where rescue was possible, the new management team – we have also extracted lessons from each case.

The attitudes that lead to decline are many and varied. In seeking to classify them, we have resorted to the concept of focus – what areas or responsibilities should every top management team pay consistent attention to in order to achieve a balanced perspective on its business? The areas we have selected may not be exhaustive, but they do encompass the majority of failings identified in our own research and in an extensive literature search. These are:

Attitudes towards controls

In particular, financial controls, but also technical, safety and other controls. Often closely allied here are the attitudes towards risk, so for practical purposes we shall consider them together.

Attitudes towards the vision

The clarity of the corporate strategy or vision and the degree to which it is shared and endorsed by people in the organization is clearly important. So, too, is the accuracy of the assumptions that make up the strategy or vision. Most companies that collapse in their first year do so because the managers have fundamental misconceptions about the nature of their business and what can realistically be achieved.

Attitudes towards the team

The key issue here is one of leadership style. It shows itself in many ways, but especially in the quality and nature of communications and in how people see their responsibilities and roles.

Attitudes towards customers

A true understanding of the markets it supplies is essential for any top management team. In many cases, the managers fail to gather the market information they need for this understanding. In others, they ignore the information they have or – more commonly – view it through a set of preconceptions that distort the reality.

Attitudes towards investors

Entrepreneurs who run public companies as if they were their own can quickly alienate their investors – particularly if profits dip. Failure to create a true partnership with the principal investors – particularly in terms of keeping them informed and involved – is a common symptom of collapse, especially in start-up situations.

Attitudes towards learning

Call it complacency, arrogance or hubris, but many businesses stop learning. By contrast, the living, vital business is continuously learning from its own mistakes and from those it observes elsewhere. It is willing constantly to audit, re-examine and revise. Usually the rot sets in at top management level and spreads rapidly down.

Attitudes towards winning and losing

Managers who are clearly in business to win tend to have a greater capacity for recognizing when something is not right and for doing something about it. The weaker the drive to win, the more likely the manager is to bury issues that need to be confronted, focusing instead on less threatening or less immediate issues that are easier to resolve – the classic activity trap. Many entrepreneurs are incapable of handling serious reversals; they ignore the danger signals that seem to undermine the dream. In other words, their love for the dream is stronger than their love of winning.

Attitudes towards competitors devolve from attitudes towards winning. A fierce interest in who the competitors are, what their strategies, strengths and weaknesses are, is an important component of a predisposition to winning. Running the competitive race blindfolded allows a company to be lapped before it knows it.

In the following chapters we will take a brief look at each of these sets of attitudes and how they contribute to the process of decline. First, however, we will examine some of the received wisdom about corporate decline.

David Clutterbuck
Susan Kernaghan

PART I
Observing Decline

In the host of cases we have studied preparing this book, we have discovered very few whose collapse or near-collapse occurred suddenly, without warning. The exceptions tend to be those where some element of fraud is revealed or suspected. Recent examples would be Ferranti's discovery of a shortfall of £200 million in the accounts of a major USA acquisition, ISC, or the tangled affairs of Eagle Trust in the UK.

The signs, in most cases, are writ large for anyone who is observant enough to see. By the time Dunlop was dismembered, for example, there was only one institutional shareholder remaining, with a mere 2% of the shares – all the others had sniffed the smell of decay and sold out long before.

So what is it about a business on the way down that makes experienced observers so nervous when they see it? After all, all businesses face crisis. Indeed, it could be argued that management is the process of marshalling resources to handle and profit from constant crisis. What is different about companies heading for the brink?

Part of the answer lies in the severity and frequency of the crises the company faces. Any business that is in constant crisis over a significant period of time is likely to be worn down – like a punch-drunk boxer in his twelfth round. Survival in the ring is related to fitness, agility, skill and stamina, both in absolute terms and in comparison to the opponent. Without any one of those qualities the only question is when, not how, the knock-out will be delivered.

The various cases we examine in this book are not all collapses. Many of the businesses were rescued from real or technical insolvency by acquisition, buy-out or buy-in. Others (a rare few) pulled themselves out of the mire, having, in a moment of last-minute sanity stopped thrashing about as they sank and seized the overhanging branch they could use to drag themselves to safety.

The common theme to all of their stories is that they have progressed through a succession of crises that eventually threatened to destroy the business, without tackling the fundamental problems that caused this debilitation.

In the introduction, we suggested that the ultimate causes were all to do with sets of attitudes. However, the usual manner in which observers refer to the causes of collapse, is as specific pieces of poor decision making, most of which can be broadly classified as poor management.

The catalogue of these failures (most of which we would describe as symptoms rather than direct causes) varies considerably among authors on the subject. Here, however, is a selection of some of the most common.

● The *Financial Times*, having carried out an informal survey among insolvency experts, produced the following list:

* Poor management. Small businesses too often lack organizational structures.
* Lack of management style. As the business climate gets colder the company finds it lacks a complete team to adapt to the changed situation.
* Lack of forward planning. You have to know where you are, and where you are going.
* Lack of financial management. That includes failure to collect outstanding debts, and too much stock lying around unsold.
* Over-reliance upon a product or a small number of customers. When the going gets tough remember that other companies can let you down.
* Government policies. However small you are, you can be affected by them – whether they be economic, planning, monetary, or 'green'. You must act accordingly to protect your business.
* Too many trappings. As one accountant put it: 'Directors must make the cream before they can skim off the fat.'

● Derek Gould, an Area Manager with Midland Bank and former member of the bank's 'intensive care' unit for companies in trouble, identifies three major problem areas currently bringing many British companies to the brink:

* problems of growth
* problems of acquisition

* problems of handling international markets.

In each case management is dealing with situations it does not fully understand. Because it lacks knowledge and experience, it makes fatal mistakes. The answer is not that they should avoid these areas – all are sensible responses to business opportunities – but rather that they should proceed with greater caution and ensure that they do acquire the know-how that will help them avoid the grosser mistakes.

● John Banham, Director General of the Confederation of British Industry, describes the causes of decline as:

* An internal focus: constant worry about organization structure, about relative standing within the organization, concern with company politics. If you look back over the past of British Leyland you can see it well. I recall being asked to join the management team at Leyland Truck and Bus in the mid-Seventies. When I got to Leyland immediately people were trying to line me up for different factions – before I even joined. Meantime, Saab, Volvo and other competitors were roaring away. Leyland was entirely focused on what was going on inside the company.

* Lack of professionalism in management. Senior managers need to be able to carry out fact-based analysis, understand strategic management, marketing design, production engineering and so on. Failure to do so is inexcusable and found in all ailing companies.

* Lack of effective leadership. I would argue that the turnaround in the fortunes of some major British companies is associated with the leadership of an individual. People like Christopher Hogg at Courtaulds or David Plaistow at Vickers or Bob Reid at Shell have made a major difference.

* A preoccupation with short-term results at the expense of long-term effectiveness.

* A failure and inability to involve all members of the workforce in working for the success of the company.

* A preoccupation with the product. Too many British companies have been managed by people who do not have an intuitive understanding of the technology they are dealing with.

● Gary Goldstick in his book, *Business-Rx: How to Get in the Black and Stay There* lists thirteen common causes of corporate illness:

* lack of planning to deal with an increase in the cost of debt

* change in the marketplace
* technological advances
* changes in the physical environment
* disruption of key relationships
* overexpansion
* overleverage
* overdiversification
* overdependence on a single customer
* inadequate control systems
* dissension in the management team
* the 'Peter Principle' as it applies to business growth
* inadequate leadership of the chief executive.

● Writing in *Top Management Digest*, Boston lawyer and management consultant Arnold Goldstein condenses his experience of dealing with failing companies into the ten 'most serious and reoccurring (sic) causes of failure'. These are:

* overleverage – too many businesses begin with inadequate capital and/or excess borrowed debt
* overexpansion – failure to generate the cash flow to cover additional borrowing made to finance ambitious plans to seize new markets. This kind of firm, says Goldstein, 'falls victim to its own rosy projections of future profits. When the earnings fail to materialize we have one more company in serious trouble forced to either reverse direction or retrench and fail.'
* overdiversification – 'companies have a hard enough time within familiar territory without journeying into someone else's'
* overemphasis on sales – as opposed to profits. Says Goldstein: 'Many companies plow ahead blindly building sales while the bottom line looks increasingly dismal.'
* inadequate control systems – 'Very few of these companies really know where they have been and hence never have the information needed to tell them where they should be going, or how to get there.'
* overdependence – relying too heavily on one customer or supplier (or, although Goldstein doesn't mention it, in our observation of small service companies, upon one or two key employees who have the ability to walk off with a large chunk of the business)
* poor location – particularly in retail, the changing virtues of

physical location can have a major impact on turnover and margins
* improper pricing – 'Many companies are in trouble today because they do not understand their costing structure and therefore operate with an unrealistic pricing strategy.'
* Government restraints – may tie a business down in red tape or close it down.
* poor planning – 'the failure to adequately plan every aspect of the business' from finance to marketing or staffing.

Goldstein sums up his list by concluding: 'Most companies do not die a natural death but are instead murdered through managerial incompetence.' Few, if any of the observers we have gathered, would disagree.

● As Ross Norgard, an Australian accountant writing in the *Chartered Accountant* in Australia puts it:

'The increased failure rate is often solely blamed on the business climate. Inflation, high finance costs, demand slumps and government constraints have all been cited as key factors precipitating business failures.'

However, case studies consistently show that the majority of business failures stem from poor management. Well-managed businesses weather economic storms, poorly-managed businesses sink.

Poor management often stems from:

* a domineering executive
* inadequate management depth
* an unbalanced administrative team
* an uninvolved board
* a weak finance function.

● Stuart Slatter of London Business School in his book *Corporate Recovery* points to twelve causes of decline:

* lack of financial control
* inadequate management
* price and product competition
* high cost-structure
* changes in market demand
* adverse movements in commodity markets
* lack of marketing effort

9

* big projects
* acquisitions
* financial policy
* overtrading
* organizational structure.

He concludes his list by pointing out: 'It is rare that any one factor by itself will precipitate the need for recovery action. The need for recovery is usually brought about by a combination of factors, although lack of financial control and poor management stand out as the most frequent causes.'

● Several writers, among them John Argenti, in his seminal book *Corporate Collapse* and O. P. Kharbanda and E. A. Stallworthy, in their less insightful but perhaps more comprehensive book *Corporate failure: prediction, panacea and prevention* review a variety of such lists, attempting to find a common pattern. Both have considerable difficulty doing so. They quote, in particular, John Argenti who produces a short-list of basic causes of collapse, which he assesses as:

* one-man rule
* non-participating board
* unbalanced top team
* weak finance function
* lack of management depth
* combined chairman–chief executive.

The problem with this list and other similar attempts to find a universal description is that it does not encompass the breadth of problems that force companies under. The reason, we believe, is that the problems quoted are a mixture of symptoms and causes. As Kharbanda and Stallworthy comment on Argenti's list: 'Surely all these are but aspects and responsibilities of management. Surveying the whole spectrum of reasons given for failure, we come back time and time again to various aspects of management. This leads us to the conviction that the nature and quality of the management is the crux of the matter.'

● Some observers feel it is useful to attempt to divide these multiple causes into internal and external problems, with the implication that internal problems are under top management's control, while external ones are not (or are less so).

Ian Mitroff of the University of Southern California and Will McWhinney of The Fielding Institute at Santa Barbara attempt to break down the causes of crisis into internal versus external; technical/economic versus people/social/organizational factors. Their studies of US companies indicate that the way companies perceive the potential for crisis depends upon the management style (in itself, another expression of attitude). They identify four main styles:

* *Inactive* organizations assume that most problems will go away if they are ignored. When a problem becomes too persistent to ignore, they react with short-term solutions.
* *Reactive* organizations follow whatever has worked in the past. Their crisis management – if they have any – focuses on traditional issues rather than what might affect the company in the future.
* *Preactive* organizations are often high-tech operations with sights set firmly on rapid growth. They have an immense enthusiasm for things new, but say Mitroff and McWhinney: 'They fail to realize ... that the new high-tech solutions themselves often are responsible for creating even worse problems.'
* *Interactive* organizations use all three styles, as appropriate. They rely, say Mitroff and McWhinney 'on ingenuity, rather than size or growth, to sustain (them) through the unending cycle of day-to-day crises'.

No prizes for guessing which style Mitroff and McWhinney recommend as the most successful. They go on to demonstrate that the choice of management style predicates the nature and extent of the monitoring and preventive actions an organization takes. Inactive organizations have very little – particularly for external issues; reactive and preactive organizations have more, but tend to focus monitoring and prevention in narrow areas (reactive organizations typically looking to short-term measures, preactive to the longer term); interactive organizations have both a better balance and broader spread of crisis monitoring.

This kind of analysis can help define whether an unexpected and severely damaging external event could and should have been predicted by top management and what the company could have done about it had the prediction been made. Salmonella poisoning in tins of salmon should have been a scenario the directors of John West could make plans against, as Johnson & Johnson had done before

Tylenol was poisoned by blackmailers. Government legislation rarely comes about without months or years of discussion. The exceptions (for example, sudden hikes in interest rates) may not easily be predictable, but the wise management ensures it is not so exposed that it cannot survive them. The 1989 crash in UK house prices, for example, may or may not have been predictable after the previous year's boom and a steady trend of rising interest rates. But the estate agents, conveyancing lawyers and house-builders whose businesses were placed in jeopardy were in general those who failed to plan against that eventuality. Those who kept staffing lean and flexible, for example by topping up with part-timers whose hours could be reduced or stopped altogether, by putting profits away for the rainy day and by limiting their own borrowings were naturally in a healthier position for survival than those who did not. It is not surprising therefore, that renowned company doctors such as Lewis Robertson put the number of business failures that have occurred as a result of bad luck at only about 2% of the total.

It is difficult to identify any patterns of industry sector or company types that are particularly prone to survival crises. In declining, mature markets there are both those companies that struggle from year to year against reducing margins and market erosion; and those that do very nicely thank you from a 'last iceman' position, earning high margins from niche products no one else can afford to make. When the dust has settled over the shrinking of the vinyl disc record industry, for example, the surviving one or two players will retain a small but highly profitable market supplying enthusiasts who insist that the only way to achieve superb sound reproduction is with a turntable and diamond stylus.

Equally, the state of the art, high-growth industry sectors are littered with the corpses of brave ventures that backed the wrong technological horse or could not handle the pace of their own growth.

Disaster doesn't seem to be a respecter of size, either. Although the large company will normally be rescued (either by selling off assets itself or by being acquired for those parts of the business that are still viable) it is just as likely to encounter crisis.

It is a sobering reflection, too, that the number of insolvencies, both in the UK and in most of our major trading partners, have increased significantly in the past decade. A boom-period dip in company collapses appears to be only a temporary blip in a general upward trend. The following table gives some of the relevant information for the past decade.

	Receiverships	Insolvent liquidations
1989	est. 1,375	est. 10,500
1988	1,217	9,427
1987	1,325	11,439
1986	1,777	14,405
1985	1,781	14,898
1984	1,803	13,721
1983	2,082	13,406
1982	2,190	12,067
1981	1,550	8,596
1980	1,350	6,890
1979	300	4,537

Source: Department of Trade and Industry.

The statistics have to be set against the massive increase in the small business sector during that period. Although the UK has a long way to go to catch up with its major trading rivals in small business generation, the number of businesses registered for VAT annually continues to rise – 1988's 230,000 was 64,000 up on 1987. But 166,000 companies deregistered in 1988. The reasons they did so vary widely. In many cases, sole traders are returning to salaried employment or retiring; in others, businesses are being absorbed into larger enterprises. Nonetheless, a significant proportion of deregistrations must be attributable to business failure. Most of these will not be brought through the insolvency process, either because the owners have dealt with the winding up themselves, or because there are no assets worth receiving.

Many of these deregistered businesses will be family businesses. A recent Stoy Hayward study of this sector found that the average life cycle of a family business was 24 years – a healthy sign. But only 30% are handed on to a second generation and only 13% survive through a third generation. Of those that do, a handful go on to become major corporations.

Every observer we spoke to had his or her own list of danger signs to look out for, that indicate the company on the steep and slippery. Many of these signs are indications of severe difficulties inside or outside the organization; others can be apparent indications of success. (One of our own favourites is when the chairman or chief executive of a large company becomes president of the Confederation of British Industry, the British Institute of Management or some other august body – a sure indication that his thoughts and commitment are no longer with his company.)

Let's look at some of these experts' lists.

● Mark Homan, national director of corporate reconstruction and insolvency with Price Waterhouse, describes his 'set of apparently frivolous danger signs' as:

* Personalized number plates on the Rolls
* Company flagpole
* Fountain in the forecourt
* Fish tank in the board room
* Founder's statue in reception
* Beautiful new offices
* Company yacht/aeroplane
* A fast-talking MD
* Directors who use military titles
* Obsession with tax avoidance
* Too many board papers
* No accountant on the board
* Too many auditors
* Too friendly with their banker
* Too many bankers.

● Patrick Wadsted, partner in charge of corporate reconstruction at the accountancy firm Hodgson Impey, is wary of company matchboxes and key rings. 'It may seem trivial, but to me it is significant that a company is spending money on disposables. If they are going to use promotional gifts, why not choose something permanent?'

He also suggests that named parking spaces in the company car park indicate a moribund culture governed by position rather than ability or usefulness. 'Why should the top executives have guaranteed spaces regardless of what time they arrive, while the people who really bring in the money have to circle the block?' he asks. Executive washrooms are another danger signal: 'One company had three: a private one for the chairman, another for main board directors and yet another for managers. I was tempted to fire a few directors to free up some keys,' says Wadsted. 'These are all examples of a

Victorian attitude to business – silly abuses of privilege and money spent on non-essentials of image and rank,' he says.

A veteran receiver, Christopher Morris of Touche Ross, finds many obvious signs in the offices and factory buildings, well before he needs to examine the books. He explains: 'The general standard of house-keeping is very indicative of how things are run. The general atmos-phere, too – for example, whether people know things they should. We once had to deal with a tannery in Northern Ireland. I asked the works director to show me round. He didn't know what was behind one of the doors – when he opened it, he fell into a limepit.'

'Another company we went into three years ago had six BMWs lined up in the forecourt. The chief executive's office was filled with mementos such as his first flight on Concorde and photographs of him playing golf with famous personalities. We knew immediately that we were going to have trouble there.'

● Lewis Robertson again:

'Besides borrowings there are other signals, some of them longer range and hence more useful, some of them subtle, many of them important and strongly indicative.

Is there a combined chairman and chief executive? Has this pre-vailed for a long time? There are exceptions, there are phases of development and of personal drive where this is right, but as a gener-alization, beware.

Is there a weak, or home-grown finance director who may not be a chartered accountant? Is the finance director largely lacking in experience in other groups, or other industries? If so, beware.

Are there no external (non-executive) directors? Or, if there is one, is there *only* one? Or, no matter how many there are, are they all very long in post, friendly with the chairman (especially if he is also chief executive), or (very important) lacking in the independence that comes from having their own base? If so, beware.

Are there (in a group of medium size) two or more sets of auditors – some surviving from before earlier mergers or acquisitions?

Similarly – and reflecting a similar failure to grasp nettles – are there, without special reason, two or more clearing banks involved? Again, beware.

Is the group proud of and reclining on – its history? Does it (or did it recently) boast the biggest, or the oldest, or the most "important" widget factory in Europe? Is it (which can be particularly doom-laden) making a virtue of riding out a major underlying market change without radical closures – "*other* widget-makers may close, but we are Bloggs, here since a century ago : we're saving shareholders' money by *not* closing, and the trade will come back". Beware, and again, beware.'

● The way organizations react to crisis also indicates how effectively they are dealing with their problems. Denys Boyle, of Tom Peters Group Europe points to two frequent signs.

* The company that cuts back on its office staff so that telephone enquiries take an inordinate amount of time to answer.
* The manufacturer that reduces stock levels to the point where customer service suffers.

These kinds of action are commonplace, and are usually justified in enormous detail on the cost savings side. But their impact on revenue generation is seldom considered: proof that, as demoralized staff quit and then, as quality and service fall, customers become increasingly dissatisfied. They either leave or begin to argue about prices. Falling market shares and profitability then lead to even greater efforts at cost-cutting. Once established, the vicious circle becomes self-reinforcing.

● Another veteran receiver, Bill Mackay, has said that among the clearest signs of impending doom are :

* offices opened by the Prime Minister
* elderly or unqualified accountants
* an annual report showing the chairman getting out of a helicopter.

The trouble with all these symptoms in isolation or even in combination is that they do not necessarily mean the business is in deep crisis. Indeed, some can equally be signs of success. For example, the company that has quality problems coping with demand may be sinking under them or actively concentrating resources to resolve them – and in doing so, may consolidate its competitive advantage. It is not the nature of the crisis or problem that matters, but how management approaches it and the skills and resources it has to deal with it.

Various more or less scientific attempts have been made to predict which companies are most likely to collapse. Among them are:

The 'Z' score, developed in the United States in the late Sixties by Edward Altman, looks at a business through financial ratios. Each ratio is given a weighting, according to how important it is to predicting failure, and scored. The sum of the scores indicates the likelihood of failure. Other systems taking a more or less similar approach are the 'L' score, and a 'decision support system' called FES. Another system called 'TIMES' focuses on managerial and administrative effectiveness rather than financial ratios.

John Argenti proposed a scoring system that is rather more thoughtful than most of these approaches. He identified early on that confusion between symptoms and causes made it more difficult to assess a company's health. He suggested a three-part sequence of decline: first come the defects, then the mistakes and finally the symptoms – but these are causally interlinked; without the defects no company would make the mistakes and without the mistakes the symptoms do not, of course, appear.

The defects are mainly in the area of management; the autocrat, a weak finance function, poor accounting data (especially costing systems, budgetary and cash flow forecasts) and, very significantly, anything that looks old-fashioned, such as the product, the factory, marketing techniques or industrial relations. Any of these, he suggests, would be readily visible to the skilled visitor to the company who should take note that these are the defects that lead, years later perhaps, to failure.

There are just three mistakes that lead to failure: overtrading, the 'grand project' and excessive financial gearing. Companies with the above defects are ripe for such errors. If the company makes them, it is virtually doomed; it is just a matter of time before the symptoms will appear.

The symptoms include creative accounting, deteriorating financial ratios and certain well-known physical signs of corporate distress.

An important feature is John Argenti's scoring system; long before the financial signs appear, the failing company may have amassed so many points for the defects and/or the mistakes that failure is easily predictable. Interestingly also; as the management takes action to avoid failure, so the 'A-Score' reverts towards the safety level.

As Slatter expresses it: 'The Z-score has been found not to be a good predictor for longer than two years before bankruptcy – which, it could be claimed, is not much use since most investors and banks know (or should know) from more conventional analysis that a firm is headed for insolvency two years before it actually happens.'

Like the pseudo-scientific scoring methods, however, Argenti's approach is no more than an interesting way of looking at the problem. It provides some useful guidelines to assessing whether a company is heading for glory or the gutter, but it is still too selective in what it measures to enable even the informed observer to make a prediction it would be safe to stand by.

To a considerable extent, this chapter has followed much the same lines as most previous books on the subject. This is perhaps inevitable, for, as we have already indicated, they are actually observing symptoms. We don't feel that is a very fruitful activity. The very fact that none of the experts can agree on even a broad set of symptoms or causes tends to support that view. Let's look instead at what lies behind these signs – the common values and perceptions that allow disastrous mismanagement to take shape and flourish.

PART II
Attitudes

ATTITUDES TOWARDS CONTROLS

Many of the earliest writers on management envisaged control as the primary function of a manager. His job was to make decisions, allocate resources, impose discipline and ensure that corrective action was taken when things didn't go according to plan.

Modern writers place much more emphasis on the value of autonomy. From this perspective, the job of the manager is to support the people 'below' him in the hierarchy in serving the customer. To do so he must delegate as much responsibility and authority as possible. Nonetheless, he must still exercise a certain amount of control, in the sense of coordination and knowing what is going on, so that he can respond effectively and rapidly to problems as they occur.

In practice, control and autonomy are two points on a wide spectrum (the extreme ends are stasis and anarchy respectively). At a corporate level, the group headquarters will exert more or less direct control according to a variety of factors, among them: the style of management, the national culture, the type of industry (retailers generally need more centralized control than, say, engineering companies) and the prevailing management fad of the time. The exact point on the spectrum may vary from division to division and even from function to function within divisions. For example, accounting departments tend to operate with considerably less internal autonomy than sales departments.

The same kind of spectrum can be applied to individual managers and to the management team as a whole. Some people take much more easily to the notion of controls than others. We can describe the two extremes as 'futurists' and 'hindsighters'. The futurist is the archetypal entrepreneur. His vision is fixed firmly on the future and today's problems are minor obstacles to be driven over. It expresses a deep-seated optimism based on an unshakeable determination not to take any notice of what is actually happening in the business.

The hindsighter is constantly concerned with the past. He greatly enjoys working out with copious statistical evidence how the company got from there to here. He is not greatly comfortable with the future, because he does not like dealing with uncertainties. He therefore acts as a brake upon innovation, experiment and ambition. He is constantly bringing discussion back down to earth.

The action-oriented manager lies somewhere in between. Typically concerned with today, he often has a sales background. To him, past and present are largely irrelevant; the one he can't influence and the other requires too much diversion of effort from today.

These characters, who are all caricatures (except, of course, that we all know people who match the descriptions perfectly) have been identified by other writers in other contexts.

The problem is that any company, where one or more of these individuals dominates the management team and/or the board, will have a biased view of what controls it needs and how it uses them. Any of these biases, used exclusively, is enough to kill a company on its own. Yet many management teams go to considerable lengths to ensure they create such damaging biases. For example, a Swedish company got rid of its finance director because the rest of the top team objected to his constant words of caution. What they regarded as being negative, however, was the voice of experience. Freed from his influence the company expanded more and more rapidly, until it overextended itself and collapsed.

The key here is balance, both among the team and in the perceptions and applications of the key players. The chief executive, in particular, must be capable of and comfortable in operating in all three time zones: of learning from past trends, of dealing with today's issues and monitoring events to handle tomorrow's threats and opportunities.

His job, and that of the management team as a whole, involves:

* understanding what controls are needed and why
* installing them and making sure they are operated effectively
* appraising them regularly to ensure they provide the information required
* *using* the information.

The excuses that executives use for not doing these things are multiple, as one might expect. High on the list comes lack of time, followed by lack of know-how. But all of the excuses we have heard boil down to one: 'We didn't think it was important enough.' Although they may have given lip-service to the need for efficient and effective control systems, their actions reveal their true attitudes. If it were sufficiently high in their priorities, they would have made the time, or acquired the know-how, either personally or by buying in the appropriate skills, which are readily available.

It is interesting here to take a quick aside to look at the special problems of the small business. In our experience, very few small businesses take on a financial director (as opposed to a book-keeper) until they reach around fifty employees. The main reason given is the high cost of acquiring what they see as a non-contributory activity – what spare cash there is should go into resources that will contribute to growth, such as equipment or production skills. In some cases, this lack of financial control is largely compensated for by having a financially-oriented managing director. But he or she has a great many other responsibilities within the company. Almost inevitably, the financial control activities become relegated to evenings and week-ends. Where the company does not have a financially-oriented chief executive, the more rapidly it grows, the more financial risks it runs. As a general rule, we suggest that any growth-oriented small business should appoint a finance director at the earliest possible moment it can afford to.

To return to our main theme, if any of the four steps of the control process is skipped over, the company becomes vulnerable. Let's look at them each in turn.

Understanding what controls are needed and why

The whole purpose of controls is to provide information that management can use to adjust the workings of the business and to plan. So, the definition of controls is much wider than finance. In practice, every activity that has a major impact on the viability of the business needs to be measured and monitored. Failure to measure any of these things is either a sign that top management does not appreciate their importance (in its turn a sign that it does not really understand its business), or that it does not take seriously its responsibilities to control them.

Says Robert Ellis, of Touche Ross's Bristol office: 'The stage comes very quickly in a company's life where, unless you have a set of accurate management information very regularly, you can't cope. A month is much too infrequent for a large company. When small companies do it six-monthly, it is criminal. The workforce relies upon the directors to run the company in a responsible manner.'

Lewis Robertson rams the point home: 'I have yet to tackle a rescue in which a complete renewal of accounting and reporting systems is not required.'

As a basic kit of controls, every company should have systems that provide top management regularly with at least the following:

Financial/accounting

Sales turnover: not just is it going up or down, but how is it performing in relation to the market as a whole? It is quite possible – and frequent – to increase sales while losing market share. Equally, if the market as a whole has plateaued, it is time to consider whether the sector has reached maturity.

Costs: Many troubled companies simply don't know where the money they spend goes. While they can generally assign expenditure to broad categories, they cannot identify how much it costs to make each type of product, or its component parts. As a result, they have little idea of what the real margin on each product is. As a makeshift measure, they often assign costs arbitrarily, for example, according to each product's sales turnover.

When (if) these companies install precise cost measurements, they often find that some product lines are much more profitable than they had thought, but are not well-promoted, while those that are promoted are losing money.

Our case study of Raleigh provides a good example of a company which had made its production processes so complex that it could not possibly establish what the real costs of producing each line were. It attempted to overcome the problem with a massive computer system, forgetting the golden rule that you should always simplify a system before you computerize it.

One recent receivership handled by Gould involved a company that on paper appeared to be doing well, but was clearly losing money. The reason emerged that its costing systems were completely misfounded.

Typical of many chief executive officers' attitudes towards cost controls is a case outlined by US company doctor Q.T.Wiles. The chief executive of ADAC Laboratories wanted to launch six new products, but was not generating enough cash from the current business. Indeed, says Wiles, he was 'shipping cash' – selling more and more medical equipment at a loss. 'The reason was the company had no controls and hadn't spent any money on improving the technology that would have allowed it to make the product cheaper – integrated circuits rather than individual circuits, double-sided boards, that sort of thing.' The chief financial officer, says Wiles, 'was still telling the CEO what he wanted to hear.'

Although the market was declining the company had a 40 per cent share. Wiles divided the business into the base business and growth businesses, and concentrated resources on getting the former into shape. Only when he had done so, did he turn to the new product ideas. But the CEO 'never could bring himself to choose which one of those six new products was the right one – he wanted to do all six. Eventually, he left the company.'

Pricing: a frequent failing is to under- or over-price. Over-pricing is usually less of a problem, because the market reaction soon provides feedback. But customers will not normally complain that you are charging too little. Monitoring price levels can be hard, time-consuming work; but it can mean the difference between healthy and unhealthy margins.

Says Wadsted: 'A lot of people just don't understand the idea of margins. They will give a five per cent discount on a ten per cent margin, not realizing they'll have to sell twice the volume for the same profit. A keenness to discount is understandable if you must liquidate inventory, and perfectly reasonable on high-margin items, but it's counter-productive to discount low-margin items because it is virtually impossible to make it up on volume.'

Cash flow: the only sure way of predicting overtrading is through a strong system of cash flow planning. In most cases, that requires an effective cost measurement system.

Cash flow management is particularly critical in times of rapid growth, says insolvency practitioner Paul Walker: 'Growth can kill if there is not enough financing to fund the expansion. As turnover grows, your cash needs increase proportionately, but many firms neglect to arrange for more overdraft facilities.'

Cash management is critical because, as another receiver puts it:

'Rapid changes in the business environment can, in only months, erode a comfortable cash position – and unceremoniously dump an otherwise untroubled company into near bankruptcy.'

Unfortunately, a surprising number of companies do not make cash projections except when required to do so during negotiations for credit lines. Other companies grind out regular cash projections that are little more than extrapolations of trends. Then their CEOs, usually intent on more exciting issues, glance at the summary reports and assume that cash is adequate.

Debtors' register: how much is outstanding and for how long? There also needs to be a system to ensure that any debt more than thirty days old is chased hard – the longer a debt is outstanding, in general, the harder it is to collect.

Although only one-third of our survey respondents noted 'lack of credit control' as a prime cause of failure, it has frequently been identified as a contributing factor in other studies.

Wadsted explains how short-term debt can get out of hand: 'If the bank grants overdraft facilities on the basis of the company's outstanding debts, it is in the firm's interest to maintain a slack ledger and maximize short-term debt. One firm, dealing in large ticket machinery, had kept the ledger so slack that it went into receivership with £2 million in book debts and only £38,000 in estimated realizable value.'

Bad debts can have a devastating knock-on effect. Walker tells of one family-run building company that learned, on the day the managing director was due to retire, that their biggest customer had failed, leaving them with a massive bad debt. Worse, the suppliers knew the firm would be in trouble as a result and had put a squeeze on credit. Though the managing director worked another three years to rebuild the business, it never recovered.

Return on investment: an essential measurement for quoted companies, but private companies may find margins and cash flow more valuable.

Gearing: banks will always encourage companies to borrow when they are in credit and look down their noses when they actually need overdraft facilities. The higher the gearing, the bigger the risk. Many companies borrow heavily when interest rates are low, then find they cannot cope when interest rates are high.

According to Wadsted, many firms fail because of insufficient working capital and rely too heavily on bank funding rather than increased venture capital, or, in the case of family businesses, family members withdraw cash and neglect to replace it. 'One family printing company that had been operating for generations went under with a share capital of £40,000 and a turnover of £30 million. They owed £4.2 million to the bank,' he says.

Management buy-outs are particularly susceptible to excessive gearing. Take the case of Hornby, for example. Hornby was bought by its managers from the ruins of toymakers Dunbee Combex-Marx in 1981. At the time, it was one of the few profitable parts of the group. The managers paid £5.5 million, which they raised as a mixture of equity and loans secured against assets. The future looked bright in spite of the massive debt the managers had to repay. The company had two of the best brand names in the top end of the toy business – Hornby model trains and Scalextric model cars. The managers predicted a profit of £2 million pre-tax for the coming year.

What they had not taken into account was the faddish nature of the toy market. Instead of buying toy trains that Christmas, parents bought video games and home computers. Sales fell to 50 per cent of forecast and the company made a £1.7 million loss. The loans continued to attract interest, raising the gearing even further. A new management team was brought in by the investors as part of their £10 million rescue package. In due course, Hornby's fortunes turned around again as the video game and home computer boom faded. But that was too late for the original buy-out team, who were a lot poorer, and perhaps a lot wiser.

Another relevant story is that of British Air Ferries. Recalls Christopher Ross: 'Standard Chartered assisted them and kept ladling out cash. But, as always, that situation came to an abrupt stop when the borrowings exceeded someone's limit. It was a good business, with good customers, but it couldn't make money because it had a heavy burden of debt. It couldn't get the volume of trade to overcome that. It was eventually acquired by a bigger organization. The creditors didn't get much out of it.' British Caledonian was on a similar path before its acquisition by British Airways.

Administrative and production

Overheads: by their very nature, overheads add nothing to the bottom line – indeed they detract from it. The efficient management team tracks the administrative overhead, with the aim of keeping it as lean as possible.

Employee turnover: most businesses are now people businesses. Employee turnover has a significant cost in terms of customer relationships, training and retraining, loss of scarce skills and reduction in efficiency. It can also be a highly accurate barometer of the health of a company (but beware the difference between a company where employees are dissatisfied enough to want to quit and one which is deliberately changing the type of people it employs).

Output per employee: not necessarily the same as sales per employee, but both figures are valuable, particularly when used as comparisons with other similar operations.

Cost of quality: the classic measurement of waste, which can compose up to 40 per cent of overall costs. Measuring cost of quality may be beyond the technical expertise of the small company, but there is ample assistance available, much of it partially funded by the Department of Trade and Industry. Many companies regard cost of quality as a more practical measure of productivity than output measures, which do not distinguish useful from useless work.

Cost of inventory: inventory, whether it be engineering components or photocopying paper, is tied cash. At best, it is not earning interest for the company; at worst it adds to the company's borrowing. Costs need to be measured not just in absolute terms (what was paid for it) but the expense of the capital tied up in it.

Throughput times: the more quickly a product or project can be pushed through the system, the sooner it can be billed. The longer it takes, the more interest the company is paying (or losing) on all the costs involved and the more vulnerable cash flow forecasts become.

Project management: large projects need well-documented, formal planning and budgeting procedures of their own. John Argenti, in particular, points to the big project as a company killer. Unless it is preceded by accurate scheduling and costing, with sufficient provision for contingencies, it can easily overrun in costs, take over the resources of the organization at the expense of more profitable operations and bring chaos to cash flow planning.

How easily this can happen is illustrated by the Channel Tunnel. The lessons of the past indicate very clearly that every previous attempt to build a 'Chunnel' ended when it ran out of money. The construction consortium working on the current attempt might have been expected to allow for this in its calculations and no doubt did to a certain extent. But it has already had to return to shareholders for a substantial additional injection of cash, with the tunnelling work far from completion.

Marketing

Market share: most useful if you are a significant player in a relatively mature market. The small business cannot usually make much sense of this as a measure, unless it defines its business as a very narrow market niche. But for the large company, market share information provides a useful overview of how customers and distributors view your company and/or its products. It is easy to over-rely on this broad information, however. Trends need to be followed up with more detailed examination of exactly what is happening within the market.

Market growth rate: more useful in general. Even the small business can work out whether it is growing at the same rate as the market as a whole.

Gain or loss of customers: not often measured, but a valuable barometer of competitive position. Used in conjunction with measurement of the costs to replace lost customers with new ones, it can reveal some of the bottom line implications of the state of customer relations. Again, the real value comes from using this information as the starting point to identify what makes customers satisfied or dissatisfied.

The loss of a customer can be devastating for small and medium-sized firms that put too many eggs in one basket. Walker tells of one electrical contractor that failed after twenty-eight years of profitable operation simply because its biggest customer decided to withhold payment.

Customer satisfaction: complaints are one of the most valuable sources of information a company can obtain about the effectiveness of its operations. Analysed data on complaints should be seen not just by the marketing department, but by the entire management team and especially the chief executive.

To these the efficient company will add other controls that relate to its business priorities. For example, oil companies measure safety performance, to ensure that every production unit is carrying out the prescribed safety procedures. Distribution companies will (or should) measure the efficiency of use of storage space.

Of course, regular reporting is not enough. The reports must be both timely and presented in a manner that makes them easy to assimilate and use. The faster a company is growing, the more rapidly it needs information. In a service business such as Kwikfit, for example, the executives receive every morning full details of the previous days trading, plotting key trends. While not every business needs this kind of timeliness, it is clear at the other extreme that three months is too long a delay to allow swift remedial action. In many of the troubled companies we have encountered, top management had never considered in any depth what the critical time period for reporting was in their business.

Installing controls and making them work

Midland Bank's Derek Gould recalls a lesson he learnt in his early days dealing with troubled companies. A more experienced colleague asked the assembled board: 'Who here is responsible for the finances of this company?' Nobody put up their hand.

The basic requirement for making control systems work is commitment. If the chief executive does not demonstrate that he believes a control to be important, no one else will take it seriously either. Implicit, too, is the need for clear accountability, for making sure that someone capable has responsibility for generating the information and someone (perhaps the same person) for taking action on the basis of it.

Appraising the controls regularly

All systems tend to have a life of their own. Part of a manager's job is to review whether the control systems he uses provide the information he needs. But the requirement may have changed; new priority issues may need to be measured; or a greater level of detail may be necessary. A good many failed companies do have control systems, but they are obsolete or ineffective. As a result, top management – not really wanting to know any different – remain blissfully unaware and/or unconcerned that the information it is receiving does not give a true picture of what is happening. How long the company survives under those circumstances is to a considerable extent a matter of luck.

Managers must also check whether the control systems are doing what they are intended to do. Walker has seen a number of firms run into trouble because of an over-reliance on computerized control systems. 'The people who sell computers say they are the answer to everything, but what they don't tell you is it can take a year of hard work to learn how to use them properly – and many people never learn.'

He tells of an advertising agency that had been operating successfully for several years. 'All the accounts information had been entered on a spreadsheet program, but the firm outgrew that and upgraded to a database system. The operator was never taught the difference and began to take shortcuts. As a result, more than fifty per cent of the daily entries for an entire year were never entered. At year end they knew they had done a year's chargeable hours, but didn't know who to charge – customers had been getting invoices for a quarter of the real amount. The director had never in all that time checked to see if the new program was working. It had not come to light earlier because everyone had so much faith in the computer.'

In another example, a wholesaler for toy shops had so many advance orders that it was virtually impossible not to make money, but, through poor controls, managed it nonetheless. 'They introduced a new computer system and only ever understood the first three columns of the print-outs. When suppliers increased their prices, no one thought to enter an increase in the selling prices. The firm was actually selling at a loss, but management was blissfully unaware of it because of its unshakable faith in the computer system.'

Using the controls

Once again, commitment is important. We have been impressed by how frequently companies in trouble have had the information they needed to tell them about the realities of their marketplaces, but have preferred to ignore it.

A comparative study of successful and unsuccessful companies we made in 1983 touched on this phenomenon. Most of the unsuccessful companies gathered information about their markets. Some spent fortunes acquiring such information. Then they locked it away because they didn't like its conclusions. In many cases, research is used as a means of deferring decisions, because the management team cannot bring itself to admit the truth of what the controls already indicate.

Receiver Christopher Morris comments on the many top management teams who are apparently completely blinkered about the problems facing their company. He refers to the case of British Air Ferries, one of Britain's oldest airlines, where the management team would not accept that the business was not viable, until the institutions pulled the rug from under them. Adds Walker: 'Managers in a crisis have a tendency to ignore bad information. They will look at evidence of a problem and dismiss it as not important, or "just a bit of a hiccup". They all seem to have a blind belief in that big order just around the corner.'

We shall refer again to this characteristic of the behaviour of managers in declining companies. The fear of facing up to reality is a natural condition of humans under stress, but the root cause goes much deeper – to their commitment to the business goals and to the clarity with which they perceive their role.

A symptom of this confusion and fear is the way control information is packaged and presented. Managers who know exactly what they want the information for and how they are going to use it, want it on a single sheet of paper, expressed in as simple a form as possible, preferably both visually and as figures. As Sir Kenneth Cork commented in our 1983 study: 'It used to be that there was a great shortage of paper in companies, in cash flows, profit forecasts and so on. People used to wait until the auditors turned up and then looked at the results with surprise ... Now I think it is the opposite – it is a glut of paper, all printed in silly little dots that you can hardly read, on the computer.

'When I go to a company to do an investigation, or to talk to the management, I ask them simple questions. What's your cash flow? When does it peak? What's your profit forecast? What's your turnover last week? And all they do is press a ruddy button and in comes an accountant with a pile of papers a mile high. Then they shuffle them and they can't find the right one.

'Nobody can think with a piece of paper. There's only one place you can think. A good businessman will answer all your questions out of his head. The only information you want is information on which you can make a decision. If you can't make a decision having read it, you don't want it. Some board meetings are full of "Well, I never" information.' Typical 'Well, I never' information, he suggests, is 'We sent three wheelbarrows last month to Mexico.'

In some cases, too, controls may be so many, so severe that they strangle a company. This was certainly the case with the sports businesses of Dunlop, unable to invest because the parent company was at the edge of its borrowing limits. It was also the case with many of the now-privatized organizations, which relied upon the uncertain generosity of the public purse. The case of Embraer, the Brazilian airline, which lost $20 million in 1988, is not untypical. Because the owners, the Brazilian government, were in severe debt, the airline was starved of capital and unable to obtain long-term loans. To survive, Embraer purchased short-term loans equivalent to two-thirds of its annual sales, at high interest. That, however, could only be a temporary solution. Under a rescue package put together by First Boston Bank, the government has had to sell off much of its equity.

Attitudes towards risk

The deliberate or unconscious refusal to cut through the cobwebs and establish exactly what is going on in the business and its environment can also be seen in the attitudes many managers take towards risk. Rather than make them risk-averse, it often makes them foolhardy. As long as they do not have to think about the reality and can pretend that the real world is like the world they want to see, they can justify their inaction, both to themselves and to outsiders. Highly optimistic forecasts of market growth, for example, may be readily accepted by investors if the tale is coherent and plausible.

According to Derek Gould, many groups prefer to have several bankers in order to keep competition alive, and also to see continuity where acquisitions have been undertaken, thus retaining existing banks. Similarly some take on new banks ad infinitum where the banks cold call, leading to a structure that is unmanageable, and they fail to rationalize the overall banking connection when required. 'We were dealing with a large company with 200 bankers across the world, 13 in this country. It was well-publicized that this company was losing money and borrowing heavily. It only needs one or two banks to pull out for a crisis to be precipitated when the going gets rough.'

Simple ignorance also leads to unacceptable risks. Gould points to an increase in the number of companies that get into severe difficulties through exchange losses. In almost all cases, these companies have disregarded their own ignorance or inexperience and failed to seek advice, which in many cases they could have had for free.

Executives can reduce their exposure to risk by recognizing when the greatest risks occur. Critical periods include:

* when the business is going through rapid growth
* the transition from entrepreneurial to professional management, or between generations in a family firm
* acquisition or merger
* launch of a major new product or diversification
* the first moves into international markets.

The key is not to attempt to tackle more than one of these risks at a time.

In a number of cases we have observed, the management team has simply not recognized that it is increasing the level of risk. Gould provides a salutory tale of a management buyout that started with credit in the bank. Its gearing was high (120 per cent) but could have been reduced to safe levels quite easily if it had focused attention on cash flow and profits. Instead the executives put their energies into rapid expansion, for which they did not have sufficient funding. At the same time, they tried to change many of the internal facets of the business – 'too many, too fast'. In particular, they tried to move from a one-season business to a two-seasons business, through diversification. Borrowings escalated, especially as much of the extra production and marketing costs had to be incurred well before the second season began. When both sales and margins in the second season were below forecast, it precipitated a cash crisis. The company had no option but to raise prices, as these had to be published well in advance.

It might have survived this stretching of its people and cash resources if it had had sufficient financial information. But it didn't like what its finance director had to say, so it fired him and replaced him with an inexperienced junior who was not qualified and who held back information. By the time the management and the investors realized what was happening, it was too late.

Other examples illustrate the problems of launching ambitious overseas ventures without adequate resources. Rainbow Software, a small start-up company, obtained £100,000 venture capital for a computer software development. The package quickly took off in the UK and the venture seemed secure. Then Alca Berkley, the institution providing the finance, insisted that it establish a sales network in the United States, the world's largest market for software. This effort ate up most of the remaining funds (marketing in the United States is very expensive) and created relatively little business, because the established competition brought out its own product. Alerted to the presence of a competitor, the US company also attacked the UK market. Now with very reduced funds and little market presence in the United States, the British company was in a difficult position. The institution declined to advance any more cash and the software company was wound up.

Midland Bank's Gould provides another case; the managing director of a company was a salesman by background – another common symptom of failure if biased too heavily this way. He rationalized the product range and built a new product range whilst diversifying overseas. He didn't have the funding to 'do it all'.

In illustrating the risks of new product launches we are spoilt for choice. One thing is for sure: most new products will take twice as long as expected to develop and will probably cost twice as much. The more important the development is to the company's future, the greater the risks associated with it. Gerry Tuffs learnt this lesson the hard way with his company Data Type. The company had grown fast from an initial turnover of £169,000 in 1979 to £6.5 million in 1982, distributing and manufacturing computer graphics terminals. The business plan for 1983 envisaged a doubling of sales, mainly as the result of the launch of a new high-resolution graphics screen, developed in-house and delivering 60 per cent margins rather than the 20 per cent on distributed products that had formed the main basis for growth so far. Not only was the development work costly, but the whole organization had been geared up around the launch, down to hiring additional assembly workers. In concentrating on resolving this issue, Tuffs had to take his eye off the ball in his overseas sales and distribution subsidiaries. Eventually both areas of the business were giving cause for concern and Tuffs was forced to obtain a second tranche of funding that meant he lost control of the company. From here on it was only a matter of time to his dismissal as chief executive.

Similarly, there are ample cases of companies running into severe cash difficulties because they have not controlled the pace of growth. Brian Palmer built his brown goods distribution company Hinari (the name was chosen to make it sound Japanese) around importing televisions, audio equipment and video recorders. Established in 1985, by 1989 the company had £60 million annual sales – and £30 million debts. Much of the problem stemmed from the decision to manufacture fourteen-inch televisions in the UK, at Cumbernauld, near Glasgow. The factory opened at about the same time as the electronics retail business went into recession. Technically insolvent, the company called in administrators (a stage prior to receivership, aimed at finding a solution that does not involve winding the business up) in September 1989. According to the *Financial Times* a few weeks later, Palmer 'admitted last winter Hinari's fast growth was its Achilles' heel.'

Dragon's managers, too, had no idea of what was needed to control the explosive growth they predicted. They ignored advice that their plans were overambitious and lacked detailed analysis; ploughed ahead to meet massive demand; and ran out of cash as the sales failed to materialize.

ATTITUDES TOWARDS THE VISION

'All trailblazers go bust – Cyril Lord with carpets to the masses, Bloom with his washing machines, Laker with travel. If you put them in one room, you'd find a lot of similarities in personality. All of them are consummate salesmen; all of them have high opinions of themselves; all of them attract extreme staff loyalty (Laker's staff worked for two-thirds as much as British Airways)'
– Christopher Morris, receiver.

In an earlier comparison of successful and unsuccessful companies, we found that the top managers of successful companies shared a strong vision of where the company was going. They also spent a good deal of their time communicating the vision to other people in the company, using it to energize them in pursuit of business objectives. Top management in unsuccessful companies lacked a clear sense of direction among themselves and were hence unable to communicate it to other people.

Having a clear vision is of vital importance because it provides the basis for building common purpose. It also provides a touchstone, against which to measure difficult decisions. It may be encapsulated in a mission statement, but is only really useful in this form as a confirmation of where the organization is headed, rather than as a set of pious hopes for the future.

A vision doesn't have to be very long-term. In many businesses, looking more than five years ahead is very difficult. The core of a successful vision is that it enables people at any level in the organization to picture what the business will be like at a definable point in the future and to mould their actions and behaviours accordingly.

There are two main problem attitudes towards vision. One is that it doesn't matter, that it is all 'text-book stuff' and therefore unnecessary for the day-to-day running of the business. In a way, this may be true, for the management team that has no ambitions other than to survive. The trouble is that, without a guiding vision, people in the organization will tend to create their own pictures of success, to which they will work. In the medium to long term, this always either pulls the organization apart or makes it ineffectual. Neither is particularly conducive to growth. (The vision does not have to encompass growth, of course. There are companies for whom the vision – very clearly articulated – is to remain small, personalized and within a specific niche where they will be renowned for their excellence. While this is in some ways a dangerous strategy, there are numerous examples of companies that have survived and prospered for decades under such a vision.)

Failure to have a unifying vision is a common characteristic of family firms in the second or third generation and of large conglomerate-type companies, where top management has forgotten (or is unable to work out) what the organization is in business for. There are examples of both in our case study chapters.

The second problem is the assumption that because the vision is there, it must be right. The archetypal entrepreneur is successful because he will not allow impediments to his dream. But if the dream is ill-timed, or under-resourced, or based upon misconceptions (particularly about the market or what is actually possible within the relevant technology) then it is even more likely to cause failure of the company. Indeed, the entrepreneur's infectious drive, enthusiasm and commitment will normally ensure that the company pursues the wrong road with the utmost speed and vigour. A leader with a less insistent dream would have proceeded more slowly, and may well have been turned back onto the right path; but the entrepreneur is moving so fast he cannot even read the road signs clearly.

A healthy vision is one that withstands and indeed invites scrutiny and criticism. Yet, as we shall see in the next chapter, the entrepreneur often surrounds himself with people who agree with him – he hasn't time or patience to argue the toss. So fellow-travellers who might also have stopped to read the road signs are also whisked past them, perhaps occasionally peering backwards in apprehension, but never daring to suggest to the driver that he stop and check the map.

An interesting illumination of the differences between the entrepreneur and the small business person comes from Dr Fay Fransella of London University. She explained the distinction between the two types of character in the *Financial Times* as follows:

'The Small Business Person wants to create a business that he or she will work for. The business itself is the goal; the size of the business may not be the sole concern. The satisfaction for all the hard work will come from having a business that is so well-organized that it will run itself; and healthy profit margins can have a decidedly cheering influence.'

The successful small business person is a talented organizer, who enjoys making things happen. The business tends to grow according to his appetite for rewards.

By contrast, the entrepreneur 'has a dream. The small business is a vehicle to realize that dream; the satisfactions come from steps achieved along the route to the fulfilment of it ... To the true entrepreneur, cash flow and profit and loss projections are necessary evils rather than the life-blood of small business success. Goals in ten years' time are expressed in terms of the dream realized, rather than in facts and figures that show a business with a £2 million turnover.'

Both of these characters, in the extreme, can be sure-fire candidates for failure. The small business person can be too small-minded, never taking risks but overtaken by events because he has not imagined the opportunities. The entrepreneur, by contrast, may have his eyes so fixed in the horizon that he does not see the edge of the cliff before him.

The problem for the investor, and for boards of directors seeking a chief executive to develop the potential of their company, is identifying when the candidates before them have a balanced mix drawn from both character types – in other words, can operate in both entrepreneurial (leader) mould and manager mould and when they veer too strongly towards either extreme. Another approach is to look for a management team that balances entrepreneurial and down-to-earth characters in a stable manner.

The following cases each illustrate one or more aspects of a faulty or unfounded vision – mostly the latter, because companies without vision usually become gobbled up before they hit disaster.

The Midlands engineering company

Typical of the kind of company which has no real vision is the family enterprise described by one of 3i's consultants, Christopher Edge, in an article for *Financial Decisions* as an old-established family-controlled group in the Midlands making engineering components for UK-based multinationals.

The business had grown to a turnover of £20 million, and had several factories mostly financed from its own resources.

But says Edge, 'In recent years the firm's margins had decreased and, in order to keep making profits, corners had been cut. The effect had been a loss of quality, reputation and major accounts. Little action had been taken to remedy this and the firm started to lose money. The joint managing directors, determinedly optimistic, believed that the market would pick up after recession.

'The bank, which had increased its overdraft to £1.5 million, did not take comfort from this "laid-back" attitude. At the time we were contacted, the overdraft was rapidly approaching the full "cover" and the company was seeking to borrow yet more money to tide it over the coming year.

'I spent a day with the company's directors, looking at the available information and seeing the main sites. It became clear that there was a core business that could be made to work, even though its potential might not be dramatically exciting, and that the real problem lay in lack of leadership and a thoroughly disorganized approach.' Among other problems, the chairman was only part-time, yet still believed he ran the business.

Homes Assured

Homes Assured was set up in 1987 to take advantage of the boom in council house sales. The idea seemed sound. The company would assist council house tenants to purchase their homes and would obtain income from three sources. Firstly, the tenants would pay the company a fee to handle all the purchase arrangements. Then there would be income from acting as an agent for endowment policies to cover the house mortgages. Finally, it expected to earn commission for arranging home improvement loans.

The whole venture was based on an estimate that the average completion time for purchasing a property would be nine months. In the event, it took an average fifteen months. The extra six months provided that much longer for householders to reconsider their endowment mortgages. Three out of four cancelled their policies – three times as many as expected.

The company might have been able to weather this setback, if it had not overextended itself in creating an overhead structure based on its predictions of insurance company commission. In the event, reported the *Financial Times*:

> 'It had four subsidiaries, each with its own accounting and other functions (it decided to centralize these in April 1989). There were 11 branch offices and, at its peak, a sales force of 400 people (although they were paid on commission).
>
> 'The bills were impressive for such a new company: £500,000 on computers, £300,000 for postage and packing; £200,000 on advertising, £150,000 on legal fees, accountancy fees of £100,000, and so on.'

Altogether the overhead bill came to £7 million. The company posted a £6 million loss in less than two years.

Such tales of overambition – of visions gone wild – are commonplace. An estimated 40 per cent of profit warnings concerning companies on the Unlisted Securities Market concern setbacks in expansion plans.

The credit card company

Wadsted cites a credit card embossing company that operated with antiquated machines, each requiring a full-time operator. Although the firm could have fully automated for far less than the salaries saved, management chose not to – not because they wanted to maintain jobs, but simply because they weren't sufficiently forward thinking. 'The attitude was: "We have been doing it this way for forty years, why should we change now?",' says Wadsted.

Dragon Data

Dragon's vision was fatally flawed because neither the managers nor the investors understood what business they were in. They were, in fact, in both the toy and the home electronic businesses, both of which are subject to very rapid product obsolescence. The plan, if plan it was, assumed that the technical problems and costs of rapid new product development would somehow be met without any major problems – less an error of judgement than an error of vision.

Kenwood

Faulty vision is particularly acute when it comes to diversifications, mergers and acquisitions. Veteran company doctor Ian Morrow recalls when he arrived at the food mixer company, Kenwood, founded by a marketeer, Ken Wood. Wood had made a disastrous diversification into refrigerators, a very different, much more cut-throat market. Said Morrow: 'Every time you get an order for a fridge, pin a five pound note on it and send it back and you'll be better off.' Closing the fridge division went against the grain for the managers, but it saved the company.

Morrow's first company doctoring task was Brush Electrical Engineering company, which he describes as 'built by a man who was more interested in acquisitions than actually running things'.

Lifecore Biomedical

A frequent mistake by start-up companies is to underestimate the costs of achieving the vision. US company Lifecore Biomedical Inc. of Minneapolis had carried out four years of research and development on a new pharmaceutical product. Sodium hyaluronic acid (HA), a valuable material for reducing scarring, particularly in cataract surgery was so difficult to make that it cost $9 million a pound by traditional methods (extraction from rooster combs). Lifecore had found a means of producing HA by bioengineering at a fraction of the cost, using, of all things, the streptococcus virus.

It found a customer, pharmaceutical company Cilco, and set about taking the laboratory technique into production. But after a number of months, it became clear that the production process wasn't working

– it needed a substantial investment in water filtering equipment to obtain the level of purity the process demanded. By the time the company was down to its last $6,000, chief executive James Bracke knew that he had to find an investor or go bust. None of the financial institutions would put up the necessary cash. Bracke was fortunate, however. Cilco, having already invested heavily in promoting the product, eventually provided the cash to continue development to the stage where production was consistent, in return for 30 per cent of the equity. The company is now thriving. Bracke told *Inc* magazine: 'I'm confident again, but not the way I was. After being shaken like that, you lose your old perspective, and you can never really go back.'

Norsk Data

The dangers of a vision that is not open to question, is too rigid, as illustrated by Norwegian computer company, Norsk Data. Chief executive and founder Rolf Skaar, after the company's sudden drop into losses in 1988, admitted that, while he had foreseen the importance of Unix software as early as 1986, as one of the world's most profitable computer businesses, the company felt it could ignore this particular world trend. 'Some of this we saw coming but there was no way we were going to change.'

Quintex

Australian entrepreneur Christopher Skase was a financial journalist with a vision of building an international leisure empire. A university drop-out, he spent two years with a broking firm, before quitting to tour Australia in an ancient Ford car. It was then he recognized the potential in tourism within Australia's sunshine state, Queensland. He joined an investment house where he accumulated enough capital to obtain a stake in a company called Quintex, that had interests in tourism, media and property. Still in his early thirties, he soon became one of Australia's youngest chief executives.

Skase, who lived the part of the larger than life, entrepreneur to the full, gradually expanded Quintex, acquiring television channels and resorts both in Australia and Hawaii.

At this point it might have been prudent to consolidate what he had, not least because many of Quintex's assets were not producing the level of profit predicted for them. As a result, the company was burdened with heavy interest payments on the money it had borrowed for its acquisitions. The purchaser of a healthy company is usually wrong when he thinks he can supply better management than the incumbent team.

But for Skase, the vision was more important than the business. He launched a $1.2 billion bid for MGM-United Artists, the Hollywood film studio in a fierce contest with Rupert Murdoch's News Corporation. But by now, the company was overextended. When, six months after its bid terms were accepted, the time came to pay up, Quintex had been unable to raise the cash. Inviting News Corporation to take an equity share merely stimulated a new counterbid, which forced the price up again to over $2 billion.

When Quintex was unable to deliver a $50 million deposit demanded by MGM, the game was up. MGM called off the deal and a few days later Quintex Entertainments, Skase's US company filed for bankruptcy.

The cash flow problems were worsened by Skase's failure to sell some of his television interests (a necessary part of financing overseas expansion) and by a long running strike by Australian pilots, which hit tourism hard. Skase also attributes the company's problems to an increase in interest rates. In November 1989, the receivers came into the Australian company and Skase – still only forty-one – went out. The company had an estimated $960 million of debt.

There never really was much chance of creating an international empire so rapidly on the asset base Quintex had. The vision *could* have been fulfilled, given a more cautious, step by step approach. But perhaps that is part of the definition of the archetypal entrepreneur – the willingness to gamble all if the stakes are high enough.

ATTITUDES TOWARDS THE TEAM

'My strengths are in founding things and in providing technical back-up. I don't want to be a line manager. Entrepreneurs should not be involved in running businesses.'

– Sir Clive Sinclair.

The vast majority of our cases of failed companies involved problems with the team. As in so many of these attitudinal issues, the basis for problems tends to lie in extremes – particularly in either excessively strong or excessively weak leadership.

Strong leadership is valuable (indeed, essential for the turnaround leader), but at the extreme of autocracy it creates a blindness to the realities of the business world. The essence of an effective team is that it makes comprehensive use of the skills and abilities of all the members – including their creativity and critical faculties. The autocrat, by his very style of management, stifles these latter attributes. When he is right, the company may be remarkable for the pace and quality of its growth; but sooner or later, buoyed up by his own success, he will begin to make wrong decisions and there will be no one able to make him think again. As we shall see when we consider attitudes to learning, the extreme entrepreneur rarely learns, because he rarely listens.

Dragon, for example, never had a team as such. Key people kept changing, so there was little stability. The chief executive behaved like an autocrat; other managers complained subsequently that 'he never spoke to us'. Unable to share his problems, he became increasingly unable to cope. Freddie Laker, too, is described by the receiver as 'very much a one-man band, an innovative autocrat surrounded by yes-men'. A benevolent autocrat, Laker inspired intense loyalty in those who worked for him. Paradoxically, that loyalty was what blinded them to the seriousness of the company's problems, and prevented them from speaking out more strongly in favour of caution.

A major problem with strong one-boss leadership is the power vacuum that can result when that person leaves. Alfred Herbert is a case in point. The founder, Sir Alfred Herbert, ruled with such solitary vigour that middle management never gained the necessary experience to take over the reins. Without a strong successor, the firm went into decline shortly after Herbert's death.

A powerful but ineffectual leader is perhaps the most damaging. Wadsted provides the ultimate example in the managing director of a furniture manufacturer who spent more time on the golf course and at his mistress's flat than running the business. Although uninvolved with the business the MD remained the dominant member on the board. The financial director did what he was told, as did the rest of the board – to the extent of putting the green fees and the flat on the company tab.

Weak leadership, on the other hand, opens the organization to politics, indecision and an equal blindness to reality, as everyone attempts to avoid facing up to the unpalatable. Of these ailments, probably the most serious is indecision.

Wilbert Scheer, editor of the US newsletter *Human Resources Update*, reports a study of deposed corporation presidents, which found that most were vulnerable because of three weaknesses in their personal style of leadership:

* a tendency to placate and patronize disgruntled employees
* a reluctance to fire executives who oppose them
* a feeling of being invincible or at least indispensable.

This would also be an apt description of many of the CEOs of our failed company cases.

American company doctor Q.T.Wiles describes a typical situation in companies he takes on:

Most of these companies had been growing at 35% and 40% a year for a number of years, and all they knew was a growing market. Now, they've hit a flat market or a down market, and they aren't equipped for that, emotionally and otherwise. The organization, more often than not, is still the CEO and a bunch of helpers versus a genuine management team, and they have no idea how to handle the situation.

The first problem is that he underestimates the size of the problem. Rather than say to himself, 'What different management style do I need?' he says, 'How am I going to work harder in the same style I've always had?' And hell, there isn't any time for him to work harder – he is already working eighteen hours a day.

And then he hits the second problem. The company's going down, and he's faced with a series of decisions that look very hard

43

and painful for him to make. Maybe he's going to have to make some lay offs. Maybe he is going to have to fire some of his top people – people who've been with him from the beginning. Maybe he's going to have to pull the plug on a new product. But he can't do those things – emotionally, I'm speaking now – so he vacillates, or he tries to avoid them by trying other things, and that only makes things worse.

They don't see their own weaknesses, and so they can't go to work on the things that they are weak at. Remember, these are guys who start companies that go from zero to $100 million in three years. How could they be wrong? ...

They really don't want to be CEOs. They're having so much fun being the Chief Operating Officer that they don't recognize there is another job up there as the company grows. They like the operating jobs they have, but since CEO looks like the biggest job, they think they ought to do that.

'Often it's just a case of square pegs in round holes,' says Walker. 'An individual may be able to run a successful large company because others take care of running the various functions. But if the same person had to be a jack-of-all-trades in a smaller business, he'd fail.' Fortunately, there are more success stories the other way round, as many small entrepreneurs learn to delegate and to grow with their firms.

'By far and away the most frequent cause of business failure is management incompetence,' he adds. 'Many people make excellent employees, but should not try to run a business. The computer industry in particular is full of people who could write the programme to make ice cream, but couldn't sell it to starving people in the desert.'

A third area of team failure is an imbalance in the backgrounds, abilities and characters of the key players.

You may at this point argue, with some justice, that leadership is a skill rather than an attitude. But different styles of leadership predicate different types of attitude towards the executive role. The autocrat, for example, assumes that he knows better than the world at large – and is not uncommonly right. His problems arise when he is wrong, but unable to admit it. The weak manager is unable to accept – emotionally, if not intellectually – that he has a responsibility to be decisive and to make tough decisions. The members of the unbalanced team tend to assume that the demands of their own functions are most important to the organization's success and so they regard the interlocking of functions as at best a secondary issue; they fail to see the power that comes from subordinating the goals of all the individual departments, including their own, to the greater goal of the business as a whole.

The importance of sharing

Some of the key 'team' questions to be asked in any business must include:

* How do the top team members view their roles? Do they truly share responsibility and a sense of ownership of the vision? Do they have the authority and support to do so?
* How do they view the rest of the employees? Are they, too, invited to share in the excitement? Do they, too, have the authority and support to do so?

Many of the executive teams behaved corporately as if they were autocrats. They failed to communicate to other employees, often to the extent that no one else knew that the company was in serious trouble.

Walker provides an extreme example of the furniture manufacturer, employing about fifteen people, whose CEO only first spoke to them en masse on the day he came with the receiver to dismiss them.

In some cases, the CEO's refusal to share extended to their relationship with other top team members. Hoarding information became another tactic in the politics of survival, usually at the expense of the business as a whole.

Inevitably, those companies, where top management has not been able to share the good times, find it difficult to 'share' their problems. Usually, managers are unable or unwilling to talk about them, let alone ask people for their constructive ideas and support. The top team continues to take the burden and, as the weight increases, slowly buckles under.

Insolvency practitioners agree that it is futile, and possibly counter-productive, to attempt to hide the company's problems from the staff.

According to one senior manager at a major insolvency firm:

'The working man is generally far more astute than people give him credit for. There is no point pretending – the guys on the shop floor know when there's something wrong. The symptoms

occur every which way: in the factory they see supplies not
delivered, in the office they see the accountant snowed under with
phone calls from irate creditors.'

'So many companies have gone bust in the last ten years that
in any given firm there will invariably be someone who has seen
it before, especially in industries like the motor trade and
construction where insolvencies are commonplace.'

'It is generally preferable to keep the employees informed.
Handled well, you may get the co-operation and commitment you
need to get through a bad patch. Handling it badly or being
secretive can make things worse. If you tell the employees certain
information is confidential, chances are they'll treat it as such. If
they aren't told, and discover it of their own accord, they are more
likely to discuss it outside the company,' he says.

Sometimes these situations arise simply because of the characters of
the key people. But there are other causes, too – one of the most
common being that companies go through transition points that
demand a new style of management, which the incumbents may be
incapable of adapting to. For example, the management style
appropriate for a small organization where everyone knows everyone
else may not be right for a professionally managed enterprise. As
an ACAS official Chris Jones told the *Financial Times* (Jan. 24, 1989:
'A nightmare which must be confronted'):

'When a company has fewer than fifty people the boss knows everyone. Most companies of that size are not unionized and the company
is like a family. But once the company grows to 150–200 employees,
the boss can't cope, people are treated inconsistently and jealousies
develop.'

Most investment institutions say they look closely at the teams
in which they invest. But the number of failures suggests that the
examination is not as thorough as it might be. We suggest that the
viable management team needs both *balances* and *competences*.

The balances will include:

* functional disciplines (with the financial director having at least
  as much authority as say, sales or production, but not too much
  more)
* character types (particularly with a view to balancing entrepreneurial vision with pragmatism)

* experience in the industry with experience elsewhere (but with at least one very experienced 'old hand').

The competences will include:

* communications skills (listening as well as talking/presenting)
* analytical skills (essential for convincing the holder of a vision that the vision is flawed)
* other basic leadership skills, such as objective setting and personal discipline and, of course,
* team-building skills (both within the top team and throughout the next layers of the organization).

Few executive teams, or the people in them, have a perfect combination of talents. But the better the mix, the less likely the company is to make serious mistakes and the more likely it is to tackle effectively those it does make.

ATTITUDES TOWARDS CUSTOMERS AND MARKETS

Managers of failing companies typically exhibit one or both of two fundamentally destructive attitudes towards their customers and markets. Both start from an assumption that they know the business they are in. To a certain extent this must be true; it is difficult to work five, ten or twenty years in a business sector without gaining some intuitive understanding of how it works. The problems arise when managers make the next leap of logic to assume that they really understand what their customers think and feel and how their markets behave and therefore do not need to inquire into or to test their assumptions. Unfortunately, all too often those assumptions turn out either to have been wrong in the first place or to have become obsolete as customer preferences change or as new competitors enter the market.

Take the case of a very successful company, Allied Dunbar. Convinced, because everyone in the organization 'knew' it, that most sales came from existing customers, the life insurance company built its marketing activities to a large extent around that assumption. Says founder Sir Mark Weinberg: 'On training courses we had always told our salesmen that the best prospects for new business were existing customers. Everyone believed we did a lot of repeat business. But it wasn't true. The research showed that on average people had only 1.06 policies with us.'

Arrogance, stupidity and fear may all be root causes of this 'selective seeing'. Whatever its origins, it reinforces the attitudes that gave rise to it, because feedback is largely restricted to data that supports the particular set of prejudices management has adopted. Data that does not fit the mould is often dismissed as faulty or irrelevant.

Computer manufacturer ICL, a company that had to be rescued several times within two decades, suffered from this problem. Like most computer companies of the time, explains Bob Downey, marketing director for ICL UK: 'We were technology led. We built better boxes expecting the customer to buy them. There was little contact between customers and product development. We talked of "throwing new products over the wall".'

To put the two attitude sets here into their simplest terms, we can call them:

* unwillingness to listen to customers
* unwillingness to explore and question the nature of the markets they are in.

Examples of the former include:

One of the most important lessons learnt by Richard Hay from the near-failure of his hi-fi distribution company Ion Systems was to listen to customers' complaints. 'You must be aware of the criticism being made about your products. If you don't get it, go out and seek it. Without it you will drive merrily along heading for disaster.'

A similar story is attached to the severe problems at Norsk Data, Norway's biggest computer systems company. As *Eurobusiness* expressed it in March 1989: 'founder and mentor Rolf Skaar could do no wrong. Now he is fighting to save the company's life – all because he was too arrogant to see that, although his systems were technically better than his rivals', they were not what the market wanted ... Norsk Data failed to heed the demands of its customers that computers and systems be able to operate such open international standards as DOS or Unix. This would have made them compatible with machines bought from other producers.

'Mr Skaar looked at the market and concluded that the company's own Sintran software was the better product. So he decided to continue producing only proprietary systems.'

The market told him he was wrong in the firmest way it could. The company's order book took a nose-dive, a six-year track record of steadily increasing profits was exchanged for an NKr 871 million loss on sales of just under NKr 3 billion. The company's saving grace lay in its low gearing and the fact that it had put aside some NKr 1.8 billion for a rainy day. But 20 per cent of the workforce had to be laid off.

At the other extreme, managers can be *too* concerned with what their customers might think, yet still unwilling to test whether their assumptions hold water. Reports a management consultant: 'One of our clients has a major product launch. The product is based on a particular technological solution and represents a lot of development effort. But now it is clear that there is a better technology. The trouble is, having made such a song and dance about the original technology, he is afraid of losing face in the market by making a switch. So he is hanging on tooth and nail to the original approach in order not to give way on this psychologically important aspect of the product and in doing so is jeopardizing the whole company.'

Examples of unwillingness to explore and question the nature of the markets they are in include Dragon, which could not come to grips with the fact that it was in the expensive toy business, even though its parent was a toy company. So it wasn't prepared for the collapse of the boom. Even operating as a computer company it failed to understand that the market demanded continuous product innovation to survive. Raleigh only just managed to save itself from disaster when it recognized belatedly that the keep fit cycling boom in the United States was a brief-lived fad. Sports shoe company Reebok found itself in much the same situation when the aerobics bubble, on which its sales were heavily dependent, suddenly burst.

Another company, selling a single product to builders merchants, was caught in the recent building slump with a warehouse full of worthless stock. Although it should have been obvious that high interest rates would lead to a drop in home starts, management had forecast blindly on the basis of previous sales, failing to take into account changing economic conditions.

Often in highly diverse or fragmented markets, such as software or fast food, companies will shift from one segment to another without appreciating that they have entered a completely different market. Compsoft is a case in point. The firm's first product was sold successfully to end-users in small businesses. Subsequent products were suited to corporate accountants and trainers respectively. These were three completely disparate markets yet Compsoft management remained blissfully unaware that they had overstepped the boundaries of the first market.

Understanding the market also means monitoring the 'S' curve, which measures effectiveness of investment against the benefits over time. In the early days, the cost of research and development will make the payback small and usually negative. After a period of time, the new concept takes off, and there is a boom and rapid growth. Eventually, the market plateaus and begins to decline. Unless a company has some idea where on the 'S' curve its products or services rest, it can make very damaging decisions about where to put its investment. One of the clearest lessons of the 'S' curve is that companies should normally begin to diversify towards the top of the curve – the very time when all attention is normally focused on increasing capacity to cope with demand. By the time the plateau and decline comes, everyone else in the market is also scrambling for diversifications against a background of declining margins and less money to invest.

In theory, the smaller business should find it easier both to define what business it is in and to listen to its customers. What stops it doing so is usually either lack of resources or management intransigence. The bigger company has more resources, but may also have greater impediments, not least the bureaucracy involved in running the organization. The problem with bureaucracy is not simply that it reduces efficiency and adds to costs, but that it gets in the way of being market-responsive. As an article in *Management Today* expressed it ('How Businesses Bust Themselves', July 1986):

> Businesses go to the wall because of maladministration – and not just the small ones. One retail chain, a subsidiary of a major UK group, was turning in a modest trading profit each year. But the annual head office 'management charge' wiped out that profit almost to the last penny. So the retail chain made its money by selling off one or two outlets each year. Recognizable? It's not

an isolated example. In this case, the head office was so far away from the sharp end that it imposed hefty administrative tasks on the retailers so that it knew, or thought it knew, what was happening out there in the world.

But, of course, it didn't. The information flow through the admin system was irrelevant to the needs of retailing. It was used for the control of retailers by non-retailers who happened to run the bigger group. The chain is now being bought out by the managers and will, it is confidently predicted, do extremely well without the burden of the old man of the sea on their shoulders.

Of course, this needn't have happened. In this case, the group management hadn't even tried to relate the market environment, in which the chain was operating, to the main activities it had to carry out, and hence to the information that was essential to keep the business in a high state of tune.

How then, can investors identify managers with a 'good' attitude towards customers and markets? Ideally they should have:

* an acceptance that listening to customers, personally, is an important part of every manager's (and employee's) job and that the CEO must set the example in creating listening opportunities
* a strong interest in the behaviour and nature of existing and potential competitors (just how much insight do their competitor analyses show?)
* experience of (and interest in) more than just the industry in question – the best marketing innovations usually come from another sector.

ATTITUDES TOWARDS INVESTORS

'When I asked Freddie Laker why he went bust, he said: "I was borrowing money from thirty leading banks. How could they all be wrong? I'm only a simple businessman."
–Christopher Morris, Touche Ross.

This is a short section, for the simple reason that most of what can

be said is fairly obvious. Many entrepreneurs seem unable to understand the motivations and concerns of the institutions that buy an
equity stake in their business or loan them the cash to exploit their
ambitious ideas. It never seems to occur to them to put themselves
in the investors' shoes.

The basic question, 'What do investors want?' can be answered
on two levels. On the overt level, it is clear that they require:

* rapid growth in profit (with or without growth in turnover)
* the ability to extract themselves from the company as early as
  possible (while they may not exercise that ability until much
  later, most institutions have a justifiable fear of having their
  cash locked into situations from which they cannot retrieve it)
* minimal risk (while that may not seem commensurate with the
  concept of venturing, from a sheer practical viewpoint, it is an
  essential element of investment management)

If the entrepreneur cannot accept these objectives and work within
them, he should not be seeking institutional finance. Better to find
a private investor willing to take a longer term perspective – a 'guardian angel'.

On a more covert level, investors seek:

* confidence (they need to be reassured that the business is solvent,
  growing and saleable)
* peer recognition (their own careers depend to a considerable
  extent upon association with success)
* a hassle-free working environment (tolerance towards people
  who create headaches for them is low, because it interrupts the
  pursuit of tomorrow's deal).

Sometimes the problems between investors and client companies arise
from the shared distress when over-optimistic plans fail to work out.
Explains 3i's Geoff Taylor: 'People who start small companies have
to be optimistic; so do we. We tend to egg each other on. On the
other hand, if the investor is pessimistic, the entrepreneur sees him
as negative and does not want to do business with him. It's a difficult
balance to keep.'

When banks and investment companies say that they do not wish
to be closely involved in running the company, that they take a hands-
off approach, they normally mean just that. But they also have to

ensure that their objectives are met and they will become involved if they have cause for concern.

That involvement is not always benign. In several of our case studies, the appointment of people from institutions into the executive management of organizations has been disastrous – not least because the institution's objectives are so different from those of the company itself. Only a healthy company can satisfy two sets of management objectives at once, and that for no more than a short period.

The managers' objective may be very different. For example, they may have their eyes on:

* steady but modest growth in profit, with the freedom to dip in profitability when necessary, for medium- to long-term objectives
* long-term, stable commitment
* minimal risk (particularly on a personal level)
* freedom from control; freedom to manage the business towards their vision
* the opportunity to extract themselves with a large cash sum in the longer term.

The differences in objectives not unnaturally lead to differences in attitude. In some cases these can be extreme. For example, the top management team in one of our case studies clearly regarded the investors as a source of constant handouts and could not understand the recommendation by consultants and auditors not to put any more money into the business.

In effect, what happened there – and happens so often in other companies – is that top management assumes everyone else involved in the enterprise shares their vision and their enthusiasm. As we shall see in the section on attitudes towards winning, they have allowed themselves to become too involved with the product at the expense of the business. While it is rare for a top management team to be completely dispassionate about the product (and presumably this would not be a healthy sign), it is important to maintain sufficient balance so that they can step outside their personal enthusiasm and see the company and its products from an outsiders' perspective.

In doing so, it becomes much easier to meet the investors' objectives without necessarily compromising those of the business. In many cases, all that is needed is a close attention to sensibilities. In particular:

- Demonstrable financial caution. When the receiver arrived at Dragon, he found that the car park was full of BMWs and Audis. Because merchant banks tend to entertain in grand style, it is easy for the entrepreneur to assume he has to run his company in the same way. In reality, extravagant behaviour will rapidly damage investor confidence. Far better to emphasize frugality and dedication, on the grounds that every penny unspent, is a penny nearer releasing the company from its financial obligations.

- Keep the investors informed. Having to chase for information indicates to the institution either that the control systems are inadequate or that the managers do not trust them. Once again, this damages confidence.

The CBI–City–Industry Task Force in 1987 recommended that companies should be 'making more effort themselves to keep the market informed about their longer-term strategic intentions and in particular about spending on research and development, as well as training and other aspects of innovation . . .'

- Don't make sudden changes of direction without warning. One start-up publishing venture we encountered changed the positioning of its product three times in six months. The managers were surprised when they ran out of money and couldn't persuade the backers to advance more.

If the business concept does turn out to have a flaw, it is important to discuss the problem with investors as early as possible, while there is still time to pull funds behind a revised strategy. The further down the track the business is, the greater the likelihood that investors will choose to withdraw.

- Look for early successes in the areas that matter to investors. Opening a US office, or making a technical breakthrough may be impressive to people in your business sector, but not necessarily to the investors. Reducing costs, raising margins or increasing cash flow in key areas of the business will be far more likely to bring a sparkle to their eyes.

Of course, the managers cannot normally afford to make the investors' priorities their own. Again, what is required is a balance of interests. If that balance is disturbed, then the potential for disaster increases.

ATTITUDES TOWARDS LEARNING

Less than one in three executives of failed companies learns from the experience – survey result.

The results of our survey (see page 79–87) show clearly that people who have presided over the disintegration and collapse of a company usually do not learn from their mistakes. Rather, they seek to place the blame elsewhere – on the unions, the banks, the government or the market – as if these were malevolent forces ranged against them. Rare indeed is the manager who will bluntly say: 'These are the mistakes I made; and these are the lessons I have learned from them.'

Every company goes through crises. In its early years, these are likely to come thick and fast, particularly if the company is growing rapidly. Change is too swift and experienced people are too few to predict and forestall all the likely problems. Tom Ahrens' study of high-growth companies in Sweden shows that a significant proportion of issues that would be dealt with automatically in established, mature companies, simply never make it to the top of the priority list in organizations whose main focus is keeping pace with growth. This is not necessarily a bad thing. On the contrary, attending to many of these issues, such as formal job structures, would have the immediate effect of slowing growth and making the company mature before its time. Ahrens points out that many companies create their own growth plateaux by assuming that, as they become bigger, they must emulate the structures, procedures and behaviours of other large companies. As soon as they do so, they lose the very vehicles that allow them to continue rapid growth – flexibility, entrepreneurial attitudes and a focus on customers rather than on internal procedures.

On the other hand, the company that is overly focused on external issues lays itself open to problems of control. Somehow, top management has to exercise a balance between these pressures, investing enough time and energy into systems and controls to avoid major crises, while not allowing them to restrain the capacity to continue growth.

According to Walker, many businesses fail because management focuses on external issues to the detriment of control. 'There are two things involved in running a business,' he says, 'producing the product or service, and running the business. Too many people concentrate on doing the job, to the detriment of running the business.'

'Most are quite skilled at "the job", as they have invariably been in a similar business as an employee. What they lack is the financial ability needed to run a business.'

'In every case when things go bad the controls and paperwork fall behind. One decorator went insolvent, and hadn't issued an invoice for months. She was so tied up trying to get the work done, she couldn't collect the money.'

The most serious danger points arise, explains Ahrens, when growth dips or plateaus. At that stage the headlong rush for growth becomes a liability. Not only does the juggernaut take time to stop, along with all the outgoings associated with growth-orientation, but people in the company are not prepared mentally or in any other way for a totally different operating environment – one where an internal focus on costs, controls and systems now assumes much greater significance. Ahrens' study suggests that most high-growth companies fail or are taken over when they meet a crisis they cannot handle. Very, very few recover the knack of high-growth thereafter, because new management almost always bureaucratizes the organization and most of the entrepreneurially-minded people leave within a period of two to three years.

One major reason why companies – high-growth or not – do not survive the major crisis, we believe, is because they have not used the opportunities to learn from the multitude of smaller crises that have preceded them. Most companies caught in the over-capacity trap (investing in expensive plant and people for a market that doesn't grow as fast as expected, or which becomes saturated by product from other sources) have had warning signs, small dips in demand that should have made them at least a little cautious; enough to have developed precautionary plans. These minor tremors before the big quake can easily be ignored as mere blips in the fulfilment of an otherwise unmarred dream.

Why do people ignore the opportunities to learn? There are numerous potential reasons, most or all of which can be detected in our cases. Among them:

* sheer arrogance: 'I know all there is to know about this business. After all, we are the market leaders ...'
* fear: 'Things are going all right at the moment. I don't want to turn up any more gremlins ...'
* over-confidence: 'We've always coped before. We're very good at handling crisis ...'
* lack of confidence in their own ability to extract the correct lessons: 'This could be too big an issue for me to take on ...'
* lack of interest: 'I've no time to spend on yesterday's problems. I'm more concerned about how we deal with this next big order ...'

Once again, these problems are all to do with management attitude. In part, it brings us back to the issue of leadership style. One of the distinctions between leader and manager is that the manager asks 'Why?', while the leader asks 'Why not?' But sometimes it is important to ask why, to establish what happened and how and to extrapolate what the effects might be if it happened again, more seriously. The role of the leader is often to ignore potential obstacles; that of the manager to plan routes round them. That is another reason why the ideal CEO is capable of playing the roles of both manager and leader, sometimes simultaneously.

This curious but very human reluctance to take experience on board extends to external events, too. The delight, with which managers often view the troubles of their competitors, is rarely tempered with the thought that this should prompt a review of their own company's position. While some banks were stinging publicly from defaults on Third World loans, for example, competitors continued to pump out money to similarly indigent nations on the assumption that they were somehow smarter.

Is this attitude to business learning a reflection of a larger problem, a feeling that learning is hard work, dull and thus to be avoided? Ask most people what they enjoyed most about their schooldays and few will mention the learning they did. Do we therefore bring to work situations an in-built apathy towards learning? Certainly, it is noticeable that increasing numbers of companies are now spending time and money to teach managers how to learn, how to understand their own learning styles and how to use them as a prerequisite for attending senior-level training courses.

We believe that a positive attitude to learning – whether from analysis of experience and observation or from formalized tuition – is an essential requirement of the effective executive. The scope of learning may be relatively narrow but should at least extend to the industry that the company operates in. In general, the more senior the manager, the wider the learning scope should be. He cannot produce meaningful strategic plans, based on an understanding of both the internal and external environment, unless it is suitably wide. Inevitably, this breadth of scope requires a trade-off in depth, but that should be compensated for by managers at lower levels.

The attitude towards learning may often be revealed by the organization chart. Does it emphasize structure and order? Or flexibility and getting things done? Does it surround the CEO with people who will support his ideas? Or with people who will challenge them? Investors looking at requests for venture capital might well start by examining whether the proposed or existing organization is structured to encourage or discourage learning. After all, if a CEO will not learn from his own experiences, how likely is he to accept willingly and act upon good advice from his financial backers? A willing learner is presumably many times safer as an investment project than an unwilling one.

Within our case studies, there are very few examples of entrepreneurs who have learned significantly from their experience. The majority tend to reject evidence of failure, or look for some outside factor to blame. One company had £1 million in outstanding writs when the receivers were called in, but to this day the accountant maintains he could have got out of that situation if the receivers hadn't been called in.

On the other hand, Dragon's managers didn't think they had anything to learn from other people's experience. They ignored advice to stop manufacturing, for example, because they did not want to hear it. This was, after all, a manufacturing company. The board of Tube Investments (now TI Group) kept pumping money into factory improvements at Raleigh although all the experience of the previous twenty years had shown that this had no significant impact on profitability.

Others repeat old errors even in the belief that they are entering new ground. Compsoft management, after a failure in a new geographical market, launched rapidly into new product markets.

Moreover, some companies encompass the supreme arrogance of preaching to others what they do not practise themselves. The Alfred Herbert sales force, for example, sold customers on the competitive advantages of up-to-date equipment while much of Alfred Herbert's own machinery was over twenty years old.

ATTITUDES TOWARDS WINNING

'If there is a single characteristic which is found in all of our successful companies, in most cases to an outstanding degree, it is the overwhelming commitment to winning.'
– *The Winning Streak*.

Teams with a winning orientation know what they want to do (they have clear, shared vision), have the drive and energy to do it and regard setbacks as mere obstacles to be overcome, and therefore to be openly debated and resolved rapidly. They tackle setbacks head-on, immediately.

Taken to excess, the winning orientation can be disastrous. Some managers get to enjoy dealing with crisis so much that they manufacture them just to keep the flow of adrenalin going. They can also end up so focused on dealing with crisis that they lose the larger perspective. Coupled with a healthy attitude towards controls, vision and customers, however, a winning orientation can make all the difference. It's all a matter of balance, as management consultant Arnold Goldstein explains: 'Managerial failure can be summarized as being the result of extremes: too much ambition or too little, too much emphasis on centralized control or too little, an overly powerful CEO or one who is a benign figurehead.'

Teams with a losing orientation (in truth, they rarely operate as genuine teams anyway) are not really sure what they are in business for, would prefer a quiet life to an eventful one (although they may still work inordinately long hours) and tend to bury problems rather than face them. To give themselves breathing space (a euphemism for hoping the storm will pass while they take shelter), they often commission market research and consultancy studies. As Lewis Robertson, chairman of Borthwicks, describes it: 'Indecision is the single biggest cause of corporate trouble. Every case I tackle has been an illustration of management failure ... caused by a feeling of helplessness, inadequacy and not knowing what is the best thing to do. A lot of people take refuge from that in piling up additional information far beyond what they really need to make the decision.'

If members of teams with a losing orientation don't like the message from these reports, they put them aside for consideration and discussion by a committee – a guaranteed method of ensuring the issue stays buried for at least a few months more. If this sounds like playing politics, it is no coincidence. Teams that bring companies to the brink are characterized by an excessive degree of internal politicking, brought about at least in part by people's desire to avoid shouldering the guilt (and/or blame) for the company's consistent failure to perform.

Had the board of Dunlop truly been in business to win, for example, it would have taken decisive action much earlier about its tyre businesses and about the union with Pirelli. Top management's attention was so focused on peripheral issues, such as trying to make the merger work (then how to get rid of it), that it did not focus sufficiently on the primary business issues. Had it done so, it might have recognized the necessity earlier to get out of tyres and concentrate on the rest of the businesses, which were basically very healthy. But the top management was more interested in the company's glorious traditions than in winning. Whether through arrogance, short-sightedness or lack of courage it could not countenance cutting off its past. So it brought both the old and the new businesses to the edge of bankruptcy.

Other companies hang on to unprofitable products, markets and locations for sentimental or symbolic reasons. For example, the Alfred Herbert board insisted on keeping the out-moded and cash-draining Coventry site operating, simply because Coventry had been the company headquarters since inception.

Contrast this with the pro-active behaviour of consumer electronics company Amstrad, which took the tough decision to close its audio division in Southend in late 1989 after a sudden drop in its profits. The division was the original core of the company. A less determined management might have spent years searching for ways to save it. But top management at Amstrad recognized that this would not only involve continual diversion of cash flow into an area of the business unlikely to show rapid growth again, but would also require an increasing proportion of executive time. The difference between sticking to the knitting and hanging on in sentiment may be subtle, but it is vital within a fast-changing business.

Dragon's managers present a different aspect of the same problem. They were so busy basking in the opportunities for public relations, telling the world about the success of their company, that they failed to notice it was crumbling about them.

The winning attitude shines through most strongly in adversity. Managers out to win show grim determination, focusing their energy on key problems, enlisting (indeed demanding) help from any source they value and mobilizing all the resources they can to put the company back on course. They are shameless in subverting anything and everything around them to the business goal.

Managers with the losing attitude are far more concerned with saving face. They are often status conscious. They have a stronger commitment to their own egos than to the business goal. (This is perhaps the real significance of the personalized number plates and pictures of them shaking hands with the Prime Minister.) Their vision is personal, not corporate – hence the difficulty they often have in sharing it with others. Because they cannot share their vision and are afraid of losing face, they fail to share their problems with colleagues, investors, auditors, customers and suppliers – all of whom could help, if only they were involved in the right manner.

The emphasis on status is not always obvious. One frequently subtle manifestation is an obsession with the latest technology. Does a company invest in the latest portable telephones and computer systems because it provides a significant cost or market advantage or because it satisfies the executives' longing to be seen as modern, forward-thinking and dynamic? Most managers who pursue this path can provide ample rationalization, in hindsight, for these purchases. The key question is: was the need identified before or after the proposal to buy?

Do managers change from winning to losing and/or vice versa? We have not identified any examples of the latter in our case studies, although there is evidence elsewhere to suggest that a certain type of high-risk entrepreneur may go through several cycles of rags to riches during his career. (We say *his* deliberately – this appears to be an exclusively male phenomenon.) However, the consensus among receivers and investors in our survey appears to be that many entrepreneurs lose their commitment to winning as their circumstances change. It may be the result of age and maturity, the gradual grinding down of spirit over the years that makes managers give up the fight. Or it may simply be that their personal ambitions for wealth have been met sufficiently to blunt their appetite for constant challenge. Why not settle for the bronze or silver medal, when the gold demands so much continued exceptional effort?

Some business people quite legitimately recognize when the time has come to move on. The entrepreneur who thrives on the challenge of a start-up may recognize that he lacks either the competency or the motivation to run a stable, mature business. Sir Clive Sinclair, for example, chose to leave the maturing home computer market so he could focus on other research. Says Sir Clive: 'I have always seen my role as an innovator, initiating markets. I have never seen my businesses as mature businesses.'

Or it may be simple boredom. Having slain dragons before, the knight errant may be forgiven for seeking new challenges. Is it really coincidence, for example, that Sir Campbell Fraser lost his job as president of Dunlop so soon after becoming president of the CBI? Entrepreneurs with the winning attitude never have enough time in the day to stop thinking about their own business. They avoid time-consuming external activities, such as multiple non-executive directorships elsewhere or posts in industrial talking shops – for the simple reason that their own business is too demanding on its own. When these external activities become a major part of the CEO's workload, it is a sign that his commitment, his devotion to achieving the business goal, is being dissipated.

PART III
Pulling the plug

'I don't think managers have ever been educated to expect a receiver'
– Christopher Morris

'The management practices that can cure a company could have kept it well'
– John O. Whitney, visiting professor and executive in residence at Columbia University's Graduate School of Business

At some point in the downward career of a troubled company someone calls a halt. It may be parent company management, the bank, an unpaid supplier, the Inland Revenue or the Customs and Excise – the latter three in particular, because financially troubled companies almost invariably end up juggling cash flow between creditors. Although most small businesses, being underfunded for capital, tend to use credit for cash flow to some extent, a high degree of 'creative cash flow diversion' is a clear sign of a company in substantial danger of going under.

What tips the balance from concern into crisis is far from clear. There seems to be little pattern to this stage in either our case studies or those discussed elsewhere, other than that the business runs out of funds. Some go under with relatively small debts and with apparent potential to turn to profit with patient nursing. As a former board member said of Alfred Herbert: 'The firm was profitable. It just ran out of money.' Others continue to rack up bigger and bigger debts until it takes the removal of just one tin from the bottom of the pile to bring the lot crashing down. The case of Homes Assured illustrates the latter. In nineteen months, the winding up hearing in the High Court heard, it had income of £3.4 million, and costs of £9.6 million. Remarkably, creditors allowed the debts to grow and grow until finally Criterion insurance lost patience when it was owed £750,000. In the case of Microblade, a manufacturer of industrial

63

blades, the trigger was the refusal of key suppliers to deliver any more raw materials until previous bills were paid. A major customer, which relied on Microblade for its own supplies, was forced to step in or lose part of its own product range.

There do, however, appear to be some common behaviours within the troubled companies during this period. The typical case according to Walker might go something like this:

> Top management, finally forced to recognize that things are going badly wrong, takes panic action to control costs. Because it has neither adequate information nor the necessary systems already in place, this action is largely ineffective. The impact of its attempts to control costs is also hindered by a reluctance to talk about the problems with middle managers and other employees, for fear of 'rats leaving the sinking ship'; or with investors and creditors, for fear that they will react negatively. At best this postpones the problems, making all parties less co-operative and understanding than would have been the case if the company were open and frank about the crisis and what it is doing to overcome it.
>
> Instead, top management develops a siege mentality that gradually pervades the organization. Creditors are met with evasion and subterfuge; large invoices are disputed almost as a matter of course, to delay payment just a few weeks more; managers, who may or may not have spent time planning previously, now spend none on planning at all. Every senior and middle manager works long hours, attempting to fix yesterday's problems, worried sick about today's accumulation and trying desperately not to think about tomorrow's.
>
> The overall impression of all this activity is that it lacks real focus. Everyone is working on bits of the problem, but there is no coherent plan to which everyone subscribes and against which they can evaluate priorities. As a result, the really important moves, such as wiping out loss-making product ranges, which could resolve many of the problems, do not occur, because people cannot achieve the requisite kind of coordinated thinking and action.

What frequently happens at this stage, says Walker, is that directors start to 'look out for themselves'. They have been used to taking their salary and will continue to draw it even when things get very bad. 'In practically every insolvency case, directors will take the PAYE deductions from the employees and not forward them to the Inland Revenue, yet continue to draw director's salaries,' he says.

Once problems arise directors often begin to contravene – as opposed to 'break' – the law, says Walker. 'It's common for directors to have personally guaranteed the bank overdraft, so, when they see the end in sight, they will withhold payments from creditors to minimize the bank overdraft. It's a fraudulent preference, which they will be forced to repay.'

This behaviour adds to the sense of secrecy at the top. Explains Walker: 'Once people start to run into problems they try to hide and don't seek advice from those best able to help them – their accountant, solicitor or banker – because they fear incurring another bill or having their overdraft privileges cut. They really don't know where to go. Few people are aware of it but many professionals will give free advice in times of trouble because it is in their interest to keep you going as well.'

When and if troubled business people do seek advice, he says, 'I can often tell in ten minutes where the problem is, but more often than not it's too late. Had they come six months, or even three months earlier, the company could have been saved.'

The new Insolvency Act of 1986 has gone some way toward changing this situation. Says Walker: 'It is now legal to enter voluntary arrangements with creditors. Enlightened creditors will generally co-operate because the debtor's survival is in their interest. Creditors have two things at stake – the account owed, and future turnover. Many will freeze the outstanding account and only collect the current, or accept a settlement on the outstanding amount, to keep you in business and retain future turnover.'

The new Act has also put more teeth into the 'continuing to trade' clause. Says Walker: 'Directors always could be held personally liable if they continued to trade with a knowledge of insolvency, but now they can be held liable if they continued to trade when a reasonable person would be aware of insolvency. The law is now much easier to enforce, but the real benefit of the change is the way it encourages people to seek professional advice and make arrangements with creditors earlier. If the creditors agree that the business is worth continuing, management cannot be held liable. The company may still fail but at least they have been open with everyone.'

It is perhaps not surprising then that, once the shock of the appointment of a receiver has been taken in, the reaction from many people at all levels within the organization is relief that someone is at last taking charge, making decisions and providing a focus.

Calling a halt doesn't necessarily involve bringing in a receiver. The owners may arrange a merger or a sale to another company that sees significant underlying value in the troubled operation (or more likely in parts of it that can be fitted into current operations). Or it may mean refinancing, usually under a different management, as happened, for example, at model-railway makers Hornby, where the original management buyout team lost almost everything when its market underwent a temporary but severe downturn at the most inconvenient time. In such cases, the prime concern of owners and investors will be to evaluate the likely return from keeping the business going, albeit perhaps with radical surgery, against the costs or losses of closing it down. Almost invariably, the top management team insists that the company is viable, if only it can be given more time to sort itself out. Unless they can demonstrate their belief with credible data – for example, significant promises of business over the next year from a number of reliable customers – these managers simply undermine their own position with such unfounded optimism. The degree of realism, with which they face the issues, is (or should be) a significant factor in whether they are retained or fired.

Nor does calling in a receiver necessarily mean that a company is to be wound up. Indeed, compared to a decade ago, this is a far, far less likely outcome. The insolvency profession has undergone considerable change in recent years. Firstly, the number of practitioners has fallen dramatically, as a result of legislation that became effective in 1986. The main thrust of the legislation was to license 'corporate undertakers', effectively putting out of business organizations that used troubled companies as opportunities for asset-stripping. Secondly, as the trade has become more respectable, the number of large accountants with insolvency departments (usually twinned with company doctoring) has increased. Thirdly, the emphasis of receivership has switched from liquidation (once 90 per cent of all cases) to rescue.

Alongside the accountants is a growing army of specialist solicitors, who help companies sort out the legal issues of near or actual insolvency.

Most of the time, receivers are appointed by banks. Investment institutions also refer a considerable proportion of cases, and so do the Inland Revenue and the Customs and Excise. According to a survey by *The Accountant* in early 1987, Barclays Bank has the dubious honour of being the most frequent at calling in the receiver. One of the reasons, said a Barclays spokesman, was that: 'We don't want to see businesses go bust, or job losses. We feel it is better to put in a receiver in order to run the business as a going concern, rather than let matters drag on and end up in non-trading liquidation.' A number of insolvency specialists support this view, pointing out that around half of their workload is in 'pre-insolvency work' – turning the crisis-ridden company around. A spokesman for accountants Grant Thornton claims in the article that less than half the companies investigated in this way actually go under.

Most large banks and many investment institutions also have company doctor departments. Investors in Industry (3i), for example, has a 'special management unit' with twelve people which second chief executives to struggling companies for six months or a year. Hambros Bank also has an industrial management team under the control of rescue veteran Sir Ian Morrow. The credentials of the company doctors are generally impressive. The job necessitates a broad range of experience. At 3i, the rescue team are all over fifty with at least two managing directorships to their name. One of the foremost company doctors, John Briggs, former chief executive of Norcros, has dealt with twenty ailing companies and at one time was chairman of a grand total of seventy-eight.

So what happens when the receiver goes in? And what do they typically find? A typical assignment may start, says Christopher Morris of Touche Ross, with:

> a letter of instruction from a bank asking us to make an assessment. We get someone outside the team to look at the industry itself and what part this company plays in it. Is the industry on its way up, or down?
>
> We'll see the chief executive first, usually at our offices. We get him talking through his cv. Next we draw a group structure chart and establish what all the people do. Then we look at the financial information they produce. We want to know how up to date it is, how accurate, how it is prepared and how quickly we can get our hands on the data we need for analysis.
>
> Then we ask him to describe the problems as he sees them. His response can vary from 'Thank God I can share this with someone'

to 'I don't think this is necessary. I've been running this business for twenty years; what can you tell me?'

Sometimes people who purport at the beginning to be extremely helpful turn out to be dishonest. We learn to be suspicious of the person who is immediately co-operative and on Christian name terms and who turns his office over to us. The genuine people find it distasteful, but recognize the need for it.

There's always a debate about how much it will cost: 'The last thing I want is a big bill from the accountants.' If the company has a good financial administrator, however, he can do most of the work.

Nine times out of ten they have not asked the key questions such as:

* What is the forecasting record like? They may have got it wrong for several years but never asked themselves how to improve it.
* How will we use our borrowings? A lot of assessments are based upon requests for more money. But they often can't say why they need it or how they will pay it back.
* Why are credit sales rising and cash sales falling?
* Why have debtors gone up?
* How much of our stock is obsolete?

We ask if they have a five-year plan. Often they just make projections, but don't do anything about what the figures mean. For example, do they need a new building? Management information can vary from a thick document nobody can read to nothing. Or it can be garbage.

Management at this point, although not dishonest as such, can be unrealistically optimistic, says Walker. 'As a general rule if it says the assets are £20,000, they are probably closer to £10,000. If it says the liabilities are £10,000, they are probably £20,000, and they are almost always eternal optimists – there is always a big order coming tomorrow. They lie to themselves, really.'

More often than not, the board has failed to supply the kind of leadership it ought to. Explains Lewis Robertson: 'The board has probably taken a beating and is bewildered and in disarray. Part of the skill is to pick them up and get them moving positively ... The structure of the board is important in avoiding disaster and a good many of the companies who hit the rocks do so because the board of directors does not function as it should. It hasn't questioned or challenged the management, hasn't been strong enough as a policy-making body.'

Adds Morris: 'There may be non-executive directors on the board (all too often they have gone, ostensibly as an economy, but really because they ask awkward questions), but those that remain are hand-picked for their incompetence. They are often local dignitaries, often too keen on their quarterly cash to speak up.'

The first day actually in the plant or offices is often full of drama. Says Morris:

> When we go into our investigations, people in the company often don't know why we are there. We sit a junior person in the canteen to listen. People talk about almost nothing else but business in most canteens. Often we find a complete ignorance of the problem. The first the employees know about it is when their wages cheque bounces.
>
> The intelligent ones will guess when there is a delay in goods arriving. The middle managers are usually very hard-working, too few in number and don't have enough time to lift their heads from the desk to find out what is going on. They have mountainous ashtrays and very impressive ashtrays. We recruit the new management from their ranks wherever we can.
>
> As the receiver we address the workforce. We ask the managing director to introduce us, but many of them can't face it.

Charles Legolas, a consultant specializing in business turnarounds, recalls one company which, having decided to close a manufacturing plant that was losing money, could not find a manager brave enough to tell the employees. Instead, it sent in a twenty-two-year-old graduate to tell the production workers they no longer had jobs – and reportedly kept a car with the engine running at the door of the hall.

Stemming the bleeding

The appointment of an administrator or a receiver gives the troubled company a breathing space. While the creditors are held at bay, the receiver can take a whole new look at the company and decide what, if anything, can be saved and how that can best be done. He can take tough decisions that the top managers, being too close and too emotionally involved with the company, often cannot. Explains Robert Ellis of Touche Ross: 'On the first day you sit opposite a director, he is often aggressive to the receiver. Afterwards he says it was the best thing that could have happened. All the strain has been taken from his shoulders. The receiver can sort things with a much sharper cutting edge than a director. He can hold back the creditors and has the time to focus on ways to get out of the situation.'

Where the decision has been to appoint a 'company doctor' as turnaround manager, there is, of course, less protection from creditors. But the company will often have been given a period of grace through the injection of further funds, either by investors (as in the case of Dragon's first rescue) or by a parent company. The receiver and the company doctor will not have the same view or objectives – the receiver normally acts primarily on behalf of the creditors and has a relatively short-term perspective; the company doctor acts on behalf of the owners and is likely to steer the company until it is healthy enough to bring in a new management team. The company doctor will often also have some choice as to whether he wants to become involved. Says Lewis Robertson: 'Corporate rescue is a form of natural selection; because the banks and the institutions – and, most particularly for he will have his own reputation at stake, the potential rescuer himself – must decide beforehand whether the particular case is, or is probably, worth the effort, and time, and exposure to risk, financial or otherwise.'

Nonetheless, the approach of company doctor and receiver to the rescue when they do take it on, is inevitably very similar. As company doctor Colin Smith of Industrial Evolution Ltd described it in *Strategic Direction* magazine:

A loss-making company faces its moment of truth. It must reassess strategy, management, style, everything. Most often, a new management is first on the list of wholesale changes. But the new CEO – on whom hopes of a turnaround so frequently depend – is pulled two ways: at the same time as needing to understand and assimilate the operating environment and the underlying conditions which have brought about financial crisis, he must above all act fast and decisively without the margin for error which comfortable profitability normally affords.

Even if existing managers stay in place, they are unlikely to find solutions to a sudden and unexpected loss in continuing with the

established order of things. They too must face up to many of
the same issues of change as the turnaround manager brought in
as a specific response to the financial crisis.

The turnaround manager must concentrate his energies on
gaining a rapid grip on affairs, all the while keeping his thinking
flexible and constantly turning his approach to the specific context
of the company.

Stallworthy and Kharbanda emphasize the same point in *Takeovers,
Acquisitions and Mergers*: 'They have to be decisive, make quick
decisions and be strict disciplinarians. The company may be in serious
trouble and unless something is done fast, it is as good as dead.
The options at this point are very limited; there is the possibility
of survival and revival but the action taken has to be immediate
and drastic if it is to succeed.'

Bill Lifka has turned round twenty-three US companies including
Aero-Jet General and Sumna-graphics. He says: 'Basically I follow
the drill I was taught in first-aid training when I was a boy scout.
In this order you deal with bleeding, breathing, bones and shock.
Cash is the lifeblood of the company, so the first thing you do is
stop the money going out.'

This initial focus on cash is natural, given that the crisis that precipi-
tates failure is virtually always a matter of being unable to pay debts.
Mark Homan of Price Waterhouse explains how he and other business
rescuers tackle the problem:

In seeking to re-establish profitability, efforts must be concentrated
initially on the short term. In businesses with diverse product lines
no activity which fails to contribute should feature in the survival
plan. Long-term projects only come into the reckoning once short-
term survival is assured. Avoidable expenditure such as research
and development should be postponed or reduced to a minimum.
A purge will be necessary on all costs which are not essential:
surplus labour will have to be eliminated and overheads reduced.

It really is astonishing how few businesses really know the
contribution achieved from each activity undertaken. Yet often
within a struggling company is a leaner, fitter business waiting
to get out. The need is to identify the activities making a
contribution, which will carry the necessary overheads. Ultimately
a plan needs to be produced showing a total contribution from
the individual activities which covers central overheads and leaves

a profit. Without the capability of profit, the business has no future.

Once the prospect of profit is established, attention can be turned to remedies which will improve the balance sheet and cash flow. Consideration should be given to stock control procedures and whether the company can operate on reduced stock levels; surplus and unproductive fixed assets should be sought out and sold and credit control should be closely monitored to ensure that debt collection is as efficient as possible. Where a diverse company or group of companies is involved, the disposal of peripheral activities should be contemplated; operations which are not mainstream can distract management from their principal tasks and can be a drain on scarce resources.

A similar view comes from John O. Whitney, visiting professor at Columbia University's Graduate School of Business:*

Turnarounds are superb management schools. Everything needs fixing. Nothing is sure except the need to recover. The learning experience is intense. Never again will the turnaround leader assume that customers always buy, vendors always ship, bankers always lend.

In a turnaround, the CEO needs information fast – about the company's cash position and its prospects; about its customers, employees, and competitors; about its control systems and important constituencies. Only then can the decisions that give the company a fighting chance be made. Resources flow to the business units that can secure the company's immediate survival and provide a foundation for profitable growth. The plug gets pulled on those that are draining profits or show poor promise.

Turnaround leaders, however, know that cash is more important to their longevity than their management contracts. (Banks do not like surprises.) They scrutinize the assumptions undergirding each line item in the cash projection. And they ask tough questions that get their financial officers talking to division and function heads. Are purchase orders being cut or contracts signed that aren't reflected in the operations or capital budget? Are sales on plan? Has the marketing department decided on a

* *Harvard Business Review*, September–October 1987, 'Turnaround Management Every Day'.

receivables-dating program to stimulate sales? What's the financial condition of our big customers? Are they taking their discounts?

Successful reorganizations cut costs, open up information flows, and increase mobility. These improvements come from changes in both the organization's structure and its management processes. Structure is represented by the organization chart; process reflects the organization's policies, practices, and values.

During the crisis stage, the turnaround leader changes process without changing structure. Subverting the chain of command and bridging communications channels nourishes a kind of chaos that is useful while the leader is learning firsthand about the organization, its people and its other constituencies.

Although this controlled chaos is effective for a surprisingly long period, ultimately the structure must be realigned to capture and preserve the vitality of crisis management while ending the corrosive stress of disorder. This is usually accomplished by flattening the organization chart and installing an active, hands-on management process.

Cost reduction is the customary justification for flattening the organization chart. But other benefits are even greater. A flat organization presents fewer impediments to the flow of information, reduces the filtering effect of hierarchy, and opens opportunities for a dialogue between senior managers and those close to operations and market information. The shortened chain of command also facilitates mobilization, especially when teams or task forces are used to support key initiatives or changes in direction.

The interest in corporate recovery has led to a spate of studies. One of the most revealing is by Dr Stuart Slatter of London Business School, who identifies ten common turnaround strategies. These are:

Change of management
Most turnarounds require the appointment of a new chief executive. Inadequate top management is the most important factor in decline. Even if it was not a factor, the sacrifice of a scapegoat, albeit innocent, has important symbolic value to outside stakeholders. Most importantly, a new chief executive is needed to carry out the 'reprogramming' – to provide new perceptions of reality, develop new strategies and revitalise the organization.

Not every good manager is good in a turnaround situation. The turnaround man needs special characteristics and skills. All turnaround managers – whether openly abrasive or with the empathetic air of a country vicar – need to be tough and ruthless. Some of the decisions they have to make are likely to be very unpopular and there may be considerable resistance to change within the firm.

Strong central financial control

Strong central financial control is virtually a law of turnaround situations, perhaps not surprising when lack of adequate financial controls is a prime cause of failure. The control needs to be centralized under the new chief executive and his financial director (who himself will often be new). Strict financial controls need to be operational within weeks even if they are not ideal. Centralized, autocratic methods are essential, otherwise the implementation process will take too long.

Organizational change and decentralization

Organizational changes below top management level should not normally be contemplated as a short-term turnaround strategy, as they can cause confusion and direct attention away from the economic problems facing the business.

The only time organizational change should be considered in the short term is:

* to restructure (e.g. into divisions) before selling off part of the business
* to help the new chief executive gain control over key aspects of the business
* to build a new management team in a large firm
* to help decentralize an over-centralized firm.

New product-market focus

It is usually essential that the turnaround firm refocus its overall product-market strategy if sustainable recovery is to take place. A focused strategy involves the firm in selecting a narrow product-market segment in which it competes on the basis of cost leadership and/or product differentiation. The firm concentrates its limited resources on one or a few such segments and withdraws from others. Such a strategy – given the right characteristics in the firm and its industry – can provide sustainable recovery or at least a breathing space.

Improved marketing

Turnaround firms rarely if ever have well-executed marketing plans. Salesforce management is often weak. Installing new, aggressive sales management can often achieve a sudden increase in sales volume, through targetting on key products and key markets.

Pricing is a crucial area for top management attention. Lowering prices is generally dangerous and successful turnarounds are more often characterized by price increases.

Growth via acquisition

Surprising though it may seem, acquisition is quite a common turn-around strategy. It is most commonly used to turn around stagnant firms which are not in financial crisis but whose financial position is poor. The objective is to grow at a faster rate by acquisition than by organic growth.

Asset reduction

An asset reduction strategy is often an integral part of product-market reorientation. As the firm cuts out product lines, customers or whole areas of business, assets are liquidated or divested. It is not uncommon to find a firm having to sell the profitable part of its business in an attempt to survive.

Cost reduction

Cost reduction strategies are aimed at increasing the firm's profit margin and thus, indirectly, at generating increased cash flow. Cost reduction can be strategic or operational, or both. Where it is strategic, its objective is to improve the firm's cost position relative to that of its competitors. Where it is operational, the objective is to improve efficiency and bring overheads in line with volume. The main point to remember is that cost reduction always needs to be more severe than top management believes is necessary. Few companies have ever implemented a cost reduction programme that was too severe.

Investment

As a turnaround strategy, investment occurs most frequently when the turnaround firm has been acquired by a firm with adequate financial resources. Few others have the money for a strategy aimed at reducing costs by spending cash to improve physical plant and equipment or to promote growth either organically or through acquisition.

Debt restructuring and other financial strategies

Debt restructuring involves an agreement between the ailing firm and its creditors, usually the banks, to reschedule and sometimes convert interest and principal payments into other negotiable financial instruments. Short-term debt may be converted into long-term debt, loans into convertible preferred shares or even equity and unpaid interest into yet further loans. The ability of the turnaround firm to raise new capital from banks and investors is largely a function of how the financial institutions assess the new management and the firm's recovery prospects.

Characteristics of successful recovery

Whatever the strategy he adopts, there are two important characteristics of successful recovery situations that the turnaround manager should always bear in mind. First he must implement at least five or six of the ten generic recovery strategies simultaneously. And secondly, he must implement the chosen strategies quite ruthlessly.

Richard Hoffman, writing in the *Journal of General Management*, analyses more than a dozen studies of turnaround management and identifies five common, or generic strategies. These are:

Restructuring the leadership and organization/culture

In many cases (from 33 per cent to 100 per cent according to the various studies), this meant appointing a new chief executive, most likely from outside the company. The most common reasons for doing so were to remove 'a distrustful or autocratic source of decline; inaction – the inability to either recognize or cope with decline; and the need for different skills or information to manage the crisis'.

Hoffman summarizes the character of the turnaround manager that emerges from these studies as 'experience in the firm's industry or a variety of industries, self-confidence, task-orientation, and ability to inspire confidence in others'. Their management style is 'task immersion, being highly visible, and using political skills'.

Turnaround managers, he concludes, 'provide a new, different or more accurate perspective of the situation ... have systematically gathered information on the causes of decline using profit analyses or other statistical studies as well as consultants ... provided a new strategic orientation for the firm [and] developed their own management team via structural and attitude changes'. Successful turnaround attempts were three times as likely to involve restructuring as unsuccessful.

Cost reduction

Says Hoffman: 'Controlling costs seems to be the key to successful turnarounds.' Successful turnaround managers introduce more effective budgetary controls and planning. Hoffman suggests this is often a particularly effective strategy in companies where sales are within 60–80 per cent of break even.

Asset redeployment

This isn't a euphemism for asset-stripping, merely the selling off of assets and shutting down of operations needed for survival. The asset sales release cash to invest in parts of the business that have greater growth potential. Typical areas where this approach works well are 'when the chief causes of downturn include: over-expansion and low capacity use; rapid technological changes in both process and product; or rapid entry of new competitors in the marketplace'.

Selective product/market strategies

Several of the studies indicate that pruning the most unprofitable products has a significant effect. Other turnarounds supplement these defensive moves by offensive strategies that involve 'increasing prices, promotion, quality or customer service'. Hoffman concludes these strategies 'are especially relevant for turnarounds precipitated by over-expansion, external causes of decline stemming from competition, social and technological changes, operating and strategic weaknesses or operating at high capacity with a poor product mix'.

Repositioning strategies

One study in particular found that, in all cases studied, 'the new CEO brought with him a vision of what the firm should be and worked to bring it about'. Repositioning, to attack a different market or a new one from an old angle, usually involves restructuring and refocusing the organization.

Hoffman extracts a number of lessons for company directors from these studies on how to handle crisis, among them:

* When the decline is evident, the owners or board of directors need to first determine if the firm has the leadership it needs to manage the crisis. The ideal manager should have a vision of what the firm should be and have access to external individuals or resources to support his/her efforts initially.
* The top manager (new or old) should develop a management team he/she can work with to manage the crisis.
* The management team needs to systematically gather information to identify the causes (internal or external) of the decline.
* Management should then develop a two-step plan to halt and reverse the decline. Initially, one can gain relief from creditors by re-negotiating terms of payment. The first phase of the plan should be based on short-term strategies aimed at generating a positive cash flow within the first few months and profitability within twelve months, ideally. The second phase should develop a strategy to reposition the firm for long-term profitability and growth. This can be developed while the first phase is being implemented.
* Management needs to plan for implementing the changes. This requires making needed changes in formal goals and organization structures.
* The plan for change also needs to focus on changing the informal structure or culture to ensure the new activities will be accepted. The use of value clarification and positive motivational techniques aimed at developing team work and a winning attitude should lie at the core of such efforts.

Summary

The clear lesson from all of these studies and experiences is that all of the actions taken to rescue troubled companies could and should have been taken at a much earlier date by the existing top management team. Why didn't they do so? Invariably, in our opinion, the answers come back to top management's attitudes towards critical aspects of managing the business.

PART IV

The Survey

In the research for this book, we interviewed a variety of observers of company failure, from managers who had been through it at the front line, through accountants, receivers, management consultants and trade unionists, to bankers and venture capitalists. This activity provided a great deal of information and opinions, but didn't provide us with sufficient quantitative data about what happens in companies on the way down.

We decided to focus on two particular audiences – venture capitalists/lending institutions and receivers – to examine how they perceived the business equivalent of the rakes' progress. These two have rather different perspectives. The receivers are almost always brought in at the end of the saga, when the main task is sweeping up and seeing what can be salvaged. Their knowledge of how decline set in is therefore often primarily second hand. The venture capitalists, however, are usually in at the start and can watch events as they develop. By the time they hand over to the receiver, the damage is already done and they rarely have much interaction with the management team thereafter.

The questionnaire (reproduced in Appendix 1) was sent to 300 organizations, drawn from the Insolvency Practitioners Association (IPA) and the British Venture Capital Association. Altogether, we received forty-six replies, just over 15 per cent.

We first asked the respondents to identify what they thought were the main underlying reasons for business failure. The responses tended to confirm the conclusions of the previous chapters. The most frequent causes were:

* poor financial information (40)
* lack of control in general (34)
* insufficient working capital (33)

* management inexperience (33)
* lack of strategy (30)
* poor understanding of the market (29)
* insufficient margins (27)
* reliance on one product/customer (27)
* obsolete or easily overtaken technology (26)

What we might call middling causes were:

* excessive overhead costs (24)
* poor quality control (23)
* too much short-term debt (20)
* change in demand (20)
* failure to adapt to new market circumstances (18)
* too narrow or too wide a product line (17)
* competitors' actions (17)
* lack of credit control (15)
* faulty pricing strategies (too high or too low) (14)
* poor implementation of strategy (14)
* increase in materials costs (13)
* wrong choice of strategy (12)

All of the other possible common causes were scored by less than a quarter of respondents. But these contain some interesting insights. For example, only seven of the venture capitalists saw long-term debt financing as a significant problem. This may be a predictable bias, but it clearly has implications for how the institutions behave towards the troublesome borrowers, if they do not see themselves as contributing to the company's problems.

Only seven pointed to lack of commitment among managers as a prime cause of failure. If that is a true representation of what happens in reality, it could be that the filtering process in vetting borrowers rules out any management team that does not have strong commitment. Personal guarantees must also sharpen the mind of many executives, particularly in start-up and buy-out situations. But evidence from elsewhere suggests that commitment tends to decline with comfort. Once the owners have half a million pounds in the bank, the incentive to think the business day in, day out, often diminishes. Moreover, the lenders themselves are aware that the process of vetting is far from perfect. The one sure inference we can draw is that, in the opinion of the institutions, top management in troubled companies is not taking it easy; rather, it continues to put its efforts and time into the wrong things.

Allied to this issue is the weighting the respondents give to risk-taking. Only ten felt that excessive risk-taking commonly contributed to failure; none felt that insufficient risk-taking was a problem.

Divisions within management also appear to be an infrequent cause, mentioned by only five respondents. Poor employee relations were marked by only two; industrial disputes by only one; skills shortages by only five. There was a distinct perception by the respondents that the workforce was not a significant factor in success or failure. Good top management would always find the right people, with the right skills and keep them happy and motivated.

The answers to these questions lead to the conclusion that the main causes of failure tend to be focused around inadequate information and controls; poor understanding of the market and the product; and inadequate strategic vision and implementation. In practice, these three are closely linked. Creating the right strategy is in large part a matter of understanding the market and how the company's products and/or services can meet market needs in a way that provides sustainable competitive advantage; implementing the strategy depends heavily upon information and control systems that allow top management to measure progress.

All the other, less frequent causes, may be regarded as symptoms, in the sense that a victim of severe burns may die of shock or pneumonia, but the real cause of his death was burning. For example, employee relations problems tend, in our observation, to be more common in organizations where there is not a clear strategy, transparent to the workforce as well as to top management. Divisions within management (scored by five respondents) do occur because of disagreements over strategy, but are more likely to result when the organization does not have a clear strategy.

Next, we asked the institutions whether the same most frequent underlying causes tended to be consistent across all troubled companies. Just over half said that they were consistent or reasonably consistent; twelve said they were not. Some of the more specific comments here included:

* 'It is rarely any one factor that causes failure – it is usually a combination of several.'

* 'All weaknesses appear in most failed firms.'
* 'Smaller firms are, by their nature, much more vulnerable.'
* 'Change in demand and processes affects technology-based companies more quickly.'
* 'Most new businesses fail for lack of finance, sales and bad management; older ones because of bad management and outdated products.'
* 'In detail they vary, but in general most failures are the result of managers' inability to react to changed external or internal circumstances.'

Asked to select their own three most common causes, the respondents overwhelmingly chose inadequate, inexperienced or simply incompetent management as the starting point, followed by poor financial controls/information. The third most frequent choice was insufficient working capital (often combined with a reluctance to accept equity participation). A few respondents bracketed poor management with fraud as a frequent combination.

Next we examined the symptoms that the institutions look for, as indications that a business is in trouble, or likely to become so. The most common indicator – against traditional expectations – is management abilities and attitudes (thirty-seven). The financial indicators, such as margins, sales trends, turnover, or return on investments are slightly less important (with thirty-one respondents placing high emphasis on them). The explanation appears in some of the behaviours that managers exhibit – in particular, lateness or infrequency in financial reporting, 'inappropriate overhead expenditure, lack of focus'. Some investors look also for changes in demand, in working capital ratios (especially in stock levels) and 'increases in the volume of aged sales debtors'. Another common sign, says one is 'problems with the accounting/management information systems' – if management isn't getting the information it needs, it probably isn't making the right decisions.

The strong perception of management failure is reflected in the institutions' attitude towards the prospects of turning round the business with the same management team. Only two respondents estimate that a half or more the number of businesses can recover with the same management team; thirteen estimate that between a quarter and a half can be rescued in this way; twenty-seven put the figure at less than half. 'By the time they get to us, it's usually too late,' says one. 'The existing management is often unable to change,' says another. Among other relevant comments:

* 'If core management team remains, it inevitably requires strengthening/broadening to introduce additional skills and expertise.'
* 'At least some change is usually required.'
* 'It is remarkable how often businesses manage to "limp" on for several months after they should have ceased trading.'
* 'We almost always need to change/enhance management.'
* 'Most small family companies seek advice far too late for any hope of reconstruction.'
* 'It is rare for people who have got into a serious mess to have the skill to get out of it without outside/additional skills being brought in.'
* 'Usually the same team will make the same mistakes. The only exception is where the problem is due to factors outside their control (e.g. a strike; a large bad debt) and is unlikely to recur.'
* 'Most of the top management do not realize the company is in serious difficulties until it is too late.'
* 'We never back a team that has already failed if no major changes also occur.'
* 'Once this stage is reached, the problems get worse at an increasing rate until an external force applies.'
* 'The number of examples is restricted because the difficulties of the company often result in changes in the management.'

Asked for the primary reasons for changing management teams, the same answers predominated. For example:

* 'The original team lacks the skills required to manage the business.'
* 'The original team was never equipped to run the business successfully. The true quality of a management team often emerges in difficult circumstances.'
* 'The team does not have the skills/will to create a success.'

A few (four) felt that the need to instil urgency was important and one that it provided an example to others. Other common reasons included:

* 'Different management skills are required in a turnaround.'

* 'To bring to the company a skill/perspective which did not previously exist.'
* 'To complement the team with expertise not presently available.'
* 'Usually add to rather than replace in total.'
* 'To establish credibility and control.'
* 'The original team still think their strategy was right.'

Next we explored the behaviours and attitudes of failing company top managers. Does the chief executive typically face up energetically to the problems? Or does he ignore them and hope they go away? By two to one the institutions say their experience is that chief executives generally take the latter course. Typical behaviour, they explain is:

* 'They are likely to energetically seek more loan finance, which invariably is not the answer, as equity (risk) capital is needed.'
* 'People tend to defend earlier decisions.'
* 'A few will face up to the problems. Far too many think "If I admit the problem, word will get around and we're sunk" – tempting fate, if you like.'
* 'They will attack the problem frenetically and in an incompetent manner, possibly in many cases because the company is too far gone by the time the seriousness of the problem is realized. They busy themselves with trivial matters whilst ignoring the main issues.'
* 'They address certain problem areas only – ignoring the others.'
* 'All others in the company will generally (in a small company anyway) take the lead from the chief executive.'

Why, we asked, do so many managers ignore then the problems that could put their company out of business? Overwhelmingly, the respondents (thirty-four of them) believed the main reason was refusal to admit the problems exist. In part, this may be because the management information is inadequate to point up problems clearly – ignorance of seriousness, caused by lack of information – as one puts it. Other contributing causes suggested are lack of experience, leading to under-emphasis on key problem areas, problems occurring at a faster rate than they can solve them, the absence of rigorous planning and review procedures that allow prompt reaction to variances, or simply because managers are 'generally out of their depth'.

Twenty-five respondents pointed to fear of admitting failure as a major reason for ignoring problems and nine thought that lack of confidence that the problem could be resolved was a factor. Among relevant comments:

* 'Reluctance to admit someone else may have a better solution – what if their solution involves getting rid of me?'
* 'In small businesses it is surprising how many managers believe that they are entitled personally to make a living without regard to the performance of the business.'
* 'It is common to ignore the large, very difficult problem and energetically pursue other matters of less importance in the business.'
* 'Lack of grit and determination.'

When the crash finally comes, who do these executives typically blame? Only six respondents thought that managers take the blame themselves. Most (twenty-nine) thought the normal reaction was to blame external forces, such as competition or investors, market conditions, the bank or the Government. However, ten respondents have found that executives often blame their staff or the trade union. In the end, as twenty-five institutions say, the executives tend to blame anyone and everyone but themselves.

Equally depressing is that the institutions have little confidence that these executives will use the events as a learning experience to improve their managerial/entrepreneurial abilities. Seventy-five per cent of those who answered on this topic thought that less than one-third of executives used the experience in that way.

Some institutions found this a difficult question to answer, because 'there is little post-insolvency contact with directors'. Says one: 'When a small company sinks, we rarely see the entrepreneur again.'

Says another: 'Anecdotal evidence suggests that the same people may mismanage more than one business into the ground.'

There is clearly a stigma in the UK against executives whose businesses fail, say some of the respondents. But this is not necessarily reflected in their behaviour towards the executive who seeks to try again. While twelve institutions say a previous business failure would play a major factor in their decision to lend, twenty-three say it would play 'a substantial but not overriding part' and four say it would be a negligible part. Relevant comments include:

* 'We would be willing to take matters further, providing the "team" was right.'
* 'This would depend on how he handled the crisis and what (if anything) he has learned from it.'
* 'There is no stigma in failure if the manager did not have control or the failure was not his fault – i.e. change in government legislation, but if he was in control then his reactions must be assessed.'
* 'It would depend on how effective he had been in his role. He might have been excellent but continually overruled.'
* 'He/she would need a very good explanation.'
* 'This is dependent upon the part to be played in the new management team.'

Finally, we examined what happens within a troubled company as people begin to recognize things are going wrong. Sadly, only two respondents felt that everyone mucks in and helps. Rather the most common trends were felt to be that customers and suppliers lose confidence (thirty-three); employees at all levels become demotivated (thirty); key people at middle and junior management leave (twenty); internal politics and wrangles intensify (twenty); and key people in senior management leave (seventeen). In these circumstances, it is hardly surprising that the options for turnaround with the existing team is limited. Other symptoms at this time include:

* 'Optimism over ability to trade out of problems increases unjustifiably.'
* 'Management runs round "like headless chickens".'
* 'Quite often nothing happens – "perhaps something will turn up".'

Several respondents took the opportunity here to emphasie the value of a good non-executive director, to calm people down, point them in the right direction and, in some cases, to act as an intermediary in finding additional capital to invest in the business.

All in all, the survey paints a gloomy picture of the worst of British management.

What lessons can be learnt from this accumulation of dismal experiences? In Appendix C we produce a simple audit that the CEO and his colleagues in a company of any size might benefit from adapting and carrying out once every six months in their organization. We do not guarantee it will save any currently troubled businesses, but we do believe it will help focus attention at an early stage on some of the areas our survey indicates most often push companies towards receivership.

PART V
Case Studies

DUNLOP HOLDINGS

Dunlop Holdings was a symbol of the triumph of Victorian ingenuity. Founded to exploit John Boyd Dunlop's patent of the inflatable rubber tyre, it rapidly became a multinational giant, with worldwide operations. It set up a wholly-owned subsidiary in Japan in 1909. In the Twenties it expanded into sports goods and became a household name in that industry, too. Its massive Midlands site at Fort Dunlop dominated the skyline and by the Thirties Dunlop was the eighth, then the sixth largest company in Britain.

The subsequent disintegration of this proud company in the Seventies stemmed from a combination of *folie de grandeur* and basic management neglect. When it was finally dismembered in 1984, Mr Saito, chairman of Sumitomo Rubber, who acquired the European tyre business, stated bluntly that Dunlop's decline had three main causes:

* it didn't care for its customers
* it was obsessed with costs rather than quality
* sheer bad management.

David Lausen, a corporate planning manager at BTR, and part of the team that later bought the non-tyre businesses, followed Dunlop's decline for a number of years. He believes that one of the major causes of Dunlop's decline was management's lack of attention to their non-tyre businesses: 'At the top, management seemed to get bogged down by the problems of the tyre industry so that their "eye was not on the ball" in their many non-tyre businesses, and diversification lacked strategy or focus.'

Other observers add additional causes, but all seem agreed that top management allowed its attention to become diverted to such an extent that the essentials of business survival were neglected until it was too late.

Two major strategic decisions brought Dunlop to the edge. The first was – in common with many tyre manufacturers – to ignore developments in technology, in particular the steel radial tyre. The second was to embark on a grandiose, ill-considered and ultimately disastrous union with the Italian tyre manufacturer, Pirelli.

It was in the early Sixties that the Dunlop board, in one of those monumental pieces of marketing myopia that were to characterize so many of its subsequent decisions, listened to its technical director when he declared that the steel-belted radial tyre, developed by Michelin, was a marketing gimmick. He couldn't have been more wrong.

The current finance director, David Powell, a veteran Dunlop employee, who joined the company as an accounting apprentice, explains: 'At the end of the Fifties not much was going wrong. But even at that stage Michelin had commercialized the steel-belted radial in 1948. We had a big company in France but we were slow to realize that the radial was what the customer wanted.'

During the early Sixties, Dunlop and other European tyre producers invested heavily in a cheaper alternative – the radial cord tyre. It gave greater mileage than the traditional crossply but it couldn't match the performance of the steel-belted radial.

Recalls Powell: 'Even in 1973 there was still a lot of hesitation about going to steel. It was quite clear that we were far too late; we resented the investment. There were other demands on cash resources – to start new ventures, in particular.'

The result, says the current chief executive Gerry Radford, was that 'we retained a high share of a declining part of the market. We didn't get our act together fast enough in the growing steel radial market. That required a high level of investment. In the early period, before volumes were large, it was very expensive to make. This compounded the losses already being made on the supply of tyres to the OE (original equipment) market, i.e. sales to vehicle manufacturers. (Traditionally, the company lost money on our original equipment business to vehicle manufacturers on the premise – albeit a false one – that OE fitments would automatically ensure an on-going replacement market share, with profits from that which would more than compensate.)'

The move to radials had a number of implications for the tyre business as a whole. Firstly, the longer life of these tyres – up to

40,000 miles – meant that there were fewer replacements. The practice of discounting to car manufacturers and making profits on replacement sales rapidly became a liability accentuated by the abolition of resale price maintenance. Moreover, replacement tyres were now mostly bought by second owners, who had far less brand loyalty, being concerned primarily with price. So cheap foreign imports began to undermine Dunlop's market share both domestically and in its key markets overseas. For example, complaints that subsidized Spanish tyres were entering Britain while Spain imposed import duties on British tyres had little effect.

It was, says Lausen, becoming almost impossible to make a profit in the tyre market. 'It was a business of profitless prosperity. You had to spend vast sums on new technology and equipment while at the same time pricing was "cut-throat" and tyres were lasting longer.'

Because Dunlop Tyres UK was so heavily reliant on the original equipment market (OEM), sales to the aftermarket were much lower proportionately than its competitors, even though Dunlop had wholly owned distribution outlets all over the country. The problem, says journalist Robert Heller, who followed Dunlop's progress closely over the years, was that these operations were little more than warehouses. They did relatively little marketing, when price competition should have made them spend heavily on building brand awareness and stressing brand quality.

As the UK car industry contracted, so did the demand for OEM tyres. By that time, the cost of buying market share in a saturated secondary market was prohibitive.

Secondly, the radial required a heavier and continuous investment in research and development and in production facilities. This would not have been such a problem if the market had not been increasingly saturated. In fact, Dunlop was one of the first European manufacturers to start reducing costs by closing down factories. But it could only remove its own excess capacity, not everyone else's. Moreover, its then new Washington plant, employing only 500 people, and with one of the highest productivity levels in the Western world simply added to overcapacity.

In some markets, such as India and France, the situation became desperate. In India, three local competitors suddenly became twelve, many of them with excellent inside tracks to the markets, via political connections. In France, Michelin bought market share, eventually forcing Dunlop's French subsidiary into receivership. (Sumitomo eventually bought it for one French franc.) Michelin, which made a £400 million loss in 1981, was supported by the French government; Dunlop had been told unequivocally by the British government that it must stand on its own feet.

In the late Sixties the impact of the deteriorating conditions in the tyre market became increasingly serious – particularly in the UK. John Simon, who was then heading up the group's international division, was brought back to take control of the domestic tyre business where a loss of £3 million had just been recorded. The loss was turned into a profit of £6.9 million in the first year – after absorbing the cost of an expensive redundancy programme involving 3,500 jobs. This allowed a vital breathing space for recovery but it wasn't enough.

The non-tyres businesses were also under pressure, arising from increased competition. There were, for example, 120 different types of golf club circulating in the UK. The two leaders, Dunlop and its wholly-owned subsidiary Slazenger, had to fight harder and harder to maintain market share.

Lausen found that the non-tyre businesses had potential but were badly neglected by Dunlop management. 'Dunlop included all the non-tyre businesses in one massive division called diversified products. They were far too many and too diversified to be thrown in together like that, but it was an indication of how little attention management gave these businesses.'

Management's tyre obsession did little to motivate management and staff of the non-tyre businesses. Says Lausen, 'Each business needs to develop a clear strategy and have the commitment and understanding of top management in order to optimize its potential. To be part of Dunlop's diversified products group was not enough.'

All through this period, Dunlop's ability to make drastic changes in strategy had been hampered by its relationship with Pirelli. Says Radford: 'The killing blow was the effect of the Pirelli union. The first full year of the union was 1971. Despite the fact that all the figures were gone over by the accountants, in the first year Pirelli (Italy) lost £18 million and soon after that Dunlop had to write off £40 million of its investment. That was just before the next inflationary bout of 1974/5. That torpedoed the balance sheet and therefore the borrowing power of Dunlop just at the time when it should have been investing heavily in steel radial.'

The Dunlop–Pirelli union was born out of what one senior Dunlop

executive described earlier as 'an obsession for scale'. It provides
a cautionary tale for large companies currently trying to position
themselves for expansion in the Single European Market by seeking
alliances.

The reasons behind the search for alliances were varied. Firstly
there was the continued decline in Dunlop's position in the UK industrial companies league table.

Secondly, there was the fear of being swallowed up by a predator.
Any one of the big oil companies would have made a natural predator
given that oil was the basis of synthetic rubber (polybutadiene) used
100 per cent in all car tyres. There was a synergy in that both petrol
and tyres were part of the motor vehicle business in general.

More importantly was the fact that Dunlop's prime product – the
tap root of its business – was in decline.

The choice was either to diversify or to merge with another major
tyre manufacturer in complementary markets. A number of candidates were examined – among them BICC and RTZ. But the chairman,
Sir Reay Geddes, rejected all of them. Then he stunned his board
colleagues over a pre-board luncheon one day in 1969. John Simon's
recollection of what happened is as follows:

'Reay Geddes said to the assembled company that he had at last
identified the people with whom we should merge. It was Pirelli;
and to quote him verbatim he said: "They are our class of people,
our style of management."'

'He then went on to say: "It is not to be a merger in the conventional
sense of the word. It will be a coming together of two equals – as
in a marriage." I broke the silence by saying that if my experience
of marriage was anything to go by, there was no such thing as equals.
One had to be the dominant party, and that if we were ever to come
to any such arrangements with Pirelli it was imperative that we were
seen to be the dominant party from the start. Otherwise we could
only be the minor one. Geddes disagreed.'

Eventually, this clash of wills would lead to Simon's resignation.
In the meantime, however, the potential for merger was taken forward
enthusiastically by Campbell Fraser, then director of public relations.
'The deal was done by John Simon and myself. Nobody voted against
the deal', says Fraser. Certainly, Italy seemed to have a buoyant economy, growing at 7 per cent per annum. The deal appeared to have
a considerable logic behind it. Dunlop was strong in the UK, the
Commonwealth and Japan; Pirelli was strong in Southern Europe

and Latin America. Fraser explains the thinking that led the company to the union in these terms:

'Tyres had had good growth in the Sixties, but Dunlop believed the growth rate would fall rapidly as more and more companies found it possible to make radials. We were proved right in the Seventies when the rate of increase virtually disappeared.

'We knew that tyres would be a tough business in the future; but we felt that Dunlop, being one of the most innovative companies, would not be one of those to go under. Dunlop had made most of the innovations in tyre technology. One of the ways of overcoming the problems was to associate with another company, not necessarily in the same line of activity but with complementary research and development and engineering facilities and flairs.

'After a great deal of research, Pirelli seemed to match better than anyone else. It had the benefits of being in tyres and having other products like ours – and in particular having a cables operation. It looked a perfect match.'

The doubters were more concerned, however, with the health of Pirelli and the nature of the merger.

For a while, it appeared that the whole idea would be stymied by the recently introduced capital gains tax, which would have added £12 million to Dunlop's costs. But this obstacle was overcome with the help of Reginald Maudling, who was on the Dunlop board, and who made introductions at the Treasury. A small change in the Chancellor of the Exchequer's budget speech and the deal was on again.

Meanwhile, Dunlop was investigating exactly what it was buying into. John Simon again:

'We brought in Price Waterhouse to do the first ever audit of Pirelli's books. It cost us £250,000. Their brief was to recommend current accounting principles, but the real reason was to look at the books. As each stone was overturned, we found gremlins.

'By October, Leopoldo Pirelli was aware of the anti-Pirelli feeling permeating throughout the group. He told Geddes that in order to pre-empt parallel capital gains legislation from Rome, it was essential that the deal had to be completed before the year end.

'This was October, so the two sides sat up all night. Heads of Agreement were initialled at 3.00 am. The sports group was purposely omitted from the arrangements to keep the two groups' balance sheets as equal as possible, but in doing so a £500,000 tax liability was overlooked.

'The deal was predicated on a profit forecast for year one of £3 million from Pirelli (Italy). The union was approved at an AGM in the November attended by a mere handful of shareholders, in a matter of a few minutes.

'Six weeks into the new year we held our first central committee comprising the top four people from each company. It was a procedural meeting only, lasting about one and a half hours. At the end, as we were all about to go out of the room, Leopoldo pulled out a document from his briefcase and said, "Oh, by the way, Reay, here is our new forecast for the year". I leaned across and put my finger on the bottom line. For £3 million profit, read £7 million loss. All that in six weeks. I was shocked and told Geddes so.

'At that point in time the exchange of shares between the two groups had not taken place. That did not happen until the June. So, we could, had we wanted to, have pulled out of the agreement at that stage. In fact an attempt was made by the chairman soon after to restrict our holdings in each other to 5% but Leopoldo Pirelli would not hear of it. So, we went forward into deeper losses, shortly to be £9 million, then £11 million by the half-year and £18.3 million in the full year. EEC law required such losses to be made good with a capital injection. That was the beginning of the end because Dunlop had to make good its share of the loss. From that point onwards it became a rearguard action, damage control all the way.

'In October we had a central committee meeting to try to agree a management plan for the union as a whole. We talked of big investments in Latin America but there was no mention of money brought home – or return on funds employed or cash flow.'

At this point, Simon made a last ditch attempt to have the deal called off. For Geddes, this was a tough choice. To go ahead was to risk disaster; to pull out would involve international loss of face. When he decided to go ahead, Simon had little option but to vote with his feet.

A while before, Dunlop had made an opening bid of £18 million for George Angus, representing its then current net worth. Angus looked for a white knight – Turner and Newall took on that role and made a counter bid offering in addition a seat on their board for the Angus managing director. Dunlop then successfully increased its bid to £36 million. At that point, says Simon: 'For the first time I began to realize that our decision making procedures were wrong. There was no real strategy; it was all opportunistic and it wasn't all that long since we couldn't find £12 million to restore our position in Japan.'

The union with Pirelli finally went through in 1971. Under the terms of the deal, Dunlop UK held 49 per cent of Pirelli SpA and 40 per cent of Societe Internazionale Pirelli, the Swiss-based holding company for Pirelli's interests outside Europe. Pirelli SpA held 49 per cent of Dunlop Holdings.

The problems with Pirelli continued to grow. It was not just a matter of the poor financial health of the Italian firm draining much needed investment cash. Rather, it was that the union prevented Dunlop from making many of the key decisions it needed to ensure profitability. In particular, it had no opportunity to strengthen its links with its Japanese partner, Sumitomo, because Pirelli would not accept a Japanese presence in Europe. The only escape clause in the agreement was if one of the parent companies were taken over, but by the time this became a possibility, Dunlop, too, was in such a state that no one wanted to buy it. 'The union was before its time,' says Fraser. 'It wasn't that they didn't look hard at us and we at them. We did endless research and no one suggested conditions would turn out as they did.'

'The Pirelli fiasco also sidetracked the radials decision,' says Lausen.

Had the union become a true merger, it might have been possible to carry out the kind of Europe-wide rationalization that would have given this combined company an edge over its competitors. But the two companies continued to operate as separate businesses, with rationalization of Pirelli bitterly opposed by the Italian government and trade unions.

The Italians' behaviour, says Fraser, stemmed from a very different approach to management. Pirelli kept spending, with the help of government and bank loans, even against interest rates of over 12 per cent, because 'they had a philosophy that even in hard times, you should invest wisely and with a good spread.' Pirelli's gearing eventually hit seven to one.

These were only the most visible of the problems facing Dunlop. Behind the scenes lay a tangle of internal misjudgements and plain poor management. Marketing and production, for example, rarely spoke to each other. One sales and marketing manager distinguished himself for wearing smart suits and declining to visit the factories.

Says Lausen: 'Dunlop tried to run the conglomerate centrally, but couldn't. St James (head office) held the purse strings. In the late Seventies every investment proposal in the group had to be cleared through a team of twenty-nine corporate planners – but none of these planners, nor anyone in top managements really knew what was going on. The group was full of little fiefdoms, with each company trying to pursue what it could with no capital.'

Industrial relations were also mishandled. Personnel and production director Ian Sloss worked in the industrial relations department in the Seventies. He recalls: 'Bureaucracy was rife. We were told one Thursday that we should apply quality circles the next Monday. Everything was managed by remote control, with often ludicrous results.

'All our wage bargaining was centralized. By the time we (the divisional industrial relations officers) arrived at the meetings, it was usually all decided. On one occasion they were going to award a 10 per cent rise. I said we can't pay that and insisted on a vote, which I won. We were compromising on everything in industrial relations. We bought peace at any price, yet we were losing money.' Says Lausen: 'The unions were in a very powerful position as they were well aware that Dunlop could not survive a strike.'

Towards the end, in its desperation to save cash, at one stage the company tried to close down a plant in Wales without paying full redundancy money to the employees concerned. A short, sharp strike persuaded it to change its mind. The impact of these problems was concealed – in the short-term at least – by the imposition of price controls in the Seventies. Abandoned by the government eventually because they simply couldn't be policed and because they acted in many cases to legitimize price increases that would not have been possible under free market conditions, price controls gave Dunlop top management another excuse not to face up to economic reality. Says Powell: 'Their attention was focused on finding ways of justifying pushing up prices rather than on cutting costs or increasing productivity. We were taking on people and costs while the competition was getting tougher and the market was becoming saturated. When prices tumbled as a result of oversupply, we still had heavy overheads.

'One of the company's best profit years was 1978.* From then on it was all downhill. Debt became a bottomless pit into which all revenues poured. Time was not on the side of those who were trying to change things.

---

*Some doubts have been raised as to whether this figure included profits from Rhodesia, which had been de-consolidated in previous years because of the unlikelihood of collection.

'We needed to invest in equipment to make the kind and quality of product customers wanted at a competitive price – but we didn't have the money to do it,' says Powell.

The bleeding could not go on forever. 'By 1983', says Radford, 'we were losing a lot of money. Plant and equipment had been neglected because there was no finance available. Says Lausen: 'Dunlop had invested well in the early Sixties in good technical people. There were some quality problems due to poor plant – some were literally held together with sellotape – but the technical drive was there.'

Market share had begun to decline. The morale of the employees was at a low ebb. Redundancies were continuous, as one factory after another was closed. Employee numbers fell by 5,000 to less than 3,500.

Losses and debt mounted inexorably until, by the end of 1984, there were rumours that the holding company in London didn't even have the cash to pay the light bill. Meanwhile, the press reported that the holding company chairman, Campbell Fraser, had voted himself a £24,000 increase in salary. (In fact, he explains, he had taken a cut in salary to consolidate his payments from the two holding companies into one.)

Lausen describes the situation at the time: 'The firm was paralysed. Strapped for cash, management couldn't afford to do what had to be done. They could not re-invest, they couldn't even pay redundancy payments, and so had to keep running a business that any rational person would be out of.

'Yet Dunlop management would sometimes surprise us by finding millions to invest on a whim. For example, at the worst point in the cash crisis they found millions to invest in research and development on miniaturization of rubber products.'

Dunlop's response to the squeeze on its margins was to reduce its product range – a classic bungle in an increasingly segmented market. Explains sales and marketing manager Peter Soddy: 'We were making tyres then finding out where to sell them, rather than making them with customers in mind. We were not selling very well either; we cut out product after product.'

The lack of cash held up the essential development of replacement new products. The engineering department had numerous plans for product improvements that would bolster market share, but the funds for development kept drying up as each wave of cost-cutting bit home.

The combination of lack of investment, inept central industrial relations and marketing ignorance led, in the words of one close observer, to 'overmanning, dirty conditions and rundown plant, linked with an undercurrent of fear for the future. It had been a company where generations of the same family had worked, but it was a 'them and us' atmosphere.'

In a vain effort to contain costs, the main offices at Fort Dunlop – a skyline feature for Birmingham – were abandoned for all except the computer department. Everyone else moved out into one storey sheds on the huge (144-acre) site. There was a terrible mood of depression. Key people, including the chief executive, quit, seeing the light.

The Pirelli merger was made difficult by reluctance of managers on either side to commit themselves to it, and by problems of reconciling two very different financial and fiscal regimes. In this, the union fore-shadowed all the problems of cross-EEC collaboration in the Eighties.

Recognizing in 1976 that the union in its original form was a lia-bility rather than an asset, Dunlop, which by now had written off much of its investment in Pirelli's Italian operations, had suggested that the union should finally become a takeover. Dunlop Italy would buy both Dunlop Holdings and Pirelli. Discussions were protracted and as they dragged on, the extent of Dunlop's own problems became clearer. When Pirelli found itself having to take on the burden of part of Dunlop's losses, too, the union was finished.

In 1979 a new managing director, Alan Lord, was appointed. A civil servant by background, his industrial experience was limited. He explains that 1980–4 was a period of concentration. 'We had either to get the European tyre business right or get rid of it.' They had three choices:

* close down and write off
* sell
* give it away.

He made his first priority untangling the union with Pirelli. It took him until spring the next year to do so. It was too late. He explains: 'The favourable exchange rate that had kept Dunlop going in the Seventies went sour.'

Lausen pegs the low point for the UK automotive component sup-plies at April 1980: 'The automotive world came to a halt – orders fell dramatically. Both the pound and interest rates were high, and as a result the bottom fell out of the UK automotive market. The car companies held strong negotiating positions, pricing was extremely competitive and the weak companies like Dunlop could not react.'

More business was wiped out by high currency levels in 1981–2. Says Lord: 'For example, an enormous investment in market share in the hydraulic hose business was lost at $2.40 to the £1. At about the same time interest rates went up to 17 per cent. We did try to go for high value products, but so did everyone else. It was very difficult to create a unique strategy.'

'By the summer of 1982', he recalls, 'we could hardly turn European tyres into a business. I got the general managers of our tyre businesses in France, Germany and the UK together. For six weeks we studied what we could do to improve the business. We had already integrated research and development. In November 1982 I went to Japan. They didn't want to buy Dunlop at first. But I had things to offer. They would have lost their quote on the Tokyo Stock Exchange under new laws; and I could offer them the research and development for Dunlop worldwide.'

In the meantime, Lord had attempted to sell off other subsidiaries around the world, in particular its plantations in Malaysia.

The negotiations with Sumitomo, who had bought a majority share in the Japanese joint venture in the late Seventies, were interrupted by an abortive rescue attempt by a group of Malaysian entrepreneurs led by a politician, Abdul Ghafar bin Baba. Baba, the son of a rubber tree tapper, had been raised on a Dunlop plantation and, says John Simon, revered the company. It was the hand that fed him. Baba's Pegi Malaysia company bought 26.1 per cent of Dunlop Holdings at a total cost of £28 million, much of it borrowed; Baba and his colleague Eng Chin Ah, who had reputedly lost and made two fortunes already, gained seats on the Dunlop board. The problem, says Simon, was that 'what they didn't do was any homework. They thought they were buying the Kingdom of Heaven but when they got to the pearly gates, the cupboard was bare. They bought at 74p. I offered 42p later; they got 64p in the end.'

The Malaysians could not mount an effective takeover, so in the end, there was no option but to sell up the tyre business to the Japanese. In August 1983, Heads of Agreement were signed and in July 1984 a contract of purchase was concluded.

Meanwhile, in 1983 the banks had sent in a team to assess how viable Dunlop's operations were. Says Fraser, who had retired by then: 'It reported in 1984 and said there should be no more borrowing. I couldn't have agreed more.' BTR was canvassed as an alternative acquirer, but was not interested at that stage, having deliberately taken itself out of the tyre business some years before.

Dunlop at this stage was effectively dismembered. The non-tyre businesses were to stay with Dunlop Holdings. Sumitomo was to take over the European tyre factories and some of the other overseas operations. The US operations were bought out by the local managers and subsequently sold on to Sumitomo. Dunlop had virtually ceased to exist.

Lord left in November 1984, along with most of the rest of the Dunlop board and Fraser, who had become president of the holding company (and was also the sitting president of the CBI). In came Michael Edwardes and a new team, including Robin Biggam, who had recently left ICL after the computer company had been taken over by STC.

The Edwardes team had been invited by Dunlop's banks to prepare an alternative strategy for the rump of the company. At the time, the only institutional shareholder left had less than 2 per cent of the equity, the Malaysians had twenty-six per cent and arbitrageurs in New York had about the same. The rest were held by loyal small investors.

While Edwardes and his colleagues prepared their plan, the existing board also lobbied the banks to be allowed to continue. Some members of the board were invited to stay on with the new as non-executive directors, but they felt that they would then have divided loyalties. 'The company was completely demoralized,' recalls Biggam. 'There was a breakdown in communications between most of the board and the management team. The board no longer had any credibility with management and employees.'

Eventually, all the old board resigned at the insistence of the banks. The next morning, the new team moved in.

One of its first moves was to relocate to a much smaller headquarters office. Its highest priority, however, was to consummate the Sumitomo deal, which could still have collapsed even at that late date, had the Japanese company decided to withdraw. The next priority was to negotiate with the banks for the funding necessary to allow the remaining businesses to function properly and to sell off the US tyre business which, strangely, had not been considered for sale in spite of the sale of the European tyre businesses to Sumitomo.

Although the company had lost a lot of good managers over the previous five years or so, there was nothing wrong with the business managers, says Biggam. Most of them continued to head up large segments of the non-tyre operations after a substantial restructuring of the organization.

'We broke the business down into seven divisions,' says Biggam. 'The old business was made up of tyres and "Diversified Products" – the very name was the kiss of death. We released some very good names from that grouping.' One of those names was Slazenger, reformed into Dunlop-Slazenger to combine two of the best names in the sports-goods market. Altogether, these rump businesses still amounted to over £1 billion.

The availability of investment cash also made a significant difference. Recalls Biggam: 'For the previous two or three years, the company had been effectively run by the banks. Even redundancy programmes and factory closures couldn't take place because the company couldn't afford the cash layout. One of the successes was the graphite tennis racquet – a sensational development. To increase capacity the factory needed £100,000 to invest in new equipment. The old board had never sanctioned the expenditure because it was outside the bank limits. The whole organization was paralysed.

'We enjoyed the energy that was released when management were allowed to operate their separate businesses,' says Biggam. The suffocation of the previous style of management 'was all summed up by the boardroom at Dunlop House. Around the walls were portraits of all the old chairmen. It epitomized how the company had not moved forward, but was looking backwards. Michael Edwardes had his own draped picture put up, the same size. When the drape was removed, instead of a portrait there were the words: "Do it now." It was a means of getting across a sense of urgency.'

Michael Edwardes' chairmanship lasted a mere thirteen weeks. Almost before the dust had settled on the Sumitomo deal, recognizing the underlying strength of these businesses, BTR stepped in with a bid that Edwardes felt he had to recommend to shareholders.

Managing the Turnaround

Sumitomo took over on 1 January 1984, after a protracted negotiation in which Dunlop Holdings was effectively dismembered. Most of the tyre business throughout the world went to Sumitomo, although aviation tyre manufacture in Britain went to BTR and the US tyre business became a management buyout (subsequently bought back by Sumitomo from its new owners). All the sports products and non-tyre businesses were bought by BTR. The prestigious offices in St James' were sold off and Fort Dunlop was divided into three – the respective factories of BTR, SP Tyres (as Sumitomo ironically named its acquisition, after the German code name under which the Dunlop radial was developed) and an area for new development.

The turnaround process in the tyre business started almost immediately. Says Radford: 'After so many years of decline, the shock of the change in ownership acted as a catalyst for change. The old owners couldn't have put the necessary changes through – it needed a shake-up. The new owners had the necessary finance to invest in the business, as a mixture of loans and capital. There are now about eleven shareholders, mostly other subsidiaries of Sumitomo Group. The board is half Japanese, half British. All the executives are British.

'Sumitomo didn't have to make any redundancies – that had been done for us by Dunlop Holdings. So when Sumitomo said there would be no more redundancies and that things would get better there were great sighs of relief. There were few tears – people knew that if someone didn't take over they would have no jobs at all.'

Sumitomo also assured the employees and customers that the Dunlop brand name would be retained and strengthened. It was, says Radford, a major attraction to them in buying the company.

The Japanese company handled its new subsidiary with remarkable sensitivity, giving its new management team, which it selected partly from existing tyre division managers, partly from Dunlop managers elsewhere, a high degree of freedom in some areas. Recalls Radford: 'We had shadow executives for a while, as they did in France and Germany. The Japanese felt that local managers would know their own people and markets better and so they never attempted to get very involved in marketing. But they did get involved in production and housekeeping. They paid much more attention to cleanliness and tidiness than a British firm would.'

Together with the new management team, Sumitomo worked out a ten-point recovery plan. Ian Sloss explains: 'In order of priority, we had to:

Put in a rigorous system of communications
'We have pursued an almost fanatical insistence on improved

communications. All managers have to be seen talking to their people, keeping in constant contact with them, holding discussion groups, encouraging quality circles and suggestion schemes. We have a regular monthly conference with all forty key managers, to tell them about sales, profits, profit shares and other issues. This information is cascaded down the line during the week.

'We have removed as many barriers between people as possible. We talk about four-way communications (up, down and sideways). Everyone wears the same uniforms, including the managing director. We've also encouraged the different functions to come together. Sales people go into the factories. So do customers. And people in the factories go to meet the customers on their premises.

'All the directors tour the plants three times a year to tell the employees how we are doing. At first people were very diffident about asking financial questions. Now they ask very difficult ones. The directors speak to them in small groups so they are not afraid to stand up and speak out. Some of the briefing meetings we have in the factories are tremendous. We show them what we are trying to achieve, who the major customers are and so on.

'We also make sure they have all the information they need about their own department. Everywhere in the plants there are charts showing how each department is doing on various measurements compared to others in Britain and around the world.

'Nonetheless, we still have some way to go in cross-functional communications. We had a meeting recently where some people who had each been here thirty-five years needed to be introduced to each other.

'We also have a lot of catching up to do on involving people through suggestion schemes. The last manager from the Japanese factories of Sumitomo Rubber who visited us here told us his unit had gone up from fifteenth to fourth in the suggestions league. They have 200 suggestions a year – per person. They see that as a key indicator. The theory is that, if information goes down, more and more ideas will come up.'

Undertake more training than we had ever done
'Training has become a normal, day-to-day activity. Every employee has been to at least one course in the past year. Next year we will hold three times as many courses. Yet we only have one full-time, professional trainer. All the rest of the teaching is done by the

managers themselves. The person who is doing the teaching learns a lot. They have to put in extra hours to hold down their job and be a tutor.

'It means we can't calculate the cost of our training accurately, because we don't use many outsiders. All we do know is that it is both effective and cost-effective this way.'

Participation

'We have spent a lot of effort getting people involved. We put in statistical process control two years ago. Around 500 people were trained at Fort Dunlop and 300 at Washington. Many of them could not even do decimals beforehand. Now they are totally in control of their machines.'

(Radford adds: 'The secret of what we have been doing is people. There is a totally different attitude based on the concept of teamwork and coincidence of interests.')

Single status

'Anything that is divisive has to be removed. For example, we brought all cars on site because those left outside were being vandalized. We've got the space now.

'When I came here in 1979, we had seven canteens. Now we have one and the rest are all training rooms. The only difference between people is money.'

Cleanliness

'This was a big priority to the Japanese. We spent money getting the factory perfect – for example, just painting the floors and machines. 'You must have an army of cleaners,' said a visitor recently. But we have none. The employees do it all themselves. If you are going to produce quality you must start with a clean and tidy environment.'

Job security

'Everyone here has a job for life. We lose people by natural wastage, but those that stay know that if we lower costs and raise productivity, we will have the growth we need to secure jobs. Since 1984 output has gone up by about 50 per cent and we expect to continue to increase it by an average of 10 per cent per annum.'

Capital expenditure

'The £40 million investment by Sumitomo has mostly been spent on renovating and replacing old equipment. But that isn't the main reason for our increases in productivity. All of our three remaining factories are all doing equally well, although some had next to no money spent on their equipment.

'We've impressed the Japanese with the speed we have installed new equipment and changed production configurations. One year we relocated seventy presses, but still met our production targets. The Japanese couldn't believe it.'

Flexibility

'At first it was largely a matter of getting the engineering unions (we had nine, now we have seven) to do things they didn't want. Gradually, the negotiations have become much easier as we established trust.

'We now move people from one department to another with ease. There is no threat to their jobs; only the chance to add to their profit share. Currently, we are trying to give the engineering workers additional skills. We scrapped the shift system, putting them onto days and introducing planned maintenance to make sure the machines kept running. As a result, we have now reduced unplanned breakdowns from 11 to 1 per cent.

'Cynics say we've bought ourselves out, but we've only increased pay at the rate of inflation – 4 per cent in 1988, 3.8 per cent in 1987, and 5 per cent in 1986.'

Production methods

'We carry out team projects to improve layouts, make jobs easier and increase precision. The Japanese are very good at the detail of production. We send teams to Japan regularly to see what they have developed in the past six months.

'Statistical Process Control is showing us when machines are not capable of performing to spec. Now, the machine stops if the process is not perfect and the operator is responsible for finding out why.'

Rewards

'We have not paid much more money in salary terms, so profit sharing is important. Profit share is based on salary, with 10 per cent of profits distributed.'

At the same time, SP Tyres was painstakingly reviewing and revising its whole approach to its markets. Mindful of Japanese management's nostrums concerning care for the customers and obsession with quality, top management focused first on these two areas.

Explains sales and marketing director, Greg Wand: 'The old attitude was that the customer could have anything he wanted, as long as we made it. We are becoming a lot more efficient at doing short runs to make what the customer wants. We are spending a lot of time trying to understand customers' needs and providing dealer support. We are not just helping them fill shelves; we want to help them move stock and create better long-term relationships.'

This attitude extends to relationships with the car manufacturers, such as Nissan, Honda and Daimler-Benz, which import new vehicles into Britain, with Dunlop tyres made elsewhere in the world. Says Wand: 'We have to find out what they need, and what problems their customers say they are having. We try to plug into our customers at three levels: technical; sales; and service.

'We have also greatly improved our response time to complaints. Now it's all on a computer. If a complaining customer isn't satisfied when we have examined a problem tyre, the report can be on-screen in three seconds.'

Much of the capital investment went into areas such as primary processing, moulding and finishing, where it would have a significant impact on quality. As a result, says Wand: 'There was a fairly quick uplift in quality, which was reflected quite quickly in the car tyre market. There was a rapid drop in the number of tyres returned and confidence in the quality meant the car makers could fit more tyres more quickly. In truck tyres it will take longer to see the effects, because with retreading and regrooving a tyre may travel 400,000 miles before it is replaced.

'Lots of benefits flow from this. The morale of the sales people is higher and so is their confidence in what they are selling. We were receiving more returned tyres than our competitors, but now with our numbers down by more than two-thirds, we think we are doing better than they are.'

Major customers are also invited to visit the factories to talk to the employees. 'They are the best salespeople of all,' says Wand.

'When they tell truck users: "This is the best tyre there is. I've been training for three months and I know", then the customers believe them. Everyone in the company now knows what is going on and why, even down to which tyres we are short of.'

One cost-cutting option for both Sumitomo and the old Dunlop management was to chop or curtail the company's long links with motor-racing. It is a very expensive business, providing both tyres, mechanics and technical experts to a major event. To their credit, both sets of management recognized the brand value of excellence on the racing circuit. Dunlop, however, had never managed to capitalize on its investment. Says Peter Soddy: 'Part of the problem was that motorsport went its own way. We had not been very good at relating it to the rest of the business – building the bridges between that and the person buying tyres for a road car.

'It was a separate division, even though it was on the same site. Now the engineers and production people work in the same teams. There is far more transfer of technology. For example, the Denlock system, developed to allow racing cars to drive in a straight line if the tyre loses all pressure, is now used on a number of luxury road cars.

'Another part of the problem was that, in the lean periods, there hadn't been the resources to go out into the marketplace and use the motor-racing credentials to best effect. We needed to transfer the perception of excellence at the race car level to the road markets, but it didn't happen.'

Yet the story Dunlop and now SP had to tell was remarkable. Explains Soddy: 'We have motor-racing links with Nissan and Porsche in Group C, and with Formula Ford and Formula First, where the control tyre is Dunlop. We won every Le Mans race between 1981 and 1988, making a total of thirty-three since 1933. This year approximately half the Le Mans entrants will have Dunlop tyres.'

At the end of 1986, the British tyre company made a modest pre-tax profit for the first time in thirteen years. At the end of 1987, it made its first post-tax profit for fourteen years; to some extent this could be said to reflect the generally healthier state of the tyre market – the more new cars, the more tyres needed when none of the European manufacturers has invested heavily in additional capacity for a long time. But SP is gaining market share as well as sales volume. A sign of the company's renewed health is that it was able to buy a 30 per cent share in a new tyre operation with Finland's Nokia, giving ready access to Scandinavian markets.

BTR's Approach

BTR, having followed Dunlop's fortunes for some years, purchased the bulk of the non-tyre businesses in 1985. 'We would not have wanted to go for the tyre business,' says Lausen. 'BTR had been out of the tyre market basically since the Fifties, and we were not interested in re-entering it. Unless you are among the top producers and are committed to spending a great deal of money there is no point in competing in the tyre market. It would have been a mugs' game for us.'

'Dunlop's other businesses, such as automotive components and industrial hose belting, were, however, compatible with BTR. We knew the markets and respected Dunlop's exceptionally good technology. The Dunlop name is also of great value – it's still in the world's top ten in terms of brand recognition,' he says.

When BTR moved in, it by and large continued the restructuring started by Edwardes. 'We were able to accelerate the Edwardes process as we had money and knew where we wanted to invest,' says Lausen. 'We asked the company's managers to tell us what they needed and we made it available.'

BTR divided the unwieldy diversified products division into product-related divisions. A few additional changes were made, says Lausen, to those set in train by Edwardes: 'We merged some Dunlop companies with BTR firms where synergies existed.'

'Most changes were, however, made with the same people. Dunlop had good managers at the operational level, but they had been hampered by a cash-strapped head office. As it turned out many of the policies BTR wanted to pursue were the Dunlop managers' own views. Each company now does its own three-year plan and profit plan, and as long as it meets BTR's financial objectives it is free to develop the businesses as it sees fit.

'Most of the companies have exceeded my expectations. The Coventry wheel business, for example, was losing money under Dunlop and is now the top wheel maker in Europe.'

Lessons

• Dunlop management allowed itself to lose contact with its markets. It neither understood what was happening (until too late) nor how to meet the needs of a changing market – in large part because it didn't really want to know.

● The pursuit of the union with Pirelli was obsessive – a superb example of continuing to run doggedly with an apparently good idea long after it has been shown to be a bad one. As Biggam expresses it: 'Top management's attention was devoted to putting the union together; then to trying to protect Dunlop from a weaker Pirelli; and latterly, the reverse. It must have been debilitating for the whole internal organization.'

● Dunlop ignored the ample evidence that marriages of equals only work if they involve complete and rapid merging of culture and identity. In practice, neither side was willing to submerge itself in a new group – so nothing changed. Part of the original agreement should have been a timetable for complete integration. Admits Fraser in hindsight: 'The structure of the union was not right, with the parent companies responsible to different shareholders. It would have been better as a takeover from the start – but that would have been extraordinarily difficult.'

● As a result of all three of these failings, top management allowed its focus to be diverted. Instead of looking to expand into greener fields, it should have first looked to putting right its own operations. But that would have meant admitting these were not as healthy as the public face suggested; and it was far less exciting than Empire-building. In many cases, companies that pursue diversification strategies do so because the top management does not have the courage to take necessary action within the core operations. Usually this means that the core becomes starved of both management attention and resources – and the end is hastened.

DRAGON DATA

Dragon Data started out as the white hope of South Wales. Instead, its short life became a black hole for institutional investors' funds.

The company was conceived as a means of diversifying another troubled company, Mettoy. Mettoy was in the toy industry and in the early Eighties was suffering badly from a mixture of competition from imports and plain bad management. A boardroom revolt led to the appointment of a new board, which commissioned PA Technology to design a high-technology product that would restore its market position. Traditionally, Mettoy had sold toys for children aged three to seventeen. But by the late Seventies, it found that changing tastes had confined most of its product range within the two- to nine-year-old age range. They had a few high-technology toys, but these were not suitable for the teenage market.

Brian Nicholson, the technical director, described as 'a very astute, forward thinking guy' by one of the consultants who worked with him, saw a market gap for a home computer designed for teenagers. There were already adult computers on the market which could be re-engineered to produce a cheaper product for kids. PA's brief was to design a state-of-the-art home computer to sell at less than £200, while providing a full-size Qwerty keyboard and being compatible with colour television monitors.

The development programme was remarkably fast – less than four months from project start-up to prototype and an additional nine months to production start-up – and the result was a machine that offered the highest performance of any computer within that price range. It was, says Alan Sutton, then with the Welsh Development Agency (WDA), 'the perfect product. It came to the market at exactly the right time.'

The 'High Street' retailers thought it was a good product, too. The company had the acumen to persuade Boots and Dixons to take the first few hundred prototypes for sale through a single outlet each, and to obtain cash upfront. These first deliveries sold out rapidly and within weeks both chains slapped in huge orders.

Meanwhile, Mettoy had been getting steadily deeper into trouble. To raise survival cash it decided to sell off the majority ownership of this promising new business. The retailers' orders arrived half-way through the round of presentations to City institutions, then suddenly, everyone wanted in. Mettoy had little difficulty disposing of 80 per cent of the venture. The main investors were Prutec (a subsidiary of the Prudential), which put in an initial £500,000, the WDA and Hill Samuel. Prutec held 41 per cent of the equity, Mettoy 20 per cent. The deal included a ratchet clause that allowed Mettoy to increase its equity to 35 per cent if the venture met profit targets.

Dragon was, on the surface at least, just the sort of company the WDA was intended to support. It was a high-technology, high-profile company, with the potential to bring a better class of job to South Wales. At the time, the WDA was still struggling to overcome an image of propping up lame ducks – an image it had earned because the terms of its original brief had emphasised the social benefits of retaining jobs within existing industries. As the obsolete industries failed one by one, the WDA's charter gradually changed to allow it to pursue and attract newer industries. The Agency desperately needed some high-technology success stories.

At first, all seemed to be going very well. Dragon moved into new premises, a WDA factory at Kenfig Hill, near Port Talbot and took on 250 employees. Derek Morgan, who was appointed to the board as a part-time non-executive director by the WDA that September, recalls: 'That Christmas we had an amazing order book, for tens of thousands of units. As other chains and the computer boutique shops also placed orders, we couldn't keep up with demand.' Production capacity was increased, then increased again.

Several of the executive team running Dragon were old Mettoy hands. The managing director, Tony Clarke, had been finance director of Mettoy; the production director, Maurice Wilde had held the same job at Mettoy. Although they were apparently a fairly balanced team in terms of the variety of disciplines involved, they did not include an experienced general manager nor, critically, anyone with intimate knowledge of the computer industry. The chairman was the chief executive of Prutec, Dr Derek Allam.

Morgan, then head of PA's consulting practice in Birmingham, started to worry in February 1983, at a board meeting. He recalls: 'As always the board papers hadn't arrived on time. Clarke and the marketing director arrived late. When they did arrive, they excitedly produced new projections for the year – a turnover of £60 million and profits of £22 million.'

Morgan was openly sceptical that the company could sell £60 million after such a short trading history. Even if it could obtain the orders, it could not fulfil them. And even if it could fulfil them, it could not fund the increased capacity. Clarke explained that the figures were actually depressed and that the extra capacity could be gained by sub-contracting where necessary. The City investors were only too ready to believe. They, too, needed runaway successes.

Over the following months, it became clear that all was far from well at Dragon. Morgan's warnings about expansion began to come true as the production side found it could not cope. Top management spent a great deal of time out marketing – giving computers to hospitals for publicity value, when it might have been better spent making sure everything was running smoothly in the factory. Then, as the company was gearing up for Christmas, a number of problems became apparent at once.

The first problem was that the main chip in the computer had a fault that caused the operating system to crash if the computer was inadvertently overloaded. The company's initial response was to slap a sticker onto the power leads, warning youngsters not to switch on before connecting to the mains. It couldn't re-engineer the product because it didn't have time and anyway, its research and development capacity was completely taken up with increasing the machine's memory capacity.

Then it emerged that many of the orders were phantom. In true retailing fashion, many of the stores had put in double orders to ensure that they received the quantity they really wanted. Competing products were now on the shelves and – against advice – Dragon had not put any resources into easily added product peripherals. As the home computer boom showed its first signs of softening, the retailers dealt Dragon a double blow. They insisted upon a substantial reduction in price and they used the excuse of a handful of faulty computers to send back whole consignments of several thousand units. Some retailers also began to extract better credit terms by sending products back at the end of one month and reordering two or three days into the next – or simply by delaying payment as long as they could.

The company had promised to release a machine with a 64K memory by that time, with a 128K version in the autumn. In the event, neither ever emerged from the laboratory.

'The managers had so many problems, they didn't know which to tackle first,' says a consultant who helped develop the technology. 'They were running in constant crisis mode.'

It rapidly became clear that the company was having severe cash problems. The auditors, Peat Marwick, came in for three weeks to recommend what the shareholders should do. They suggested that the existing shareholders double their investment, with a new rights issue for £1.5 million in June 1983. Unable or unwilling to pay its share, Mettoy saw its equity stake further diluted. The WDA also allowed its equity share to fall rather than invest further.

Within three weeks this new money was gone, soaked up to pay suppliers. The company was on the verge of insolvency, unable to pay its bills. An emergency board meeting was called, appropriately, at the Dragon Hotel, Swansea. Clarke was told to be there, but did not show.

The board meeting appointed Morgan temporarily as deputy chairman and chief executive and asked him to do a consultant's report on the company within two weeks. His first action was to find Clarke, who was clearly abject and depressed and agreed readily to take a leave of absence that inevitably became permanent.

At eight o'clock on Monday morning Morgan explained to the managers how deeply in trouble the company was. An hour later, he was negotiating with the banks to provide the credit needed to keep Dragon afloat. Instead of a consultant's report he offered the board a survival plan that recommended no further investment and a rapid sell-off to another manufacturer. 'We don't have a company,' he declared. 'We have a limited product range. We must be absorbed by someone with a bigger product range.' Negotiations were started with GEC MacMichael.

To counter the problems of returned orders, Morgan whipped up sufficient enthusiasm among the managers and other employees to test and send back several thousand machines within forty-eight hours. Very few had any real faults. But the problems in the marketplace remained.

Morgan brought in Touche Ross to substantiate the projections of sales, which had been revised down to £17 million. In the event, even this was an overestimate, as the Christmas sales figures reflected the beginning of the end of the home computer boom. Having effected a temporary reprieve at Dragon, he turned down the offer of the permanent post and returned to his normal job as a management consultant.

Given the scale of the problems he had found, this seemed a pretty wise move. Explains Touche Ross's Robert Ellis: 'Our report said there were low sales; an incomplete product; and that some or all suppliers had the company on stop because credit terms had not been met. We told the board that if they put in more money, it would only pay off the credit already granted and that it needed still more investment to get the product right.'

The shareholders appointed a new chief executive from GEC, Brian

Moore, who set about trying to diversify around the existing product, while putting on the pressure to release the more powerful versions. In September 1983, Morgan resigned from the Dragon board, having already advised the WDA not to put in any more money.

GEC, while willing to market the Dragon computer, would have nothing to do with the company itself. In the end, Hill Samuel lost patience in May 1984 and called in Touche Ross as receivers.

Ellis as receiver summarizes Dragon's situation as 'a classic Catch-22. The new product was far from complete and those computers that did go out into the market had technical problems. They were working on getting the technology right, under great pressure from the investors to get the product onto the market.' There were so many returns from retailers that that year's sales were negative.

Ellis rapidly reduced the workforce from 250 to 100, to reduce the 'unsustainable weekly drain in wages', leaving only what he perceived to be 'the core of the company – enough people to fulfil the few orders the company had and some technical experts – so we had something we could sell'.

Several interested buyers appeared, among them Tandy and Hitachi. But it was a subsidiary of a Spanish regional development board, Eurohard, which bought the assets of the company, paying just over £1 million for them (rather more than Ellis had expected). The Spaniards had the intention of emulating the successful BBC micro project, to produce a relatively unsophisticated, reliable learning machine. They bought the patent rights and the entire factory contents: plant and machinery, testing equipment and work in progress. Dragon was boxed into containers and shipped to Spain, leaving only an empty building for the WDA to rent again.

'All I wanted was a factory left clean and tidy,' says Ellis. 'I got paid in a series of tranches, depending on how many containers arrived at the dock.'

The WDA lost £1 million and Prutec lost nearly £7 million. Other losers included the Water Authorities' Pension Fund. Ellis is philosophical about it. 'That's the cost of research and development investment. In all these failed hi-tech companies the asset value is small compared to the investment.'

Lessons

• Dragon's management placed too much reliance on the original product. It assumed it would have a much longer lifetime than was in fact the case. It also decided it could handle the development of future versions itself, but lacked the skills to do so. There was no contingency plan for delays in bringing product enhancements on stream.

Comments Ellis: 'You should never start something in a relatively new field if you can't complete it. In any venture, the assumptions in your plan have to be wide enough to cover these kinds of uncertainties. The investors, too, should be assured that if all these uncertainties go against the company, the business will still make a profit.'

● Top management didn't understand either the computer business or the toy business. The latter is subject to sudden fads that disappear as quickly as they arrive; the former was and is subject to rapid product obsolescence. As Chris Lewis, a consultant with PA Technology, expresses it: 'If you don't have the resources to run with the rest of the pack, you shouldn't enter the race.'

'It needs a special kind of fast-moving management to prosper in the home electronics industry,' adds another observer. 'Dragon didn't have that sort of team.'

● Research and development resources were pulled in two directions. Lewis again: 'In the computer industry in particular you must segregate your development activities from product support. You can't afford to take the development people off the next product to support the current one.' A logical course for Dragon would have been to subcontract the new product development while concentrating in-house efforts on getting the current product right.

● The project was underfunded from the start. Comments a former manager at the plant: 'We didn't have the technical or financial backing to maintain a lead in the technology.'

● Inadequate financial controls, particularly in the contracts with retailers, made it difficult for top management to know how serious matters were, let alone to deal with the problems.

● Top management refused to face the reality of the situation. Although Morgan advised them to stop manufacturing, in favour of having the product made more cheaply in the Far East, both Clarke and the then chairman dismissed the idea, on the grounds that Dragon was a manufacturing company. Yet this one decision could have saved the company had it been taken early enough.

RALEIGH INDUSTRIES

When Ian Phillipps took over as chairman of Raleigh Industries in 1974, the finance director told him: 'When you own the biggest white elephant in Britain, there are only two things you can do with it – feed it or shoot it.'

The white elephant in question was Raleigh's vast sixty-four acre manufacturing site at Nottingham. So long it was often not possible to see from one end to the other on a dull day; it crossed two railway lines and a road. It had the largest ballroom in Nottingham, and the second largest (after Fiat) chrome plating shop in Europe, capable of turning out an acre of plate a day. It also used forty miles of steel tube each day. It was capable at full stretch of turning out 8,500 bicycles a day – virtually every component of which was manufactured on site.

In the end, the white elephant drained Raleigh of resources so effectively and for so long that it brought the company to its knees.

Had the decision been made then – or even a year or two later – to shoot the elephant (by eliminating most of the component production on the Nottingham site and concentrating on frame and fork manufacture and assembly) Raleigh might still have been at the top of the world cycle industry.

Like several other of our case histories, Raleigh was a piece of British industrial history, a name known and respected the world over. The company's origins go back to the late nineteenth century. Explains a company history written by his descendant Gregory Houston Bowden, 'Frank Bowden bought a little firm of bicycle makers in 1887, in Raleigh St, Nottingham. Sir Frank died in 1921, by which time Raleigh was the largest bicycle manufacturer in the world.

'Frank Bowden was a lawyer just returned from Hong Kong where his health had failed. He bought a bicycle for exercise – and his health remarkably returned. Bowden realized there must be an enormous potential for this in Britain and abroad – not simply for leisure but for work – so he bought the company and called the product Raleigh after the street where it was made.'

Bowden took his bicycle (actually a tricycle) on a tour of France, Switzerland and Austria, all the while thinking about the commercial possibilities of cycle power. He moved the company almost immediately into a bigger five-storey factory and soon employed 200 people. By 1890, there were twenty-three models of Raleigh bicycle and three models of tricycle.

Then he made his master stroke. He hired G. P. Mills, civil and mechanical engineer, who had recently won the Land's End to John O'Groats race on a bicycle of his own design. Bowden offered him £1,000 a year to be his chief designer. This was a fortune at the time, but it was more than repaid. Superb design and engineering rapidly took Raleigh cycles to international dominance by 1910.

By 1974, Raleigh was owned by Tube Investments Ltd, which had acquired it a few years before as part of a diversification strategy. TI's business plan was that its lighter products were counter cyclical in profit terms to the heavy engineering industries such as steel tubes and it could not afford to let Raleigh establish tube making, which was then in train.

Phillipps came with the later acquisition of Radiation Ltd, makers of Ascot fires and Jackson boilers. He was asked to take over Raleigh by the TI group chairman Lord Plowden, who admitted that he had doubts as to whether Raleigh was a viable long-term business.

On arrival at Nottingham, Phillipps found a number of very serious underlying problems that were affecting profitability. The four most critical were:

* the cost of vertical integration
* lack of technological development
* industrial relations
* market myopia.

In the Twenties, Raleigh had to make most of its components itself because there simply weren't suppliers who could provide the quantity and quality of components it needed. It bought in only tyres and chains – and some factories overseas made them, too.

But later entrants to the market didn't need to buy all or even most of their components, because specialist suppliers gradually sprang up around the world. The problem became acute in the Sixties when there was a great surge in availability of components. Developing countries moved in, as demand for bicycles grew across the world, because bicycles were one of the first and easiest industrialized products they could make. They started by assembling kits, then moved into making components. Bicycle manufacture was and is a very labour intensive operation, not least because one model has to have several sizes and colours. Says Phillipps: 'We were the biggest jobbing shop in the world.'

To a considerable extent, Raleigh had created the problem itself. As the present managing director, R. A. L. Roberts, explains: 'From 1948, when it entered into its first licence agreement with the Sen family in India and took a 27 per cent interest in Sen-Raleigh Ltd for the manufacture of bicycles in India, the seeds of Raleigh's own destruction as a company as it then was, were sown.

'Raleigh's export achievement, which was remarkable, was founded on a 'follow the flag' principle and therefore as the Commonwealth countries became independent and sought to provide work for their indigenous population, they started a process of import replacement. One of their earliest selections was always the bicycle because it was normally a significant item on the import bill and with Raleigh's dominance in the marketplace, was a fairly sure-fired economic success, and as Morris was able to demonstrate in Oxford, was a marvellous nursery for light industrial development.

'One by one, between 1948 and the late Seventies, all Raleigh's principal overseas export markets, with the exception of Iran and the USA, reverted to one form or another of local manufacture. Raleigh followed these local manufacturing requirements by setting up its own subsidiaries, by establishing manufacture in association with others, or merely by licensing.'

Competition began to affect Raleigh's international sales as local producers assembled cheaper bicycles using parts produced in, say, Taiwan. To maintain quality, Raleigh insisted that its dealers, distributors and licensees should use only Raleigh parts (unless they made their own, to Raleigh standards). Says Phillipps: 'Raleigh licensees were facing disaster from local competition who could buy from the cheapest source. Some sources were inferior, but not all. One of the earliest decisions I had to make was what to do about this. I took the decision to release these people from their obligation. We still had to defend quality and brands – so we insisted on being satisfied with quality of bought-in parts. This made it possible for these people around the world to survive, but it imposed great problems on the Birmingham and Nottingham factories – it removed a great part of their tied work load.'

Attempting to do everything, when niche competitors could concentrate all their resources on one or a family of components, meant that there was never enough cash to invest in keeping the factory up-to-date technologically. The film *Saturday Night and Sunday Morning* used the lathe shop at the Nottingham factory as the backdrop – the dreary environment and ancient equipment provided a suitably bleak atmosphere. 'They didn't have leather belts any more, but not much else had changed,' says Frank Ruhemann, who took charge of Raleigh in 1986.

It also created a nightmare of production control. There were 7,000 variations of bicycle in the Raleigh range when Phillipps arrived and 50,000 finished part numbers. Although he reduced the model variations to nearer 1,000, the logistics were still difficult. Some bikes were assembled in Nottingham; others were crated up as CKD (Completely Knocked Down) for assembly overseas.

To cope with the constant pressure for particular parts, further factories were set up rather than buy in from component competitors. In 1973, for example, Raleigh opened a new plant at Sleaford in Lincolnshire. It didn't seem to occur to anyone that specialist component manufacturers might be useful allies.

There simply wasn't any way to sustain competitive advantage through technology advances. The nearest possibility was an offer to buy the Moulton patent for small wheeled adult bicycles, in the mid-Sixties. But Raleigh – probably rightly then – turned it down on the grounds that the market was not yet right for such an innovation.

The archives of the *Nottingham Post* are littered with stories of industrial relations problems at Raleigh.

Recalls Phillipps: 'It was a labour intensive business, with a lot of trade unions, and a powerful works committee. Ten out of the 140 shop stewards were on the committee. At that time, the majority were continually fighting the management and defending restrictive practices – not difficult in a factory of that size. There were very poor communications between management and shop floor. I was helped by a far-seeing man, Ken Baker, an engineering officer for the trade union GMB.'

'During the Seventies we had two major strikes. During the first day at Raleigh when the convenor came to see me, he stood there, put the toes of his shoes up to mine, looked me in the eyes and said he'd draw a white line on the floor and fight with any man. "Let's give each other six months" I said. After six months he called a strike. 1500 people on the gates in picket line. Someone punched him on the nose. The strike fizzled out in the rain.

'A few years later there was a longer strike. In the end we reached agreement with the national officers. The next day the shop stewards committee ratted on it. The strike lasted five weeks. Eventually, a new convenor was elected and things calmed down. There was a gradual improvement in industrial relations by the end of the Seventies.'

G. H. Somes, the local organizer for GMB, believes that management attitudes were an important part of Raleigh's problems. He explains: 'Raleigh, like many other companies, could have got far closer to its workforce than what it did during the Seventies and early Eighties. Whilst there was a fair amount of communication through the joint union committee and consultative arrangements, they were plagued with other matters to do with wage issues, piece-work, bonuses, etc. If they had encouraged the workforce through the consultative arrangements and negotiations, they may not have suffered to the extent that they have.

'I am not aware that the company took notice of the views and experience of the shop floor workers. For example, they were never consulted about any form of technology or computerization, and I believe if they had, they could have prevented management from making many mistakes which brought about the decline. There was a large amount of knowledge on the shop floor and in the offices, where employees may not have held any managerial position, but could have told those who were managers where they were going wrong. However, they were very seldom asked what their views or feelings were.'

The history of confrontational industrial relations was one more impediment to rationalizing and reducing the scale of the Nottingham site. The TI board knew that every step it made to reduce manpower would be resisted. Says Phillipps: 'During the Seventies no one dared to make people redundant. We were still getting demand for CKD sets. It was a difficult decision to spend a lot of money to make Nottingham's enormous complex smaller when it was full of work and had very strong trade unions, especially when the unions were common to other TI factories. TI employed 175,000 people – the idea of stirring up the whole industrial scene was totally unacceptable. We were locked into this situation.'

Progress in this direction did happen, however. Between 1974 and 1983, manpower fell bit by bit from 8,000 employees to 3,200. But the reduction had limited impact on productivity because the factory was not designed for smaller numbers. 'All we did was increase the space between people,' says Phillipps.

Nevertheless, some increases in productivity did occur, as management and unions began to work together. Says Phillipps: 'In the Seventies we completely changed the assembly shop. We'd had long Charlie Chaplin style lines, where you could have a highly complicated sports bike and a boy's standard bike one after the other. It meant a lot of people were doing nothing a lot of the time. We changed to a herring bone type system of small teams. Bonuses were paid to the team who could stand in for each other. Productivity leapt up by 26 per cent and morale went up too.'

In fact, in early 1974 sales were looking good. The US was going through an unexpected cycling boom, with 70 per cent of Nottingham's production going to North America at one point. A lot of this production was unbranded, and therefore low margined; so top management decided to reduce numbers shipped to about 500,000 a year, but with the Raleigh name and higher margins. All this was very well, but the company had misunderstood what was happening in this key market. From a steady base level of 8 million units a year sold mostly to children, the US market had soared rapidly to sixteen million, as adults caught the health fad. Trumpeted the *Nottingham Post* at the time: 'Raleigh is looking for 20 per cent growth in the US cycle market "their prime cycle market". The Nottingham factories meanwhile are working flat out to keep up with a worldwide export demand that was worth a record £25 million last year. America is Raleigh's biggest customer ...'

The trouble was, says Phillipps, that 'they were all buying sports bikes, riding them once round the block, then putting them in the garage. I got to Raleigh when that fad was just going over the hill. In six months the market dropped to six million bikes.'

Raleigh was all geared up for continued strong US sales. A tour of the US distributors soon convinced Phillipps to revise the estimate downwards – and even that turned out to be heavily optimistic. He explains: 'Imports fell away virtually to nothing because there was an indigenous capacity to serve the children's market. We had two years bikes in stock in the US – awful turnover for the next year.'

It didn't help that the previous management had attempted to capitalize on the boom by building a US production facility, to overcome US tariffs on lightweight cycle imports. The facility at Enid Oklahoma was very modern and efficient – a highly mechanized assembly plant. The local authority provided the land and incentives. The president of Raleigh's US operations boasted to the press that the company had 25 per cent of the US specialist bicycle market. It soon dropped to almost nil. Recalls Ruhemann: 'Raleigh put a factory into Enid Oklahoma in the middle of nowhere. The only way to get there was for the managing director to collect you in his own plane from the nearest airport. It just got going as the US market collapsed.'

Over the next five years, Raleigh was kept afloat by its CKD trade, which blossomed unexpectedly. It had also bought some well-run factories in Holland and elsewhere, that provided much-needed cash flow.

But the basic problem remained. Raleigh could never compete effectively unless it focused on making and selling bicycles rather than components – and this was a decision no one wanted to make.

The crunch came in 1979, when several calamities coincided. The *Nottingham Post* warned readers in September of that year 'A major review of TI Raleigh's UK operation is currently under way, following the Nottingham company's announcement of a major loss in the first six months of this year ... a move that marks the start of a grim fight back to profit. That fight – made difficult by world economic conditions, a strong pound and problems in two major markets – has now taken on the appearance of a mammoth struggle because of the current national engineering strike.

'The workforce of 7,500 at Nottingham will have to be cut.'

The key markets referred to were Iran and Nigeria. Iran was going through its Islamic revolution; Nigeria ran out of money. In its heyday, Nigeria took 8,000 bicycles a week from Nottingham. Raleigh had been looking to grow its business in Europe but this was small beer by comparison. Food for the elephant ran out as the high value of sterling made the CKD trade less and less viable.

Says Phillipps: 'Between 1979 and 1981, the house came down about our ears. It was very clear to me that there was no long-term future for Raleigh as it was. Seventy per cent of our production was for export. The factory was four times bigger than was needed to supply the UK. You had to have volume to feed the elephant and it just wasn't there.'

But the TI board was not yet ready for such a drastic step. Phillips quit and a new chairman, Michael Boughton, stepped in, warning immediately that there would be further job losses. And there were. Before long the workforce was down to 2,400.

Raleigh was losing money heavily at this stage – £14.4 million in 1981 – and short-time working became inevitable as orders dried up. In December of that year TI was doing no better. It posted a £13.7 million loss for the first six months of 1981.

The BMX craze provided a short reprieve, although Raleigh – mindful of its earlier experience in the United States – was very cautious about investing resources into a temporary product. Phillipps expressed concern that the BMX – a US invention – would undermine Raleigh's established product, The Chopper, which had already sold one million units, while Dr Paul King, the marketing director, told the press, 'The last thing Raleigh wants is to get its fingers burnt in another skateboard-type "boom".'

One positive event during this period was bringing all the overseas subsidiaries together under the umbrella of Raleigh International in 1979. Previously, responsibility had been parcelled out among the Raleigh directors. Managing them as a group on their own made the difference that restored most of them to health.

In spite of its cash difficulties, the TI board agreed to put more money into improving the productivity of the Nottingham site. Managing director Roland (Roly) Jarvis presided over a major programme of modernization and computerization that was intended to solve all Raleigh's production problems. Recalls Ruhemann: '"Sandman" was the code name of a giant computer. It took orders, batched them, ordered materials and so on and tried to keep track of where things were in factory. It was a failure – only as good as the dirty bits of paper being fed into the system. They had tried to computerize the chaos.'

Robert Heller in his book *Supermarketers* also followed the course of Sandman. 'The automation project, when (ostensibly) completed, refused to operate as planned. The entire plant became hopelessly entangled in one of the most infamous fiascos in factory history. Production came to a full stop, and Raleigh returned to grievous losses that once again placed its parent under heavy financial pressure.'

Investment in the paint plant alone was £3.75 million between 1981 and 1984.

It was all too much for the TI board. Says Ruhemann: 'Some £70 million of cash had disappeared into the business in losses and investments in computers and paint plants etc. None solved its problems. We kept telling shareholders the problem was solved, but each time it wasn't. In the Spring of 1986 we were having to report it had lost £8 million for the second year running. It was embarrassing and stopped us doing other things – for example, making a big acquisition in the US. Our credibility was being undermined. Out of the blue the chairman called me in – would I go to Raleigh and fix it. He said: "Do anything you like – close it, give it away, turn it round – but fix it." This was October 1985. The board needed a plan by early 1986 so as to have something to tell the shareholders with the preliminary announcement.'

Raleigh was becoming too much of a liability. Moreover, the industrial climate had changed. What was unthinkable in 1978 in terms of the possibilities of rationalization, was now commonplace.

It was, Ruhemann recognized, something of a poisoned chalice. Of the previous chairmen, one had been fired and two had quit.

Managing the Turnaround

'I thought what the hell, it's a new challenge. To start with I was to take over as chairman as well as keeping my other activities. Then half way through 1986 it was decided that it was such a big job that we promoted other people to take over my specialized engineering companies so that I could concentrate on Raleigh alone.

'On my third day I got the directors all together and said: "This is the end of the line. What are the options?"

* We could walk away. What would that cost us? £40 million write off *but* a positive cash flow and the site was worth something. Anything else we did had to be better than that.
* We could sell, though that would be difficult. We listed who could be interested. We even went to see Peugeot in Paris, but they were in a mess as well and not ready then to contemplate a merger.
* So what would we have to do to run it successfully?

'We set up a task force, bringing together bright people in Raleigh and from elsewhere in TI. McKinsey came in as a catalyst to give an objective view from outside. It was a fun thing for people to do – like sending them to business school while simultaneously working on real issues.

'We started off by asking: Who are the best bicycle makers in the world? We wrote them down: Huffy in Chicago; Merida in Taiwan; our own profitable factories in Holland and Canada. We sent a team to each.

'When the project team reported back they had found that Raleigh, by comparison to the best in the industry, had:

Factory labour costs	30–40% above competitive levels
Overheads	2 times
Stock levels	2–4 times
Site area used	3–4 times

On lead times, Huffy had it down to three days, Canada and Gazelle ten days; Raleigh thirty days. On stocks, Raleigh had eighteen day's worth, Gazelle four. Huffy used 0.3 sq.ft./bike. We had 1.8, which fell to 1.1 as we cleared bits of the factory.

'Prices were already at the limit of acceptability, so we couldn't price up to get out of trouble. We couldn't rely on being floated off the rocks by volume either and the market was getting more difficult to predict because it was getting more faddish. Our market share had drifted down from nearly seventy to forty per cent (having dipped at one stage to 28).

'Our material specifications, on the other hand, were very good – they were at least at a competitive level. So there was not much we could do there either.

'We were up the creek totally on costs due to the inefficiency of our factory. Roughly speaking it should take sixty minutes to put a bike together; we were taking double that. What were the causes? Handling, waiting, setting and rectification were killing us. Rectification was built into standards – five minutes brazing and six cleaning off.'

'The paint plant was even worse. When McKinsey looked at it, there were twenty-one handling operations in painting. In the best of our competitors it simply went on a conveyor in the paintshop and out the other end.

'We investigated, for every 100,000 bikes, how many people were not working on manufacture? Huffy had nine people, Raleigh Canada twenty-two, Raleigh UK fifty-one. This was exciting because we could see the reason for the overheads – it was keeping track of the chaos. We had kept adding more people to deal with it, but it hadn't worked. The cost of complexity was enormous.

'If we could reduce the time orders took to get through the factory to one week or less we'd save £15 million in work in progress. So we said, "If we were to start a greenfield site to build one million bikes, how would we do it?" We'd have a just-in-time process factory, with everything made in 500 of one colour. We set up small cells in each department to make 500 sets each per day. This had the enormous advantage of simplicity even if it was not necessarily the most efficient way.

'We planned to make the same number of bikes with half the people in one third of the space. This would enable us to get out of the area south of the rail-line and develop it.

'We got all the employees together – 2,300 of them (we finished up with half of that) in batches and took them through the highlights of this. It was really very positive. They realized that the alternative was the end. Generally speaking everyone entered into the spirit of it. We had only one strike – the assembly department went on strike for one week. They were the highest paid with loose times. The rest of the factory resented it, so the strike collapsed.

'Morale was low because they had been through so many reorganizations before. They were pretty cynical about it the fourth time around. We were starting from below rock bottom.'

This time, everyone could see that Raleigh was at the very edge of the cliff and the fundamental issues had at last to be addressed. The results were rapid and dramatic.

Says Ruhemann: 'We had weeks not months to get things right. We set ourselves the goal – if we can't make 1000 bikes/man/year we are not in the right ball park. It was an easy measure for our people to grasp. When we started out we were in the 200s.

'We got rid of individual piecework and paid on the number of good bikes that went out of the door. We established a variable manufacturing year to cope with the cyclical demand, but we paid employees for thirty-nine hours regularly and agreed with the unions the use of temporary workers at the peak.

'We had to rationalize the bicycle design to fit into the JIT ('Just-

In-Time") concept. A massive effort went into that. We tried to build them so variations were left until the latest possible moment on the assembly line after painting. Suppliers now had to deliver boxes of 500 pedals the day they were wanted. Under the previous system we used to have a massive store where a picker would have an order to collect twenty-four or whatever sets for assembly. Now we were ruthless about not letting them cut any tube that was not going to be welded or brazed the following day. Some cells stopped for weeks while we were using up bits which came out of stores and from all sorts of corners.

'We got the lead times down to ten days. The aim was to get to five with thirty orders going through the factory at any one time rather than 500.'

It seemed that the corner had been turned.

The Cycle Division (of which Nottingham was by far the largest part) had lost £6.6 million in 1985. That halved to £2.6 million in 1986 and in 1987 it made a small profit which has continued to improve since.

More than £10 million was extracted from working capital leaving a handsome surplus over the costs of the reorganization.

Halfway through 1986, however, a new chief executive arrived at TI and started to work on a new mission for the group. Recalls Ruhemann: 'We argued through what we should try to do. Could we be both a successful consumer product company and a specialized engineering company? They were different cultures. In theory we could do it, but in practice was it on? TI came to the conclusion it should get out of domestic appliance products – at that time our most profitable division. It had high market share in the UK but no visibility overseas. We could see all around us the sector was falling into global groupings around Electrolux, Philips, Bosch, Siemens etc. The cost of catching up would be high. So we decided to get out and focus on areas where we were world leaders.' Raleigh would be one of the operations to go.

Then came the Derby International bid. Ed Gottesmann, an American lawyer in London and head of London/American Chamber of Commerce, put together a consortium to take over the business. Says Ruhemann: 'By the autumn of 1986 I knew we were winning.' The big breakthrough was after Christmas 1986. They'd relaid all the assembly cells and they were running. The rest of the main building was empty. The workers could see it was working too. That was the key – the Derby International people could see what they were going to get. Nottingham was on the way back into profit.

The deal was made in March 1987. TI received £18.5 million from the sale and wrote off £45 million in that year's accounts. Since then, the profit recovery has continued and the new owners have invested in further acquisitions, including Raleigh Cycle Co in the United States, a cycle distribution business based in Los Angeles, and Germany's number two cycle maker, Kalkhoff. In 1989 it also acquired Peugeot's cycle interests. Both of the latter businesses had been loss-makers. The Nottingham site has now been rationalized down to forty-two acres and generally modernized at a cost of around £10 million. In 1988, the UK operations made their first profit in a decade.

Raleigh recovered, but it could as easily have failed. Even now it is not an immensely profitable business – few if any bicycle manufacturers are – and has to fight constantly to contain erosion of its market share by using imports from Taiwan, Japan, Thailand and Indonesia. The question for TI directors must surely be: why did the holding company hang on to Raleigh for so long without tackling the real problems?

Lessons

• Above all, Raleigh is an example of failure by successive holding company managements to authorize what they knew had to be done. Instead of tinkering with the production lines, they needed to face up to the realities of the bicycle market and rebuild the company accordingly. But there was always a good reason for trying to improve the mess they had rather than start again from scratch. Says Phillipps: 'Raleigh's situation was as remorseless as that of British Shipbuilders. It was the last remaining large cycle manufacturer in Britain. But you could not convert it into building anything but bicycles and the world did not need to buy bikes from England.'

• In part, this must also be a failure of vision, or strategy. At no time, in more than a decade did the holding company seriously examine why it was in the bicycle business at all, nor what value the bicycle business could add to the group when it became clear that the original intention of counterbalancing the heavy industry trade cycle was invalid.

• Failure to keep up with the state of the art. Says Ruhemann: 'Although the company invested (they'd come along to TI for massive sums for a new paint plant, computers etc.) no one calibrated the operation against the best of the competition or addressed the basic issue: 'What's the best way to make a bicycle today?'

• Says General Municipal Boilermakers and Allied Trades Union organizer, Somes: 'Raleigh lost touch with the market. Over a number of years, it attempted to give its customers too great a range, and by doing so, lost its way and allowed competitors to take over a large part of its market share.'

• Phillipps adds another poignant lesson: 'Never agree out of the kindness of your heart to command the slowest ship in the convoy. After a while, if they go wrong, people look at you as if it is your fault. When the pound turned against Raleigh in 1980, people at TI didn't want to know. No one else in TI wanted to be identified with Raleigh at that point.'

In other words, if you take the career risk of running a declining company, make sure you have the resources and support to do what needs to be done.

ALFRED HERBERT

'Alfred Herbert', wrote a *Financial Times* analyst, 'presents the classic case of a British company which, after the war, seemed to be in an unassailable position, both in the UK and world markets, but has been unable to maintain its position in the face of the more competitive conditions that developed since 1969.'

Alfred Herbert was, in its heyday, one of the most powerful and best known industrial companies in Britain. When Sir Alfred Herbert died in 1957, the firm he had founded almost seventy years earlier was one of the largest machine tool organizations in the world. Its international branch network and reputation for quality meant 'that its employees effectively carried an international passport as engineers' (*Machinery Magazine*). In the late Sixties, with a twenty-five per cent UK market share and £40 million in annual worldwide sales, Alfred Herbert was the undisputed industry leader.

In 1970 Alfred Herbert paid its last dividend on ordinary shares and, the following year, announced a £3.3 million loss. It floundered from cash crises to nationalization and – some said long overdue – insolvency in 1980. By the time the receivers were called in, the workforce, once as high as 12,000, had shrunk to about 750, and the firm had lost millions of pounds of both private and public funds.

The Machine Tool Trades Association (the MTTA) echoed the industry's sentiment with the comment: 'It seemed inconceivable that Alfred Herbert Ltd should ever fall; but in the end, and even after the government had moved in, it could not be saved.' A less sympathetic writer awarded it the dubious status of 'top star in the team of great British industrial lame ducks'.

What happened? How could such a large, profitable and long established firm suffer such an irreversible decline?

Perhaps the saddest part of Alfred Herbert's failure was its more than symbolic place at the head of the UK machine tool industry – and that industry's fundamental role in the nation's industrial base.

In 1963, the UK was the world's third largest exporter of machine tools. In 1988 it ranked eighth, with only 3.5 per cent of world production, according to the magazine *American Machinist*, trailing such industrial powers as Switzerland and the Soviet Union.

The Machine Tool Trades Association in repeated editorials blamed the nation's long decades of chronic underinvestment. The lack of forward planning hurt not only the UK's competitive stance, but also served to dry up the market for machine tools. In a 1972 leading article the MTTA noted: 'a situation is rapidly developing such that when new plant is needed by our metalworking industries, home sources will be inadequate to meet demand. There is no doubt that any further attrition of the sector through lack of support will have serious consequences for the national economy.'

A 1972 MTTA study showed that UK investment in machine tools per employee was only $560 compared with $1810 in West Germany, $1560 in the US and $1080 in Japan. 'We shall rapidly become a fourth-rate industrial nation', thundered *Machinery Magazine* in a 1972 editorial, 'unless our manufacturing industries start seriously to re-equip without delay.

'The need to replace a large proportion of out-dated manufacturing plant has never been more urgent. Without re-equipment of our manufacturing industries on a massive scale as rapidly as possible we are remaining on a course that must inevitably lead to disaster.'

Others blamed the machine tool producers themselves, citing an unwillingness to adopt new technology, a lack of marketing orientation and chronic underinvestment in their own plant and equipment.

Among them was the then Labour Minister of Technology, Frank

Cousins, who accused the industry of being 'insufficiently forward looking, short of capacity, lacking in productivity, weak in research and development and generally backward compared with its counterparts in Europe and the US' (*Machinery Magazine*). What the machine tool industry really needed, said Cousins, was to be 'picked up and shaken'.

Whatever sector was to blame, the decline of the machine tool industry did correspond with a severe drop in its major market – the motor industry. During the Sixties, the motor industry accounted for 50 per cent of Alfred Herbert's business, says Keith Bailey, a main board director of Alfred Herbert between 1976 and 1980. 'We used to say "when the car industry catches a cold, we get the flu".' The motor industry verged on pneumonia, having declined in volume by 60 per cent since 1966.

Bailey believes that the British car industry didn't stand a chance. The American automakers, Ford and GM, concentrated their investment in Germany and Spain for political reasons and the UK government policy did not protect the domestic industry. There was minimal tariff protection and, says Bailey, 'the on-off-on-off government policy with respect to hire purchase regulations meant we had to keep laying people off and hiring them back again – that's both very expensive and very disruptive to the people involved.' The government policy, says Bailey, effectively gave the UK market to the importers.

Another MTTA survey, carried out in 1971, determined what had long been suspected – that the industry is subject to a four- to five-year cyclical order pattern. Says Bailey: 'We faced a plus or minus 25 per cent business fluctuation every five years, and the amplitude was increasing. Many of the industry's difficulties, among them waves of lay offs and rehirings and overly high inventories, can be traced back to this cyclical order pattern.' The MTTA suggested that the government adopt a scheme for ironing out the peaks and troughs – but the suggestion fell on deaf ears.

A five-year business cycle can make it unrealistic to try to meet the City's expectations of annual results, says Bailey. 'As a limited company, we had to show results every year. This was a major disincentive to planning and investing for the five-year term that we were really operating in. When the firm was still private Sir Alfred could do what he liked – he could plan for the long-term without having to answer to the City.'

Also in the late Sixties, the machine tool industry worldwide was on the brink of a technological revolution. The Americans, and to some extent the Europeans, were producing new numerically controlled (NC) machine tools. These allowed for far greater precision, and saved time and labour in retooling.

British industrialists were buying these tools from abroad and were prepared to pay a premium for the greatly improved performance. As a result, Alfred Herbert was losing orders to overseas competitors just when the machine tool industry was entering its first really vicious downturn.

In 1966 R. D. (later Sir Richard) Young took over as chairman and moved to expand the business. One of his first moves was the purchase of the Birmingham Small Arms machine tool business, partly because of government incentives encouraging industrial rationalization, partly to acquire BSA's numerically controlled machine tool capacity. 'NC tools were not terribly reliable', says Bailey, 'but BSA's were as good as any of the others available – certainly better than those produced in the States.'

The purchase soon proved to be a strategic error. It meant broadening an already too broad product line just at a time when the market was demanding specialized equipment. As a *Times* writer noted: 'The Herbert salesman may have been able to offer any type of machine, but could he offer, for example, the best grinding machine in the world? The specialist could, and did.'

Alfred Herbert's profits topped £4 million in 1967. At that point they began to slide. The slide was never halted.

Alfred Herbert was lagging in technological development. In 1968 management attempted to overcome that weakness through a joint venture with the US based Ingersoll Milling Machine Company. The new firm was to muscle in on the growing market for computer controlled machines, primarily for the motor industry.

Herbert Ingersoll was, according to the *Birmingham Post*, 'an experiment to establish a special company that would be geared to meet the challenges of advanced technology in the machine tool field. With the economic picture much brighter, there is every reason to believe that Herbert Ingersoll's confidence in the future is well-based.'

It wasn't. Herbert Ingersoll lost £1.3 million in its first two months, and from then to October 1969 it registered a further loss of £1.5 million. Management claimed that, because the heavy start-up and development costs were included in its trading account, the firm couldn't make a profit until it had recouped its original outlay of

£5.25 million, even though it had a £7.5 million order book.

In 1972 Herbert Ingersoll went into receivership, citing a serious and sustained lack of orders for special purpose machine tools and automated equipment. 'There was no business at the time – British Leyland could hardly afford new equipment and Ford and GM were producing in Spain and in Germany with German specified machine tools,' explains Bailey.

The venture was, according to a *Times* analyst, 'a victim of one of the most vicious slumps in demand the machine tool industry had ever experienced. Whether or not it would have borne fruit, the experiment, which had lost £4 million for Alfred Herbert, had to be sacrificed for survival'.

Herbert Ingersoll was, if anything, ahead of its time. The uptake of numerically and computer controlled machine tools in British industry was well behind that of competing nations. By 1970 they still represented a mere 0.2 to 0.3 per cent of the machines in use.

According to a *Machinery Magazine* leader: 'The technology gap in Britain yawned dangerously wide. The chasm between the technology that was commercially available and the technology in use was enormous. All the efforts of the Ministry of Technology – and salesmen – failed to reduce the gap sufficiently through the Seventies. It was into this black hole that many of our traditional industries fell victims of uncompetitiveness.'

The market downturn had hit Alfred Herbert hard. When Neil Raine joined as group managing director in 1970, his first steps were to stop the cash haemorrhage by cutting the workforce, inventories and debts. These necessary short-term measures saved Alfred Herbert at the time, but left it weakened for the long-term.

'Having piled up nearly £9 million of losses and seeing its debts mounting, Herbert had to destock at the very time it should have been building inventories, ready to take advantage of the upturn in the demand cycle which history assured was on its way,' wrote a *Financial Times* analyst – with hindsight.

Richard Young, who took most of the blame for the Ingersoll disaster, resigned in 1972. Raine then took over as chairman, made further cuts in the workforce and closed some factories in the North.

The 1973 coal strike, which forced British industry on to a power crisis, a three-day week and a national ban on overtime, hit the engineering sector particularly hard. To make matters worse, the strike was followed by rampant inflation. Raw material prices jumped 50 per cent in three months. Alfred Herbert weathered this relatively well, however, not least because 64 per cent of its orders were high-priced exports.

The decline continued. During 1974, Alfred Herbert cut its work-force from 11,300 to 7,000 and saw a 70 per cent drop in domestic orders. 'During this time', said Neil Raine, 'seven top and middle managers had coronaries and some died. That's the kind of stress we were under.'

Alfred Herbert was, to all intents and purposes, insolvent in 1974. The firm had racked up £9 million pounds in debt and announced neither profit nor dividend for seven years. It was desperately short of cash and unable to afford the £3–6 million pounds needed for new plant and product development. Alfred Herbert was, according to the *Financial Times* 'feeling the effects of a decade of capital starvation'.

Facing a liquidity crisis brought on by high interest charges, heavy losses, inflation and escalating inventories, Herbert sought to increase its borrowing power in the summer of 1974.

John James, who held a substantial stake in Herbert's preferred shares, attempted to block the borrowing increase. Had he succeeded, the firm would have been wound up then and there. The government stepped in, effectively nationalizing Alfred Herbert through its offer to buy up James' preferred shares.

Anthony Wedgwood Benn, the then Secretary of State for Industry, gave his reasons for the government help: 'It was now clear that the company was unable to secure its long-term commercial future on a sound basis against a background of long-standing problems.' Aid was given under section eight of the Industry Act to 'enable the company's business at home and overseas to continue normally while suitable arrangements are worked out to meet its long-term financial needs.'

Even in this debilitated state, Alfred Herbert remained one of Britain's most important machine tool producers. Help under the Industry Act was inevitable, in view of the firm's still significant contribution to employment and export. As *The Economist* observed: 'Since Alfred Herbert employs 6,000 people, no government is going to allow it to collapse overnight.'

Shortly after the change of ownership, Alfred Herbert became the first company to be taken under the wing of the new National Enterprise Board (the NEB). *Investors' Chronicle* echoed the City's consensus with the comment that 'the government could not have chosen a much more sickly animal to rescue'.

When, in early 1975, Alfred Herbert forecast a profit for the final quarter, the announcement was greeted with scepticism. The firm had after all lost £11 million in less than four years, and had, apparently, done nothing to change its operating style. As the *Financial Times* put it: 'Alfred Herbert has done nothing but stagger from one crisis to the next since 1969'. The *Daily Mail* commented: 'Alfred Herbert is always a good buy – after the next results.'

Nationalization was complete in October 1975 when Neil Raine resigned and the government bought all of Alfred Herbert's outstanding shares.

Relations between the original Herbert board and the new administration were not good. 'The NEB was really a bit of an old boys' network,' says Bailey. 'We (the board) were beginning to show our teeth and disagreed with some of their plans. The NEB reacted by creating another board above us, called the "Herbert Board" and reporting directly to the NEB. The original board was effectively neutralized.'

In 1974 the Industrial Development Advisory Board (the IDAB) advocated receivership for Herbert, but this was rejected by Industry Secretary Benn as unsuitable. 'For the next six years Alfred Herbert pursued a strange kind of posthumous existence', wrote Patrick Sargeant in the *Daily Mail*.

Although the firm did manage to turn in modest profits in 1976 and 1977, it remained desperately short of cash. In 1978, the reorganization of Herbert's Edgewick plant in Coventry and the sale of its grinding business together added extraordinary costs of £4 million. As late as 1979, the pathetically optimistic Herbert announced that it was 'confident of recovery', despite having lost £16 million that year alone.

And still markets for machine tools were weak. Despite a clear recognition of the problem of underinvestment in the Sixties, the situation had changed little in a decade. In 1978, Sir Frederick Catherwood, the then chairman of the British Overseas Trade Board, described investment in UK industry as ridiculously low. In the previous seven years for every £1,000 invested in Britain, the Americans had spent £1,445, the Canadians £1,642, the Germans £1,648, the French £2,079 and the Japanese £3,769.

In early 1980, Alfred Herbert, under the chairmanship of Peter

Rippon, launched a major rationalization programme in a last ditch attempt to save the company.

The newly elected Conservative government, through the National Enterprise Board, made it clear that the programme had to be self-financing. 'It was a very tense situation,' said an NEB spokesman, 'but the group will have to implement its rationalization programme without recourse to NEB funds.'

The plan involved cutting back production of conventional machine tools and concentrating on advanced technology products – a loose category covering machine tools with numerical or computerized controls – the only growth market in the industry at the time.

'Everything', commented a *Financial Times* writer, 'is staked on this programme of disposals, slimming down and probably some closures.'

Several observers suggested that Herbert was entering the market too late. Imports of Japanese numerically controlled lathes had soared in recent years, and their prices were very competitive. Furthermore, Herbert could not produce enough to compete. Its annual production of CNC (computer numerically controlled) machines equalled just one month's production of the leading Japanese exporter. As the *Financial Times* commented, 'with all the hurdles Herbert still had to surmount it would be unwise to see the programme as anything safer than a gamble'.

The gamble did not pay off. The receivers were called in in July 1980, after the NEB refused a request for a further funding.

By this time it had become abundantly clear that it would have been better to have put Alfred Herbert out of its misery in 1974, or financed a massive capital investment programme, rather than to have sentenced it to a lingering death by capital starvation.

After such a long illness, mourning was understandably subdued. It was, said Rippon at the time, 'very sad indeed. Since the rationalization plan was conceived, economic conditions have deteriorated and the plans involved entering a very highly competitive market.'

Many analysts at the time diagnosed Herbert's problem as a desperate shortage of cash. In reality, the liquidity crisis was only a symptom of Alfred Herbert's long-running, underlying problems.

Any failure, even one with such a history of bad luck, bad timing and dying markets as Alfred Herbert's, comes down in the end to management decisions. It wasn't market decline, inflation and foreign imports that killed Alfred Herbert; it was the way management approached these challenges that led to the downfall of the firm.

Alfred Herbert presents the classic case of the dangers of one-man rule. It was Sir Alfred, described as 'a towering figure of exceptional energy and vision' (Chris Powley, *Machinery Magazine*), who built Alfred Herbert Ltd into the market leader of the Fifties. As with so many entrepreneurial firms, 'the company's disproportionate dependence on the man was both its great strength and ultimately, its fatal weakness'. (MTTA)

Sir Alfred ruled with such vigour that the firm never had the opportunity to develop a layer of professional management. 'The directors on the whole were ex-Herbert apprentices and engineers,' says Bailey. 'Professional management skills were sorely lacking – especially in terms of finance. One financial director had only trained as a company secretary – he had no financial training whatsoever. Financial management was so incompetent, even under the NEB, that the firm spent a million pounds on a new headquarters at Coventry within months of the receivers' arrival.'

One symptom of the financial ineptitude was a dangerous lack of production control, explains Bailey. 'They bought more raw materials than they could possibly use in production, and not surprisingly, ran into liquidity problems. Alfred Herbert was profitable until 1974. It just ran out of cash.'

There was so much money tied up in inventory that the firm was harder hit by inflation than its more prudent competitors. Too much money was poured into unnecessary inventories, while far too little went into badly-needed plant and equipment.

The *Financial Times* draws an image of the Alfred Herbert board fiddling as Rome burned: 'In the six years up to 1968, Herbert paid out £11 million in dividends to ordinary shareholders – this was £11 million not put towards badly needed plant, equipment and new product development.'

A *Guardian* writer found that 'well over half of Alfred Herbert's own machine tools were more than twenty years old in the late Sixties – and many were museum pieces. This would have been bad enough for a run of the mill engineering firm, but it was a fatal advertisement for a company which relied on other companies investing in order to sell its own products.'

Even the government resources poured into the ailing operation failed to address this need. Most of the £43 million of public money spent between 1975 and 1980 went to paying off debts, buying out shareholders and building up inventories to meet orders that never came.

'The saving of Alfred Herbert was one of the most ill thought out rescues of its kind ever undertaken,' wrote a *Guardian* analyst. 'Substantial capital investment was a necessary, if not sufficient, condition for a long-term revival of the company but it was not forthcoming.'

The NEB's decision to pay off Alfred Herbert's debts, but not invest in new plant and equipment meant that everyone – the taxpayers, shareholders and employees – lost. 'Lame ducks', noted one analyst at the time, 'cannot survive on starvation rations.'

Says Bailey: 'The money wasn't used wisely. Part of it did go to investment, but this was wasted as the cash-draining Coventry site continued to operate.'

The Coventry headquarters had gone beyond the need for re-investment – by 1974 it was overdue for closure. 'Our biggest problem was that the Coventry plant was losing millions a year, while all of the other locations were at least breaking even,' says Bailey. 'Had we closed it, and moved our operations into the modern Lutterworth and Birmingham sites, even as late as 1979 or 1980, we could have kept the firm going.'

The dispute about the future of the Coventry plant was a very divisive issue on the Herbert board, divisive enough for one director to resign over the issue in 1979. 'I suggested they close it, but you couldn't say that to the board,' explains Bailey. 'The management and the directors were all Coventry lads. Their attitude was "this is where we are – it's our headquarters"; Herbert would be alive today if they had not been so narrow-minded.'

Inflexibility, intentional or otherwise, was a major factor in Alfred's demise.

When it became obvious, in the late Sixties, that the industry faced a major change, Alfred Herbert was already under fire for being too inbred and conservative in its design. 'But it was felt that with its great financial resources and manufacturing skills it was capable of making the transition', reported the *Financial Times*.

This was not the case. During the Seventies, Alfred Herbert's domestic market share fell from 25 to 10 per cent, because it could not move quickly enough to meet shifts in customer demand. For example, having established itself as the largest maker of cutting tools, Herbert had difficulty changing tack when manufacturers demanded more exacting specifications and switched to grinding rather than cutting metal. At the same time demand for computer-controlled machines, which Herbert did not produce, was rising rapidly.

Successful machine tool concerns the world over concentrated on a particular activity and remained profitable even in the worst economic downturns, while Alfred Herbert's massive organization could only prosper in an extremely healthy economic climate.

'We probably could have survived if we had been prepared to size the business to the new, smaller market, and take better advantage of the opportunities that presented themselves,' says Bailey. 'For example, even when new machine demand was at its worst, the spare part sales were fantastic – we could have made profits on that alone.'

A number of other opportunities that might have saved the firm were passed up because of inflexibility on the part of the board, says Bailey. 'For example, we could have taken advantage of our network of overseas outlets and sold other peoples' products on an international scale – it would have been very profitable – in fact some reps risked doing it on the sly because there was such demand, but the board wouldn't stand for it.'

The companies that survived in the machine tool sector were those that could adjust quickly to changing market forces – in most cases these are the smaller, specialist firms. 'Managing a firm the size of Alfred Herbert is like steering a freighter – you turn the wheel and it takes half a mile to react,' says Bailey.

'Of course, the present British machine tool industry is a much leaner and fitter industry as only those able to react to technological change in the marketplace have survived.'

Lessons

In summary, the lessons to be learned from Alfred Herbert include the following:

• Alfred Herbert is an illustration of the dangers of dictatorial management. Without a strong team of supporting managers, able to develop the founder's vision, the company was ill-equipped to tackle a difficult future aggressively.

• Poor attention to financial and production controls led inevitably to liquidity problems.

- Even under the receiver, the company failed to recognize and take advantage of the market opportunities surrounding it.

DATA MAGNETICS

Data Magnetics survived three years almost to the day. It died, says its former chief executive Denis Mahony, just as it was finally coming right. It had dragged on too long and was already in a downwards spiral, say the investors. This start-up company is a classic case of a new technology venture that attracted enthusiastic initial support from investors, but was unable to sustain their patience and interest long enough to overcome the initial development problems.

Perhaps uniquely among our cases, the company's demise was not due to bad management. Says Geoff Taylor of 3i: 'They were all experienced. Mahony had pulled together an outstanding technical team. I find it difficult to think of a management decision of substance they should have made differently.'

The concept for Data Magnetics came from 3i itself. It had financed a Scottish Winchester disk drive manufacturer, Rodime. Rodime was buying its thin film disks from the United States and Japan. 3i saw an opportunity to establish a domestic supplier for the European market and looked for a management team to back. Mahony, then running a manufacturing facility using similar technology for Control Data in the United States, had seen the potential for a new player in this evolving market and even had a business plan in embryo.

Two particular aspects made this an attractive market niche. The first was that supplying to a long-distance market was fraught with difficulties, because, obtaining high performance from the combination of drive and disk demanded very close working between drive manufacturer and disk supplier. As the only supplier in Europe, Data Magnetics could be expected to seize the lion's share of the European market. The second was that new technology, replacing the iron oxide coatings with nickel cobalt, would change the nature of the game. The first to perfect production of nickel cobalt coated disks would be in a strong competitive position.

None of the participants was able to foretell that these apparent advantages would turn out to be a liability. It could not have been predicted that, in due course, most Winchester disk manufacturers would conclude that the problems of dealing with distant suppliers were so great that it made better logic to manufacture themselves, in-house. This is now the case and even the disk industry leader, US company Domain, has experienced market difficulties.

It might have been easier to predict that the technological break-throughs in nickel cobalt would take longer than expected, while the existing iron oxide technology hung around longer, as manufacturers constantly tweaked up its performance. But, admits Taylor: 'The markets were misread by all of us.'

Mahony met 3i on St Patrick's Day, 1984 and soon afterwards set about putting together a management team. The key appointment was an American colleague, who had experience in thin film plating, a critical technology. Other appointments included a marketing man, also from Control Data, a manufacturing director, a finance director and a couple of Ph.D.s with relevant technical experience.

3i agreed to finance initial development in November 1984, but it took until 18 April the following year to raise the £5.1 million start-up capital – then the largest hi-tech venture capital start-up in the UK. Mahony and his colleagues spent most of the time knocking on City doors. He recalls: 'Raising the money was more traumatic than the failure.' In the last weeks, the Coal Board Investment Fund (CIN), which had been in for £500,000, dropped out. The shortfall was made up; then, at the signing, Metal Box, a key industrial investor, objected to one of the clauses. Data Magnetics' lawyers eventually brought about a compromise, more than justifying their £70,000 fees on that day alone, says Mahony.

Finally underway, the new company rented 50,000 square feet of industrial space in North Wales from the Welsh Development Agency. It spent heavily on equipment and facilities, including a 20,000 square foot clean room. It also bought expensive manufacturing equipment and started to build up a workforce that eventually numbered 160. Remarkably, it persuaded all of the cleanroom staff to shower and change clothes every time they entered the clean areas.

From this point on, the problems came thick and fast. Firstly, the technology proved much more difficult to master than expected. The engineering director had thought he could crack the technical problems of producing a consistent quality of ultra-thin magnetic films, and had predicted it would take fifteen to eighteen months to get into production. In the event, by that time, the company was not even close.

Part of the problem was that the technology was not standing still. The tolerances required grew tighter and tighter until they reached 20 ångströms* (about a single molecule thickness) on a film of only 380 ångströms thickness. Another contributory problem was that all the leading edge experience in the technology was in the United States. The British Ph.D.s needed time to come up to speed and eighteen months was not long enough. 'As soon as we developed a product,' says Mahony, 'it was out of date.'

Equally problematic was that it looked as if Data Magnetics had backed the wrong technology. The competing technology, sputtering, was drawing ahead. The company invested £600,000 in a sputtering machine, which never worked. Even in the plating technology, there were disappointments. Mahony had bought new equipment from British suppliers, who failed to deliver on time, introducing further delays.

An additional set-back was introduced when the company attempted to work alongside Rodime to produce an eight-inch disk for ICL. The computer company had wanted a cheaper, home-grown product that would replace imported drives from Fujitsu. This failed experiment distracted top management at a time when it needed to concentrate entirely upon survival.

With no production and a continuing need to invest in developing the technology, Data Magnetics went back to the institutions for a second round of financing, of £2.5 million. Only £2 million was raised and most of this was tranched against achievement milestones. The investment took many months to put together and by the time it was in place looked very much like 'too little, too late'.

Unfortunately in the month immediately afterwards, the company produced no income. But, says Mahony, 'We cracked the technical problems. From then on things began to look up and output started to increase rapidly.' But the company was continuing to eat cash and the board started to look around for a buyer. 3i suggested that Rodime should take the company over, a view strongly supported by the WDA; Mahony disagreed, believing that the Scottish com-

---

* 1 ångström = one hundred-millionth of a centimetre.

pany had enough troubles of its own (a prophecy subsequently fulfilled when Rodime itself got into financial difficulties). The argument boiled over in March 1988, when Mahony was fired.

'We were caught by shifts in the technology that added at least a year to the "dead" period before making any sales. That doubled the amount of the planned investment in Data Magnetics,' says Taylor. The important issue in any capital intensive operation is to get product out of the door as rapidly as possible. Data Magnetics did start to ship some high quality product to Rodime (and Rodime was prepared to accept some disks with visual blemishes), but there were no signs that the factory could sustain high volume production of consistently perfect disks. At the same time, it became clear that expected sales to the very small number of Continental European Winchester disk makers – basically Siemens and Bull – were unlikely to materialize in the near future.

For the rest of 1988, the company continued to conquer the technical problems and would have eventually broken even operationally that year. By then, it had swallowed £14 million in investment capital. More would have been needed to make the venture a success, but the investors just weren't prepared to go through yet another round of financing. An administrative receiver was called in on 28 April 1988 and Data Magnetics was sold to an Israeli consortium that July.

Lessons

As a former management consultant, Denis Mahony is disarmingly frank about the mistakes he and the board made. In hindsight, he believes, they should have:

* held off investing in equipment for a few months more. The US market was due for a shake-out. When it happened, up-to-date equipment that had already been bedded in became available at knock-down prices.
* invested in someone else's technology through a joint venture or alliance with an American manufacturer.
* taken more note of the 'S' curve. 'We hit the wrong end of the curve,' he admits. 'We went under as it started to plateau.'
* arranged a different form of equity incentive for the managers. As is normal in such large deals, the managers were given a small shareholding, which would be ratchetted up if the company

performed to plan or better. But high-technology start-ups are notorious for taking longer than expected to deliver the goods. 'Once we had missed a couple of years, there was no chance of catching up,' he explains. 'The longer the business went on in a mediocre fashion, the less likely it was that we'd get anything out of it. So there was no incentive for the mid-range of successes – we couldn't go through a blip and still benefit as an owner. I don't think the investors could ever see that.'

3i's Taylor is also frank. He sees the main problems as stemming from an understandable misreading of the global market for this particular high-tech product and of the technical effort that would be required to make the company viable. 'It's a common situation with high-tech start-ups,' he explains. 'There is a joint miscasting of the rate of market growth and you end up having to support the company for two years more than you expected. There's only one thing you know for sure when you draw up an operating plan for such ventures; and that is that it certainly will not work out the way it is planned.'

SINCLAIR RESEARCH

'If you don't try new things you'll never know where the limits are; if you don't fail a few times it means you're not trying hard enough,' is Clive Sinclair's own summation of his successes, failures and lasting impact on British technology.

Sinclair, often credited with single-handedly masterminding the home computer boom, earned his place as the working man's boffin when he was declared by *Sun* readers to be one of the country's greatest inventors.

He dazzled the British public during the Sixties and Seventies with a succession of technical wonders. His real impact, however, lay in making the new technology available to the 'High Street' consumer.

Through Sinclair Radionics and Sinclair Research, Sir Clive (he was knighted in 1983) and his research team claim to have invented the world's first pocket calculator, the first affordable home computer and the first digital watch – arguably all products we could live without, but products that have nonetheless touched our lives. Few developed-world consumers could now imagine a world without Clive Sinclair's inventions.

Unfortunately, changing the world is no guarantee of business success. In 1986, after debilitating losses, Sinclair sold the computer stock, related patents and the rights to the Sinclair name on computers to Alan Sugar of Amstrad for £5 million.

Sinclair Radionics

In 1962, the twenty-two-year-old Clive Sinclair formed Sinclair Radionics and produced a line of miniature radios and audio amplifiers in his garden shed. The products, although essentially gimmicky, sold like hot cakes through skilful mail order marketing. Quality control was uneven; but the low prices kept returns to a minimum.

Sinclair moved the business to Cambridge in 1966 and six years later launched the world's first single-chip pocket calculator. The Sinclair Executive, as it was called, was an immediate success, but still essentially a prototype and not without its teething problems.

A more pragmatic and less innovative entrepreneur might have worked the profits back into improving the basic technology – making the calculator cheaper to manufacture, more reliable or easier to use. Sinclair and his colleagues, however, preferred inventing to fine-tuning, and went ahead with several bold new products – all based on the same imperfect technology.

So, while Sinclair developed the first pocket calculator to use memory, the first with scientific functions and the first programmable calculator, Japanese manufacturers were perfecting the technology. Sinclair was soon at a cost disadvantage with the product he had originated and it was the Japanese producers who ultimately reaped the benefits of the pocket calculator boom.

In 1975 Sinclair brought out the 'Black Watch' – the world's first digital watch. It was extremely popular – until consumers found that it drained batteries in a matter of days. Again Sinclair had discovered a market, but couldn't satisfy it. Other products, such as the hi-fi sets and microvisions, were also bought up quickly, only to falter as consumers found they often didn't work.

Mick Mclean, editor of *The Electronic Times,* believes that many of the quality problems could have been solved easily: 'Clive's obsession with compactness was a big mistake. He tried to cram too much circuitry into too small a space. The products would have worked far better if they had been just a little bigger.'

By 1979, Sinclair Radionics could no longer support this series of failed products and was abandoned to the National Enterprise Board. Sinclair, however, was back in business within the year.

The new firm, Sinclair Research, will be remembered as the company that triggered the home computer boom. The Sinclair ZX80, launched in 1980, was the first computer to break the magic £100 price barrier. Although often touted as the product that opened the world of computing to the public, many later writers credit Sinclair computers with little more than teaching millions of eleven-year-olds to play computer games – and annoying many parents to the point of never buying another computer.

Many analysts now question whether Sinclair machines could rightly be called computers. As one *Guardian* writer put it: 'taken at face value, the first two ZX machines were little more than over-priced video games. But at a time when the whole country was going computer-mad they offered an introduction to this new area of hi-tech that was unlikely to hurt anyone's pocket.'

Sinclair's promotional practices have also been called into question. 'Drawing on his considerable experience as a mail order marketeer, Sinclair promoted the computer as an essential element of the hi-tech lifestyle. Full-colour spreads pushed the educational promise of computers and computing. Feeding on the potent mix of consumer ignorance and parental guilt, increasingly aggressive campaigns promoted the dubious contention that a home without a micro was a child without a future', wrote one *Guardian* analyst.

The price and promotion combination was effective – in six years the British public snapped up five million Sinclair ZX80s and its successors the ZX81 and the Spectrum.

The City shared the public's faith in hi-tech for the home. In 1983 institutional investors bought a 10 per cent share in Sinclair Research, though many ultimately came to regret it.

The market for cheap home computers was insatiable. Sinclair's sales continued to climb despite the kind of technical and quality control problems that had quashed demand for the Black Watch and the Sinclair Executive.

Even the magical sub-£100 price was somewhat misleading. Although the ZX80 and 81 were usable without accessories, they needed additional interfaces or RAM (Random Access Memory) packs to bring them up to the basic specifications of many rivals.

Return rates were particularly high, at close to 25 per cent of output, with some dealers reporting even higher figures. Amstrad's return rate was 1 per cent, Acorn's was five. The discrepancy, says Sir Clive, could be accounted for by Sinclair Research's generous returns policy: 'Unlike our competitors, we accepted back all machines at any time without question for exchange. Almost all the faults were caused by the inevitable hard treatment that children give to such machines. Amstrad and Acorn refused to accept such returns.'

Other firms, most notably Dragon and Acorn, tried to muscle into the booming market, but couldn't compete with Sinclair's high-powered promotion. Sinclair's market dominance was taken as an indication that the public did not want to pay more for a truly useful home computer. Cheap, recreational computers were what the public wanted, it was assumed, and they were all the public got.

It was only when personal computers became commonplace in offices that consumers became aware of what the machines were capable of. No longer intimidated by the mystique, they began to demand home computers that could perform practical tasks.

As one analyst noted, one of Sir Clive's most significant mistakes was his failure to note the point at which the mysteries of computing became an impediment rather than an asset to sales.

The logical response to this market shift would have been to build on the existing brand name and distribution channels and develop a more practical and powerful Spectrum. Sinclair, however, was never one for gradual developments and reacted instead with a completely new product.

The Sinclair QL aimed straight for the top of the home computer market, offering a portable workstation with modem, flat screen, spreadsheet and word processor. Although the QL was initially well-received, technical and distribution problems soon combined to choke off sales. At the same time dozens of the new competitors, including Amstrad and Commodore, entered the market.

Yet Sinclair Research still retained the market lead. In 1983 profits hit £14 million and looked set to double the next year. A private share placement raised £12 million, bringing the firm's net worth to £136 million.

Sinclair computers suffered a major blow with the disastrous Christmas of 1984 when the market collapsed by 25 per cent virtually overnight.

Says Sinclair: 'The retail chains over-ordered for that Christmas, having under-ordered for the previous two years. The retailers got it wrong and of course we had no way of unravelling the situation. It's a classic problem with new markets – there are no goal posts.'

Having stocked up for a sales boom that never materialized, Sinclair Research finished the financial year with stocks and debts of more than £50 million.

The C5 car – a visionary vehicle?

Hot on the heels of that bleak Christmas came the January 1985 launch of the C5 car. Fuel for chat show jokes for years afterward, the C5 was both Sir Clive's enduring ambition and one of the greatest débâcles of marketing history. Financially the C5 had no connection with Sinclair Research's cash crisis as Sinclair financed it personally, but, he says 'It certainly had a lot to do with my own problems.'

The C5 grew from what Sinclair saw as a genuine need for a non-polluting and efficient private vehicle. Many would agree with his comment that 'there is chaos in our cities and chaos on our roads. I don't believe that the forms of transport we use today can long serve us.' He was, however, probably alone in believing that the British public was ready for his particular vision.

The trike version was launched in January 1985 at a retail price of about £400 in the hopes that it would eventually fund the development of the C15 – a full-sized electric car.

It didn't. Production was halted just three months after the launch, with 5,000 cars sold. The mid-winter timing, together with a labour dispute and what Sinclair refers to as a 'specious campaign saying the C5 was unsafe', combined to severely dampen demand. 'Which is not to say it would have sold like hotcakes otherwise', he admits.

In the year ended March 1985, Sinclair Research lost £18 million after writing off £23 million against excess stock. Yet the firm still held a strong market position – its turnover of £103 million in the same period indicated that demand for the Spectrum remained buoyant. Even as late as 1986 Sinclair was the highest volume home computer vendor in the UK with a 40 per cent market share.

During the summer of 1985 Sinclair managed to postpone collapse with a series of delayed payment deals with his suppliers and a sales arrangement with the retail chain Dixons. He cut the workforce by 20 per cent and dropped nine directors from the main board, while hoping to find the £10 to £15 million needed to save the company.

Robert Maxwell, publisher of Mirror Group Newspapers, offered a £12 million rescue package in June 1985. 'Robert Maxwell was completely aware of the losses at Sinclair Research when he made his offer,' says Sinclair. Despite that, however, Maxwell changed his mind later that year.

Sinclair Research was still badly in need of cash, particularly to develop new products and maintain its market share. Another rescue, however, seemed unlikely, especially as relations with the people he most needed were poor. Clive Sinclair had created what one analyst called a 'credibility gap' between himself, his creditors and the City. As Liz Sharpe, a partner in Edinburgh fund managers Baillie Gifford, told the *Sunday Times*: 'Information flow from the company to its outside shareholders has been non-existent. The point was raised at an investors' meeting and the response so far has been under-whelming.'

Shareholders had more reasons to be disgruntled. Sinclair shares, once valued at £34 were trading at only 60p in 1986, capitalizing the whole company at less than £2 million.

In February 1986 Sinclair's chief executive Bill Jeffrey told *The Times* that the previous year's financial problems were over. A rebound in the company's home computer sales in Britain had permit-ted it to pay back nearly £10 million of its twice rescheduled £15 million debt load. 'However, it still left a cash gap,' says Sinclair, 'as we sold a lot of stock at cut prices to get the cash.'

It was then conceivable that Sinclair computers could survive and even prosper in a secure games niche, providing the firm could raise enough cash to develop new products it needed.

Sir Clive believed it was time to move on: 'Sinclair Research had reached the point where it needed new products in its own markets. That, unfortunately was in games machines, which didn't interest me at all.'

On 1 April 1986 Sinclair sold the computer business to the newcomer Alan Sugar of Amstrad for £5 million, leaving Amstrad with 85 per cent of the UK home computer market. Sugar's production and marketing skills, together with the still powerful Sinclair brand name put Amstrad in a perfect position to make the most of it.

'The deal is good for both of us. Sinclair is good at research and this gives him cash to press on with it; we are good at marketing and this gives us another wonderful product to sell,' said Sugar at the time of the sale.

Alan Sugar was not the only bidder for Sinclair Research. The *Sunday Times* reported only a week after the sale that another firm 'was poised to make a rescue offer of £5 million for a 30 per cent share of Sinclair Research. The offer would have enabled Sinclair to stay in business and was fully supported by his management team and all the non-executive directors. For Sinclair, though, it would have meant a dilution of his 83 per cent shareholding and relinquishing control. He refused.'

Bill Jeffrey told the *Sunday Times*: 'I pleaded with Clive to accept the offer on the table, which would have supported the business as it was.' Another senior manager, who resigned over the issue, added: 'It was totally clear that Clive had the option of keeping the company going, retaining the trademark and people's jobs and he chose not to do so. I find it very distasteful.'

Sinclair, however, saw it as a choice between the research activities and the computer business, and to him, there was no contest.

'At that time we had two options,' he says. 'The other company offered to buy a minority share of the business. They were happy to put money into the home computer business but didn't want to support the other projects we were working on at the time – wafer scale integration, portable phones and so on.

'The way I saw it, accepting that offer would preserve the home computer business, but would impair the research side, as the company concerned would want to focus on what they believed to be the profitable business. Although the other directors wanted me to accept it, to me it would be like a throwing out the baby and keeping the bathwater,' he says.

'Alan Sugar's offer was the reverse of that: it would mean getting out of computers altogether, but would enable us to carry on with our new projects.'

As Sinclair is quick to point out, the sale to Sugar did not mean the end of Sinclair Research: 'To the outside world it looked as if Sugar was buying the entire firm because he was buying the most visible part of it. I decided the thing to do was to take up Alan Sugar's offer, unravel the resulting confusion and set up all the technology we were working on as separate companies.

Sinclair Research remains viable, if barely recognizable, as a holding company for Sinclair's various high-technology projects.

These include pocket telephones, a portable computer, and research into wafer scale integration. 'Each firm has its own management, so I'm insulated from the daily running of things,' says Sinclair.

Whether a rescue or a sale would have been better for Sinclair Research in the long run, the fact remains that the computer business failed as an entrepreneurial venture.

Lessons

Sinclair Computers were a victim of the 'Inventor Shake-out' of 1985–86, when most of the pioneering companies in the home computer market, including Apple, Acorn and Commodore as well as Sinclair, were forced to abandon the maturing home computer market to the marketing experts.

Sir Clive had always taken an inventor's, rather than a marketer's, approach to new product development. As he once described it: 'I invent things when I perceive people's needs – it is then a matter of convincing people they need it.' For Sinclair, this proved to be an extremely effective route to new markets. It is not, however, the way to meet demand in the long term.

Sinclair himself is well aware that a full-grown market is no place for an inventor: 'I'd always seen my, and Sinclair Research's, job as initiating markets; I'd never seen my businesses as mature businesses,' he says.

The maturing home computer market demanded an altogether different set of skills. It favoured business people like Alan Sugar who work by discovering what the consumer wants and then find a cheap way to produce it. These buyers do not want state-of-the-art technology: they demand only utility and reliability at the best possible price. It makes for an altogether duller – and healthier – place to work.

COMPSOFT–HEADLAND

The UK software market of the mid-Eighties was volatile, fragmented and, for those with a marketing edge, very lucrative. During the peak of the boom, net profit rates of 25 per cent – on 95 per cent gross profit margins – were commonplace.

Several million-pound firms sprang up virtually overnight. In many cases, however, the pace of growth proved to be more than management could handle; many of the shooting stars fell victim to their own success.

Compsoft is a case in point. Launched in 1979 by husband and wife team Heather Kiersley and Nick Horgan, it lasted only six years before succumbing to crippling losses. Compsoft's story is an example of the damage an inexperienced management team can do to a promising firm. Now, under new management, and renamed the Headland Group, a redirected Compsoft is thriving with annual sales of over £8 million.

In 1979, Compsoft's one product, an advanced database management system called Delta, was unique in that end-users (i.e. customers without expert knowledge) could put it to work without calling in a programmer. Dr Geoffrey Bristow, chairman of the Headland Group and part of the turnaround management team, explains that Compsoft started in a safe niche: 'in the early Eighties Delta was the only product of its kind in the UK that could be used without programming. Compsoft really had the field to itself.'

'Power without programming' was Compsoft's slogan and its strength. Delta won industry awards and prestige customers and by

1985 had 40,000 users in the UK. With a 10 per cent market share, it was second only to Ashton Tate's DBase in the PC database market and certainly one of the leaders among PC software vendors as a whole.

In 1984, Compsoft launched a public share offering. 'With a turnover of £2 million, it was a very small company to float, but, during the PC boom, £500,000 of that £2 million was profit,' says Bristow. High profits, then typical in the software market, made Compsoft attractive to city investors.

Ironically, these profits also meant that the flotation was not strictly necessary. Kiersley and Horgan, who together retained 75 per cent of the business, did not really need the outside financing for expansion. In fact, says Bristow, 'If they hadn't gone public, perhaps they could have ploughed more of the profits back into product development.'

Perhaps the partners, like other successful entrepreneurs, saw going public as an end in itself. A plc after the name can be as much a motivating factor as the capital raised.

By 1985, success in the UK encouraged Compsoft management to expand to the Continent. In doing so, says Bristow, 'Compsoft broke all the rules of foreign expansion. They didn't really know the European market, but that didn't stop them from opening five subsidiaries in the space of a year.'

The normal route to European markets, especially for a one-product firm, is through a distributor. 'You must be able to achieve critical mass in terms of market share, staff and sales in the new market to warrant running direct subsidiaries. Otherwise you use a distributor,' says Bristow. 'With a distributor, all news is good news – a sale means a royalty. But even if a direct subsidiary does make a sale, that doesn't necessarily mean a profit – you have to get in there and control it very, very hard. You must trust a manager at that distance far more than you have to trust the guy sitting next to you.' Unfortunately, Compsoft's European operations did not have the calibre of managers needed.

Moreover, Compsoft's one and only product was written in English. English may be acceptable in products aimed at computer literate people, but Delta was for end-users who rightly expect software to be written in their own language. Although Compsoft did eventually supply products and support material in the relevant European languages, the cost, time and attention required for the translations were far greater than expected.

Overall, European results were far worse than expected: all made substantial losses and Compsoft's £0.5 million profit of 1985 became a £1.28 million loss in 1987.

Back in the UK Compsoft was now facing severe competition, primarily from Paradox, which had also developed a 'power without programming' facility.

In 1986 Compsoft found it needed to develop new products to maintain sales and protect its niche in the domestic market. This is as far as many firms get, says Bristow. 'Often software companies find that having made one successful product, it can be tricky to make another.'

Compsoft's two new products were very well-designed, but failed dismally in the market place. Debut and Domino, as they were called, shared little with Delta beyond the initial 'D'. Aimed at different markets – from each other as well as from Delta – neither could benefit from Compsoft's name, goodwill, marketing or distribution channels. Further, management did little market research before either launch. 'Although they tested the ideas with a few big clients, they never really tried to find out what people in general wanted or how well competitors were servicing these markets,' says Bristow.

Debut was a very sophisticated spreadsheet programme for use by large multinationals in consolidating subsidiaries' financial information. Its market was specialized and required very different distribution arrangements from the excellent dealer channels already in place. Whereas Delta could be sold over the counter through distributors, Debut required a two-hour presentation from a highly trained salesperson.

Domino, a computer-based training package, had similar problems. According to Bristow: 'It was a very good product, well-supported and well-received, but it didn't rely on Delta's expertise, name or distribution network. It meant entering an entirely new market.'

Nonetheless, in the original market the positioning that Compsoft had developed with its 'power without programming' image was a valuable asset. Although competition had increased, Compsoft did retain a market edge for end-user products. A sound approach would have been to create more products that built on Delta's strengths, in particular products that could run on the new PCs then becoming popular. As Bristow sees it: 'Compsoft management could have put the money spent on research and development into products which built more on the firm's position in the marketplace.'

In introducing the new products, Compsoft management broke a cardinal rule of marketing. An expanding firm can take one of three routes if it is to build on its strengths: it can penetrate deeper into an existing market with an existing product; it can take an existing product into a new market; or it can introduce a new product into an existing market. One thing that can rarely be done with any success is to launch a new product into an unknown market, and that is exactly what Compsoft tried to do.

The new products were complete departures from the original line in part because Compsoft, like many software firms, was driven by research and development. Programmers want new challenges and designing gradual enhancements to meet market needs can be very dull work. This attitude, says Bristow, is 'very, very common in this industry'.

Meanwhile, Delta was enhanced very little, even though some new versions were in demand – for example a Delta product that could run on the new Unix or OS2 operating systems, or a relational version of Delta.

A relational database is essentially a free-format database that allows the user to specify and change the relationships among the data at any time. Because Delta lacked the power and flexibility demanded by some users, it lost sales to Ashton Tate's relational DBase.

By January 1987 Horgan and Kiersley knew they were in trouble and approached Octagon Industries, a consultancy firm specializing in turning around troubled software firms, for help on a consultancy basis. In particular, they wanted assistance in finding other products to help achieve critical mass of sales in Europe. Unfortunately, Octagon was unavailable for another six months.

Meanwhile, Multisoft, a rival accounting software manufacturer, approached Compsoft with a reverse takeover offer. The deal would involve Compsoft buying the much larger Multisoft and effectively disappearing – leaving Multisoft with Compsoft's stock exchange listing. The deal was not particularly welcome at Compsoft as it would mean redundancies at board level. It was, however, the only offer on the table.

'Only a week before completing the deal with Multisoft, Kiersley and Horgan came back to Octagon and asked them to match the Multisoft offer,' says Bristow.

They could. In August 1987 Octagon and Compsoft signed a

management contract by which Octagon management would receive share options tied to earnings in return for managing a turnaround. The firm was later renamed Headland with Dr Bristow as chairman and chief executive.

'All of this was done in a week. We then got on with the turn-around,' says Bristow.

Managing the Turnaround

Octagon's turnaround involved cutting overheads and increasing UK sales.

'The company had a very weak balance sheet and didn't have any money to close down the overseas subsidiaries,' explains Bristow. So, after a rescue rights issue to raise the necessary cash, Bristow closed all the European operations in the space of six weeks – for a profit improvement of over half a million pounds.

Sales in 1987 were so low that losses would have continued even after the cost-cutting measures. It was necessary to overhaul the UK marketing operations as well. Steps included appointing a new marketing director, providing better support for the dealer channels, making more use of the training facilities, using a telesales team to follow up on user-registration cards and doubling the salesforce.

Octagon also changed the product line, releasing a relational version of Delta, dropping Domino and repositioning the spreadsheet product. 'We quadrupled the price of Debut and aimed it at a corporate level customer, instead of as a dealer product,' says Bristow.

Compsoft had marketed both a budget and a pricier 'professional' version of the database; and had differentiated the two by making the former look very low budget indeed. Bristow's team discontinued the budget range and made the professional range look far more up-market. 'Doubling the product costs meant eroding our profit margin from 95 to 90 per cent. But it was money well spent – if people are going to spend £600 pounds for a product, they want it to look like more than a floppy disk,' says Bristow.

'Overall, we concentrated on profit rather than sales. Sales actually declined from approximately £2.2 million to £1.7 million because of the closure of the European operations,' he says. The closures, however, enabled Headland to reverse 1987's loss and show a 10 per cent profit for the following year.

Lessons

The Compsoft failure was by no means inevitable, explains Bristow. If played differently, Compsoft's 'power without programming' niche could have stood the firm in good stead well into the Nineties. 'Compsoft's real power lay in its easy-to-use man-machine interface,' he says. 'They could have profited from that even after the database battle had been played out, by grafting the screens, training and consultancy on to the new, standardized, database packages of the Nineties.'

'To compete in the software market, you must either find a niche and be everything you can to one group of customers, or you can try to compete on a global scale,' says Bristow. A niche strategy may be less glamorous than attempting to take over the world, but it can be just as profitable.

Horgan and Kiersley apparently did not see it that way. They chose to abandon Compsoft's niche and aim for a share of the larger market, in direct competition with some very large firms. And, that, says Bristow, 'is not a comfortable place to be in for the long term'.

ROLLS-ROYCE

The failure of Rolls-Royce was, to many, the beginning of a decade-long crisis of confidence in British industry. When the receivers arrived at the Derby engine plant in February 1971, the company's founders, the Hon. C. S. Rolls and Sir Henry Royce, must surely have revolved in their graves. Headlines, industry watchers and even Rolls-Royce management expressed shock that such a symbol of stability could fail. As Tom Allan, then an executive at Derby, put it: 'We had always thought of Rolls-Royce as the epitome of what was sturdy and infallible.' It is not surprising that John Argenti chose Rolls-Royce as one of his two core cases of invincible companies that collapsed.

Rolls-Royce, although best-known as a symbol of excellence in motor cars, has produced aero-engines since the First World War.

By 1945 most of its 47,000 employees were making engines for war planes. Peace brought a return to luxury car manufacture, but jet engines retained centre stage. By the late Sixties Rolls' 90,000 employees made the engines for over half of all jet-engined civil aircraft in the western world.

How could one of the world's most celebrated companies with the most famous marque in the motor industry reach such a low point? The demise was sudden – triggered as it was by the failure of a major project – but the underlying weaknesses were long-standing.

In 1968, Rolls-Royce, in an effort to gain a toe-hold in the American civil aviation market, committed itself to orders and development cycles that put immense pressure on the organization.

The firm's finances at the time were both badly managed and over-extended. A history of poor cost control dated from wartime government contracts that included an automatic profit margin for the manufacturer. There had been no incentive for cost control then, and the engineers in charge since had never seen the need to change. Finances were particularly strained in 1966 with the purchase of Rolls' only UK competitor, Bristol Siddeley, for a punishing sum.

Rolls-Royce's position was further weakened by the sudden death in 1967 of Adrian Lombard, the board's technical adviser. No replacement was appointed, and management was left to make a number of fateful engineering decisions without the benefit of board-level technical expertise.

One such decision was the authorization to manufacture seven prototypes of the RB211–06 engines in an effort to win a contract from Lockheed, the American civil aviation manufacturer. The number of prototypes promised turned out to be impractical given the time and resources available.

The decision was, however, successful in so far as Rolls-Royce did win the huge Lockheed order – it was in fact one of the largest orders ever secured by a British manufacturer. However, the contract, to supply engines for Lockheed's Tri-Star airliner, called for the more powerful RB211–22 engine, not the RB211–06 that had already swallowed so much investment.

This meant producing an engine around twice the size of anything the company had previously made and involving new technology, such as fan blades, made from carbon fibre instead of metal. Although the extra power specified had not been achieved when the contract was signed, the design engineers presumed that the necessary technology would be discovered during the development process.

In an effort to re-direct resources to cope with the new order, Ernest Eltis, then director of engineering at Derby's engine division, attempted to cancel four or five of the RB211–06 prototypes which were then almost complete. However, political pressures intervened and the development process continued.

The project put a severe strain on company resources. Workshops were operating at full capacity to keep up with the glut of work and the top designers had to neglect the RB211–06 project in favour of the RB211–22. David Andrews, former chief engineer of the company's rocket engine department, described the situation in late 1970: 'There was a total shortfall of 1,000 hours in engine-bench development running, and the minimum contracted design thrust had still not been attained.'

The company had committed itself to the development of two engines in the timescale and using the resources intended for one. The improvements the designers had expected to find in the development process of the RB211–22 were not forthcoming. A last-minute design modification did give the required power, but too late to meet Lockheed's delivery dates.

Seeking a way out, Rolls asked for a credit extension of £60 million, but the government and bankers made this conditional on a change in management. Unfortunately, the chairman and chief executive who replaced Sir Denning Pearson and Sir David Huddie both lacked industry experience. They lacked the time needed to understand the problem, let alone solve it.

In February 1971, the receiver arrived at Derby and the government bought Rolls-Royce from its shareholders for £87.9 million.

The receiver did nothing to placate the workforce when he said to the *Derby Evening Telegraph*: 'I'll preserve as much as I can, but substantial redundancies are inevitable.'

The Minister for Trade and Industry appointed R. A. MacCrindle, Queen's Counsel, and P. Godfrey, a chartered accountant, to investigate and report on the demise of the firm. The 1973 report concluded, erroneously according to some experts, that Rolls' demise had been caused by lack of financial control and a series of engineering problems.

The investigators criticized Sir Denning and Sir David for making a 'rash commitment' to develop the two engines. Ironically this decision later proved to have been the right choice at the wrong time. It was, paradoxically, the RB-211 engine that saved Rolls Royce.

By persevering with the 211 and improving it, albeit with a good deal of government investment, Rolls-Royce was able to break into the vast North American market, which still constitutes two-thirds of the world market for civil aero-engines.

Lessons

Rolls-Royce failed in 1971 not, as the report would have it, because of rash development decisions, but because it lacked the financial and organizational agility needed to take the opportunity that presented itself.

As John Wragg, head of the military engine division commented later: 'The essential thing we learned from the failure was that the company was not just a playground for engineers to amuse themselves.' Rolls-Royce learned the hard way that technical excellence without commercial competitiveness was simply not enough.

Sir Kenneth Keith, chairman in 1972–79, operated a relatively autonomous management team under government ownership. He brought home the concept that, if Rolls-Royce was to regain profitability, it had to operate less like a research institute and more like a business. Sir Kenneth introduced stronger financial controls, a realistic marketing strategy and, most importantly, a management framework, within which the engineers could get on with what they did best. He also prepared detailed cost analyses and comparisons with Rolls-Royce's American competitors, concluding that to survive the firm had to make drastic improvements in productivity. Changes in production methods, including a major reduction in the number of component parts used, meant that, over the years, productivity improved to the point where 4,000 employees could produce more than 6,000 had in 1971.

These changes were just beginning to take effect when the civil aviation industry was hit with the worst recession in its history. A combination of oil price hikes and US airline deregulation meant that demand for aircraft and components all but disappeared in the early Eighties.

It was at this point that Rolls-Royce gambled on a revival of the industry and, while the production facilities were little used, made major investments in plant and production. The firm was able to reduce its costs below those of its competitors by investing in machinery, research and development and in an overhaul of the whole manufacturing process.

This was, perhaps, as big a risk as the project that caused the 1971 downfall, but this time the gamble paid off. Rolls Royce is now back in the private sector and a leaner, more competitive operation better suited to compete on an international scale.

STONE PLATT

Stone Platt was a large diversified engineering group, one of Britain's largest textile machinery manufacturers. It came into being in 1958 with the merger of J. Stone Holdings and Platt Brothers Holdings. The new holding company manufactured textile machinery, pumps, ship's propellers and electrical equipment for air conditioning and transportation. In its most successful years (the mid Seventies) the Stone Platt group had a turnover of about £200 million and pre-tax profits of over £15 million. It also had over 13,000 employees worldwide and operated from over fifty locations. The company exported about 70 per cent of its products overseas and won Queen's Awards for this and for technological achievements in the Sixties and Seventies. In 1982, Stone Platt's bankers called in the receivers and the group was dismantled.

Stone Platt's striking collapse was one of the low-points of the recession of the early Eighties.

The background to the arrival of receivers in March 1982 was the decline of the British textile machinery industry as a whole. Whereas the sector had employed 47,000 people in 1970, by 1979 this figure had been reduced to 24,000 and, by 1982, less than 20,000.

At the latter end of the Seventies, demand rapidly declined and British companies were faced, not only with a highly competitive market, but with the added disadvantage of an unfavourable exchange rate against the two most important currencies, the German Deutsch-mark and the Swiss Franc.

The decline in British textile machine manufacturing was undoubtedly dramatic in an industry already full of dramatic history. Between 1970 and 1985, the value of British textile machinery exports was almost halved from SFr 1.18 billion to SFr 655 million. As exports traditionally accounted for 80 per cent of the industry's sales, the affects were disastrous. By 1985, Britain lay sixth in the world league table for textile machinery exports with a mere 4.8 per cent of the market.

For Stone Platt's textile machinery division, Platt Saco Lowell (PSL), the decline in exports was particularly devastating. In 1974, 82 per cent of PSL's sales were from exports (£55 million out of £67 million).

Even so, PSL was established as a world-leader in open-end spinning as well as having developing interests in worsted spinning through the Australian developed Repco spinner. Its place in the world market had, it seemed, been thoroughly secured through the acquisition of the American spinning machinery company, Saco Lowell in 1973. In the following year, textile machinery sales accounted for £67 million out of SP's total sales of £111.4 million. The 1975 merger with Ernest Scragg, another British textile machinery company, produced a textile machinery company with a turnover of more than £70 million and a far wider product range than previously.

Scragg had 30 per cent of the world market in its highly specialized texturizing machinery. Ominously, Scragg's profits in the year before the merger, at £2.96 million, were less than half those of 1969. In the first half of 1975 Scragg was, in fact, reporting a loss following a 50 per cent drop in turnover to £10 million. It was also heavily reliant on exports, which made up 89 per cent of its sales in 1974.

However, Stone Platt's group profits rose consistently during the Seventies. In 1978, for example, it posted a profit of approaching £10 million from sales of £200 million.

Stone Platt had, it was thought, the advantage of a diverse product range which would insulate the company from the worst of the decline in textile machinery demand. Its other divisions were involved in pumps, propellers and electronics. It was not until 1979 that the group's first loss was reported:

Stone Platt Industries pre-tax profits 1971–9

£million

1971	3.58
1972	4.65
1973	7.04
1974	7.89
1975	11.14
1976	15.61
1977	14.43
1978	9.51
1979	−2.94

(Source: *The Times*, 19 March 1982)

The Road to Collapse

● April 1980: The first rescue begins. Stone Platt defaults on borrowings and is forced to rearrange loans of nearly £40 million. The Bank of England is involved in co-ordinating talks with bankers.

● November 1980: Leslie Pincott is brought in as Stone Platt chairman. The group's pump division is sold for £11.5 million.

● March 1981: As part of the second rescue operation, £10 million is raised through a share issue.

● April 1981: A third rescue package is rejected by the company's small shareholders. City institutions meet all the costs of a £10 million cash injection, but Stone Platt announces losses of £15 million for 1980.

● May 1981: The group's fixed pitch propeller business is sold for £3.5 million.

● October 1981: Chief executive, Robin Tavener, resigns after a boardroom dispute.

● March 1982: The receiver is called in.

The reasons behind the demise of any company are likely to be diverse. In the case of Stone Platt, argument and debate has been particularly fierce. As Graham Searjeant of the *Sunday Times* observed at the time of the company's collapse in 1982: 'If the Stone Platt rescue had succeeded, some subsidiaries would have still lacked the resources they deserved for expansion. Yet this was no rotten organization.

It reacted too slowly to rapid changes. But it fell from grace mainly because the special virtues common to its diverse businesses – worldwide exporting, metal-working technology, engineering skill – suddenly became liabilities. Its home customers, notably in textiles and shipbuilding, faded away, while its exports faced a super-high pound and a worldwide hiatus in demand for capital equipment.'*

Indeed, many of the problems confronting the company in the Seventies and early Eighties mirrored those of the Sixties – declining profits and return on capital, lack of central control and excessive manpower. Between 1965 and 1968 Stone Platt's profits fell from £3.2 million to £800,000 and return on capital employed from 11.2 to 4.3 per cent. The magazine *Marketing* commented in 1970: 'There were too many people, too many plants, overlapping of production lines and a management structure that was unsuitable because it could not easily derive any strength from central direction.' Re-organization in the late Sixties attempted to offset these deficiencies. Under Edward Smalley, the number of employees fell from 9,000 in 1967 to 7,000 in 1970 and the textile works area was reduced from 4.5 million to 2.5 million square feet.

These changes failed to create foundations for long-term success. In some ways the company sowed the seeds of its own destruction. Its export orientation created an over-reliance on developing international markets in the Far East and Third World. By selling the machinery for complete mills, Stone Platt created the competition for Britain's textile companies. Having supplied the mills, Stone Platt also failed to provide an adequate back-up service. The company did not even know where most of its machines were in the world.

The warning signs were already there, with increased technologically advanced competition from Germany and Switzerland. A 1975 report by a senior Stone Platt executive, Jimmy McKinnon, exposed the company's shortcomings. McKinnon recommended that the three Lancashire factories should be reduced to one. His message of rationalization was not heeded. The company's diversification strategy was regarded as the only means of progress.

The closure of Platt Saco Lowell's Oldham and Bolton plants in 1980 and 1981 brought the group's problems to a head. Almost 1,000 people lost their jobs. The depth of the company's difficulties had been brought to the public's attention in April 1980 when Stone

* *Sunday Times*, 28 March 1982.

Platt defaulted on borrowings and was forced to re-arrange loans of nearly £40 million. In fact, due to a default clause with an American bank, the company's £30 million debts became immediately repayable – Stone Platt was technically insolvent. As problems mounted, Leslie Pincott, former managing director of Esso Petroleum and chairman of the Prices and Incomes Board, was brought in as chairman. A 'total outsider' is how he described himself. Pincott entered with the classic strategy of redundancy and retrenchment. 'I had to get it straight in a year or it would go down. I felt like a white knight,' says Pincott.

What he found at the company certainly seemed to require drastic action. Says Pincott: 'The board was complacent. It seemed to think that the worst was over. They had a running sore and thought everything was alright.'

As he examined the state of Stone Platt in late 1980, Pincott's concerns grew: 'I went through the order book and was aghast,' he recalls. 'Capacity was committed, people were cutting metal for non-existent orders.' Over £12 million of goods were eventually stored by Stone Platt with nowhere to go.

Reports commissioned by the company offered little solace. The Shirley Institute found that Stone Platt remained in second place in most of its markets. The markets, moreover, were generally only half as large as five years previously.

Despite the sale of the pump division in November 1980 for £11.5 million, Stone Platt made a loss of over £5 million for that year.

With continuing losses, a second rescue operation was launched in March 1981 when the City rallied round with a £10 million capital injection and new borrowing facilities totalling £40 million. The company hoped to break even that year. Instead, losses increased in the first half of the year to £3.5 million before tax. With the banks standing to lose £12–£16 million there was understandable concern about the company's prospects. Disagreement was rife.

The banks now began to become jittery. A participant in the rescue attempts comments: 'I think the banks lost confidence when Stone Platt did not meet its projections for 1981. But I don't think they ever really understood the very real difficulties for a company of this kind in trying to forecast its likely sales and profits.'

Morale could not have been helped by the resignation of chief executive Robin Tavener in September 1981 after a boardroom disagreement.

The Platt Saco Lowell textile machinery division, in the Sixties the company's star performer, was hit particularly hard. Says Pincott: 'The textile business was almost in freefall.' By 1982, *The Times* was able to label it 'the running sore which is largely responsible for the company's problems'. It lost £2.97 million in 1979 and a further £2.82 million in 1980. Against fierce European competition, this division alone lost £10 million between 1979 and 1982.

Other divisions of Stone Platt were not in such a precarious position. The electrical division registered a £4 million pre-tax profit in 1981 and had a turnover of £60 million, mainly generated by its 2,000 US employees.

By January 1982, however, there were less encouraging signs when the group announced a loss of £805,000 for the half year. The *Financial Times* commented: 'Stones are not renowned for their aerodynamic properties and these figures from the systems engineering group reveal a breathtaking plummet into loss.'

Stone Platt 1979–1982

	1979 Actual	1981 After PBSE	1982 Stone International
Turnover worldwide £m	212	153	95
Operating locations	52	21	13
Employees	13,000	7,100	4,500
Shareholders' funds £m	60	16	20
Net borrowings £m	37	20	15
Net capital employed £m	97	36	35

In March 1982, receivers were finally called into Stone Platt after a traumatic week of discussions with bankers. The shock of the 120-strong receivership staff arriving remains with Leslie Pincott. 'Suddenly everything is taken away from you,' he says.

The banks involved – Midland, Barclays, NatWest, Williams and Glyns and the Bank of England's industrial finance unit – had finally had enough. They refused to provide the further support asked for by the company, which was, by this time, at the limit of its agreed borrowings, at around £34 million.

The chairman, Leslie Pincott, observed: 'The banks were not able to accede to the company's plans, even though four leading share-holders were prepared to offer indications of assistance. I do not blame the banks. I am just worried about the fact that the system cannot help an engineering company with technology and hard work-ing people.'* He concluded: 'Something is deeply wrong with the system.'†

Ernst and Whinney's receivers, Bill Mackey and Bill Roberts, found Stone Platt attempting to launch yet another rescue package. The loss making textile machinery subsidiary, Platt Saco Lowell, was to be sold to an American buyer, while the Altrincham factory was about to be sold for £4.5 million. These deals would have reduced the group's borrowing to £22 million and would have left the remain-ing parts of Stone Platt at break even level. The company would then have gone to its main shareholders for a new rights issue of £5.5–7 million.

With Stone Platt's second half losses running at around £7 million, the same as in the first half of 1982, the short-term prospects were undoubtedly cloudy. Even so, the company envisaged a return to profit in 1983. To support this, optimists pointed towards the electri-cal side of Stone Platt's business which, when the receivers were called in, had orders from around the world totalling £43 million.

Central to the controversy surrounding sending Stone Platt into receivership, was the question of whether the banks had given the company long enough. Says Pincott: 'With a re-branded range, one factory and some help, it could have been a small electrical engineering group which could have grown again.' It appeared to many investors, not surprisingly, that they had been let down by the banks. One of the leading Stone Platt shareholders – Brian Dean of Equity Capital for Industry – complained at the time the receivers were called in: 'ECI is shocked and dismayed that after so much time and effort and money over two years the banks should have run away, just when a final solution was in sight.' The strength of his feeling is demonstrated by the fact that Equity Capital for Industry is a wholly owned subsidiary of the clearing banks.

Representatives of Stone Platt's major shareholder, unit trust group M&G, which lost £1.5 million through the engineering company's collapse, were similarly critical. Said M&G's managing director,

* *The Times*, 19 March 1982
† *Sunday Times*, 28 March, 1982.

David Hopkinson: 'I am sad that with a company that would have been profitable and viable in 1983, the banks were not prepared to have patience.'

Hopkinson called on the Bank of England to exercise closer control over the big banks: 'The institutional shareholders, with the Bank of England, worked the whole of last weekend to try and arrange a rescue package. They have been bloody-minded ... When a consortium is trying to rescue a company, you have to have some way of controlling individual members so they do not act solely in their own interests.'* Hopkinson pointed out the need for more long-term perspectives: 'Everyone knew that companies in trouble take two to three years to turn around. If anyone had said the banks were going to withdraw support so soon nobody would have subscribed.' He may have added, that during the weekend of final discussions before the receivers were called in, the clearing banks and institutions dealt through intermediaries rather than face-to-face. It was also significant that the company had a confusing array of thirteen banks prior to 1980.

A City observer added an even more uncomplimentary comment on the role of the banks: 'Frankly they ought to stick to lending money for houses. Industry would be better off going to the building societies for risk capital. I really do feel the banks would have acted differently six months ago.'

And Leslie Pincott's criticism has not altered with time: 'The banks lacked will and were not orientated towards industrial risks. They forced the sales of assets at knock-down rates.' Time-consuming meetings with the banks to some extent prevented management from getting on with the hard work of saving Stone Platt. Says Pincott: 'We spent so much time visiting banks that we ceased to sell the company's products. Eventually they became stonily silent and I realized I was talking to a wall.'

Midland Bank's chief executive at the time, Stuart Graham, had a different point of view: 'I don't like being told by other institutions how to run our business. Why don't they put their money where their mouth is?'†

As if to emphasize what the banks had thrown away, the Stone Platt Industries group was quickly split up and sold off.

* *Sunday Times*, 21 March 1982.
† *The Times*, 20 March 1982.

Platt Saco Lowell was sold, less than a month after the receivers arrived, to the South Carolina company, Hollingsworth On Wheels for £12 million. A total of 450 jobs were immediately lost.

In May 1982 Stone International, the group electrical division, was bought from the receiver in a management buyout for around £15 million. Robin Tavener, former Stone Platt chief executive, became chief executive of the new company. Stone International returned to the Stock Market in February 1984 and was, in June 1987, taken over by FKI Internationals for £36.6 million.

The experience of Platt Saco Lowell since it was sold off provides an example of what the Stone Platt group perhaps should have done earlier. The companies, which have survived the recession in the textile machinery industry, have generally done so through specialization rather than diversification. PSL has pioneered friction spinning and other British companies have also had to seek out market niches. Mackie of Belfast, for example, has reduced its workforce from over 5,000 in the Sixties to just over 1,000 and has specialized in 'long staple' spinning machinery for wool, jute and linen. Cobble of Blackburn has followed a similar pattern in the carpet tufting machinery market. The mass markets, once dominated by the likes of Stone Platt, have been left to the West Germans, Swiss and Italians.

The company's collapse may have had a silver lining in that it obliged the City to re-examine its attitudes towards troubled companies. Borthwick's chairman, Lewis Robertson, believes that the case has increased the resolve to save companies rather than letting them go down. Says Robertson: 'The financial world feels that the Stone Platt case ought not, if possible, to happen again. There is a definite feeling that Stone Platt marked a turning point at which the will to find a positive solution became dominant.'

Lessons

● Procrastination by management allowed problems to develop into crises.

Leslie Pincott explains: 'Rationalization and make or buy decisions were not taken in time. It was very sad because Stone Platt was worth saving. It was a marvellous company.'

● Controls were inadequate, particularly in the production area, where unrequired stocks of finished and semi-finished goods were allowed to accumulate.

• The company had a strong production orientation and a very weak marketing orientation in an industry where such demand as there was was increasingly market-led. A strong customer focus would have forced the issue on much of the necessary production rationalization.

WARDLE STOREYS

When Brian Taylor arrived at the Bernard Wardle company in May 1980, the situation was desperate. 'It was losing £300,000 in a good month, £400,000 in a bad one. The company was on the short road to bankruptcy,' he recalls. In the winter there was no heating oil to heat the offices, managers had to wear overcoats. In an effort to save money, water was taken from a stream to avoid paying water rates.

Since 1980 the company, now Wardle Storeys, has been transformed. It has been called 'Britain's sharpest industrial turnaround'. As managing director, Taylor has transformed large scale losses into sizeable profits. There is heating in the offices, a Bentley Turbo R outside and the water rates are paid on time.

Taylor was brought in by Graham Ferguson Lacy, who had paid £6 million for the ailing plastic sheeting manufacturer earlier in 1980. Lacy, the 'millionaire evangelist', entrepreneur and financier, anticipated that Taylor could manage a turnaround of Wardle within six months.

This optimism quickly gave way to the shock of reality. Taylor recalls his first day: 'I arrived at 7.30 on a Tuesday morning and I sat and went through the latest set of management accounts. By about 10.30 I'd come to the view that it wasn't a matter of how long it would take to turn the company round but whether it could be saved. If you set down the figures now you would decide it was plain crazy to try to save it.' Taylor's initial view was borne out by a £5 million loss in the sixteen months to the end of March 1981.

Bernard Wardle had previously been relatively successful. It had expanded by acquisition throughout the Sixties and Seventies. But, in 1980 Wardle Storeys felt the brunt of the recession that hit the automotive industry.

Taylor provides a forceful insight into the mistakes that were made: 'By 1980 it was in a much worse state than anyone realized. It was very clear what had gone wrong. Some things were internal, self-inflicted injuries. Others were external over which it had little or no control. It was heavily dependent on the automotive industry and, in particular, on the British automotive industry. Because of that, when the industry virtually stopped producing cars in 1980–1, volume obviously got hit very hard.' In fact, over 60 per cent of Wardle's sales were to the automotive industry.

Wardle's attempts at diversification had also been unsuccessful. Argues Taylor: 'It could have reorganized in good times and cut down the number of production facilities much earlier. It need not have gone off on some of its diversification projects with borrowed money. Wardle had got into a plastic bottle company in Holland which was losing a lot of money. It also had a noise insulation business, which really had very little value.'

Wardle had also diversified into garden and leisure products with little understanding of those markets. It fully equipped itself with expensive overheads before the sales materialized. As most of the products were manufactured outside the company, margins were wafer thin.

These problems were worsened by speculative, long-term agreements for raw materials, which the company had entered into. Wardle had a large forward commitment to raw materials stock, which it had agreed to buy at prices which were higher than the market rate and at volumes larger than the company could generate. Management had, in effect, gambled on raw material prices and inflation.

Taylor sums up: 'There were enough stupid mistakes for a large company to make and hit trouble. For a very small company, it really was a strong and almost successful attempt at suicide.'

Solving the problems was a challenging task. Taylor closed the factories at Caernarvon and Blackburn, as well as the company's head office at Knutsford. 'It was clear what had to be done: some of the factories had to be taken out, the head count had to be reduced very fast, some of the products we had to get out of and we had to get rid of the Dutch subsidiary,' he says.

The discipline of managing an ailing company provided a valuable lesson for Taylor: 'Running a business for cash gives you a different approach to life altogether and it's one most managers are not used to.'

But it wasn't just a dynamic life-saving operation. The long-term survival of the company was the real challenge, claims Taylor: 'We couldn't just say, cut it all back and that's that. Within eighteen months or two years the whole thing would have drifted down a bit further. We had to prepare for the future.'

By 1982 Wardle was breaking even, but had substantial borrowings to contend with. Taylor realized that future growth into profitability depended on overcoming this difficulty. He recalls: 'The borrowings were huge. New money needed to be brought in and the only way I could think of was to do a buyout.'

In fact, the idea of a management buyout had materialized towards the end of 1981. It was not until October 1982 that it went ahead. The buyout from parent company NCC Energy was financed by a consortium of leading institutions and the Wardle management team. Taylor himself put in £70,000.

Not surprisingly it was difficult to convince institutions that a company, which had been spectacularly unsuccessful just two years previously, was now a worthwhile investment. Says Taylor: 'We had only shown that we could save a business from ruin. We hadn't shown that we could make it successful. It was the early days of buyouts and many people wanted proof positive that you could produce gold bricks out of cucumbers. Lots of institutions threw us out.'

It didn't help that Wardle was in unfashionable businesses, such as pvc sheet production. But the buyout team had some cards in its hand.

It was basically selling proven management capability; and it had a plan, unfulfilled at the time, to buy a competitor, Storeys Industrial Products.

In the end Citicorp Venture Capital, Electra Investment Trust, Fountain Capital Development Fund and the British Rail Pension Fund were sufficiently impressed to finance the buyout, taking 63 per cent of the equity. If profit targets were met, the management were then to take over 51 per cent control.

The key to meeting the profit targets was the acquisition of Storeys, which had been a Turner and Newall subsidiary since 1977. Says Taylor: 'It became obvious that if we could put Wardle together with Storeys we would have a strength of market sector and product type and be able to create a potent force in the market place which didn't rely too heavily on commodity products. It was an integral part of the recovery. We were making use of under-utilized capacity and bringing it up to utilization. It made Wardle less reliant on the automotive sector and, of course, it also brought in the physical possibility of value added products we could put into our marketing effort.' Negotiations had been going on simultaneously with the buyout. In February 1983 the deal finally went ahead and Wardle Storeys came into being.

Again the problems were large. Although production, logistical and efficiency advantages, as well as the relatively cheap price, made Storeys an attractive proposition, it, too, was losing money – around £300,000 a month.

The purchase and integration of Storeys cost £4 million. Almost £3 million of this was spent on redundancy costs – the Lancaster plant was closed and a total of 1,500 jobs were lost. Merger and rationalization took just six months, including the transfer of technology, product lines, relocation of large machines and reorganization of transportation. Some of the plant and equipment and most of the product lines were transferred to the Wardle factories at Earby and Brantham.

The process of recovery reached another landmark in November 1984 when Wardle Storey returned to the Stock Market with a price tag of £20.4 million. The sale of seven million shares was heavily oversubscribed and Brian Taylor turned the £70,000 he had borrowed in 1982 to £6.6 million just two years later. He observed at the time: 'The consistent factor has been management style, working for profits and cash, and now we are going public, for earnings per share.'

The most striking feature of the company's recovery has been its financial management. Taylor previously worked on the turnaround of Wilkinson Match's Safety and Protection Division. In six years, return on net assets was raised from virtually zero to 60 per cent. He believes in 'good sound old Victorian management principles' and provides a simple management philosophy. 'Management is the same as it always has been,' he says. 'It's just that the aids to management differ. At one time someone ran the East India company before there was such things as computers. But they evolved a management style which was successful. This is no more than the Japanese, Germans or anybody does. They pay great attention to detail and quality. They do not chase marvellous strategic concepts all around the sky. They actually get into the business and run the hell out of it.'

In the half year to the end of February 1988 Wardle Storeys' pre-tax profits were up 38 per cent to £7.6 million. Its technical products division almost doubled its operating profit.

This has been achieved through organic growth and a number of successful acquisitions. In April 1987 Wardle acquired Weston Hyde Products' coated fabrics business. In June 1986 Wardle acquired RFD, a manufacturer of life-rafts, dinghies and parachutes. This 'gave us a wider segment of business interests and got us into the defence industry', says Taylor.

The only blot on the company's recent record has been the abortive £62 million bid for Chamberlain Phipps, the shoe components and adhesives company, early in 1987, which cost the company £1.5 million.

Year to 31 August	Turnover £million	Pre-tax profit £million	Stated earnings per share (pence)	Gross dividend per share (pence)
1984	39.8	3.15	16.7	–
1985	40.5	4.02	19.1	7.14
1986	44.8	5.6	23.6	8.45
1987	69	12.7	35.2	12.33

Wardle Storeys remains firmly rooted in a traditional manufacturing sector with 35 per cent of its sales being coated fabrics and laminated products with the rest plastic sheeting. The automotive industry now accounts for 24 per cent of sales with Wardle making plastic and sound insulation for Jaguar and Rolls Royce as well as sun visors for the Ford Sierra. The level of its diversification can be seen in the nursery market where Wardle is the leading supplier of washable linings for prams and push chairs to companies such as Mothercare. It also sells shop awnings, floor tiles, protective clothing, bath panels and a range of stationery products.

The company has recently been described as a small version of BTR. Brian Taylor remains a realist: 'It may sound smug and pompous but there's no such thing as yesterday's hero. You've got to make it work next year.'

Lessons

Most of Bernard Wardle's problems can be summed up as a failure of vision. Faced with declining demand in its core markets, the company switched attention to a series of investments in areas it knew nothing about and to which it could bring little in the way of special expertise. While top management's attention was diverted by ill-judged, unhealthy acquisitions, the rationalization and modernization of the existing businesses was neglected. Acquisitions appear to have been opportunistic rather than part of a carefully developed growth plan.

• Even a very healthy company is ill-advised to expose itself extensively to the fluctuations of the commodities markets.

CURTAIN DREAM

One of the acclaimed attractions of franchise operations is that they have a much better survival rate than start-up businesses in general. Curtain Dream could have been designed to bring down the averages.

The vision behind Curtain Dream belonged to managing director Christopher Whitehead. He envisaged a nationwide chain of franchised retail outlets, selling first curtains, then a range of matching furnishings, to working-class customers. In July 1986, he and a colleague, Paul Lister, began trading from factory premises in Bradford, producing curtains to order. By the end of that year he had three shops in the North of England and was sufficiently confident in the business concept to move into franchising. During the first six months of 1987, he opened another nine shops, all through franchisees. These were the relatively lucky ones – they paid only £7,000 for their franchises; shortly before the end, new franchisees were paying £65,000. The shops carried very little stock, other than for display and demonstration; they mainly served to take orders, which would then be made by the factory.

Curtain Dream's financial year ended on 30 June, at which point it showed a profit of £14,000 on turnover of £216,000. Two expansionary moves followed rapidly. The first was to enlarge the range from curtains and curtain accessories to matching furnishings such as sofas, carpets and wallpaper. This increased the average sales volume per customer by about 50 per cent, to around £750.

The second move was to seek institutional backing to increase the number of franchisees more rapidly. At the end of 1987, Curtain Dream had a cash injection of £350,000, via a Business Expansion Scheme fund. Against fierce competition, Quester Capital Management won the beauty parade to acquire 35 per cent of the equity in what was, to all appearances, a solid investment. A year later it took in another £1.5 million from Quester and a variety of other institutions, including Paribas, with arrangements for a further tranche of the same size in 1990, to assist it in obtaining a USM listing. Reported turnover in year two shot up to £2 million.

Plans were put in train for a doubling of the Bradford factory space to 160,000 sq. ft. and, in February 1989, Helen James, Curtain Dream's marketing director, was telling *Carpet and Floorcoverings Review* that 'We have forty-two shops up and trading and are opening three per month nationwide. Franchisees are expected to make £25,000 in the first year of trading and, with a group turnover predicted to be in excess of £5 million for the financial year 1989/90, I would expect the UK market to hold 250 such stores before saturation point is reached.'

In expansive mood, Whitehead told *Today*, in mid-1988, that the company had little to fear from the entry into its market of High Street stores such as Next and Marks & Spencer. 'They don't understand their customers like we do ... We listen, then we supply people with what they want.'

By mid-1988, the main business of the company was manufacture in its Bradford factory (by now employing 207 production employees) and the sale of franchises. As with all rapid expansion programmes, however, there were inevitably a number of problems. Difficulties in obtaining the kind of shopfitting the company needed led Whitehead to start his own shopfitting operation. This was the start of a major phase of empire-building for Curtain Dream. Instead of focusing on the core business, top management diverted its attention to a host of peripheral activities. Rather than hire in a photographer as needed, it created Curtain Dream Studios. The company began to print its own fabric; it set up a carpet-fitting service to fit the carpets it supplied; and a consultancy service that visited franchisees twice each year and advised on improvements to the window display.

Another problem was that the company had been insufficiently discriminating about who it took on as a franchisee. Stuart McKellar, of receivers Cork Gully, says that 'There is no record of them having turned anyone away.' The only qualification required, it seemed, was the cash to pay for the franchise. Whitehead had aimed the recruitment deliberately at what he described as blue-collar people; his ideal franchisee was an ex-miner with a substantial redundancy cheque and a clever wife. The reasoning was to some extent sound – such people would better be able to relate to the working-class customers than the middle-class couples managing competitive outlets. Unfortunately, many of them had no commercial experience or acumen. Indeed, the company emphasized in interviews that previous retail experience was not essential. As one publication reported: 'What makes for success is hard work, operating by the book – and no previous experience. So far the most successful Curtain Dreamer is a structural engineeer, who earned £30,000 in his first year. And the least successful was – you guessed – a salesman who knew it all beforehand.'

In the race to fit franchisees with premises, Curtain Dream also approved a number of unsuitable sites. Some were simply so out of the way that custom was limited; others were in expensive town centre sites where the rent and rates were so high it wasn't possible to obtain an adequate return. Seven franchisees failed and gave up. Curtain Dream took over their operations, in the (not always justified) expectation that it could do a better job of making these locations pay.

Debt collection from franchisees was badly handled, too. Failure to collect receivables rapidly enough exacerbated the cash flow problems.

As demand from the retail outlets increased, the factory found it more and more difficult to cope. It didn't have the production management or systems to produce relatively customized products in large volume. Order to delivery times gradually stretched out to twelve weeks.

All these problems were fairly obvious, even to a top management that preferred to largely ignore them. Less obvious was the fact that the company was insufficiently capitalized to handle the pace of its growth. By mid-1989 it had seventy outlets, of which sixty-six were trading. An inadequate accounting system (the accounting function was extremely weak) failed to show that the company was actually bleeding to death.

The seriousness of the financial problems was disguised in part by the way in which the company handled its retail property portfolio. *Retail Week* described the practice as 'buying freehold properties, charging the franchisees inflated rents and selling the freeholds for large profits.'

The bubble burst when Curtain Dream applied to the investors to have the second tranche of £1.5 million brought forward by a year. Barclays Bank, which was already concerned that the company had exceeded its overdraft for a considerable period, asked Cork Gully to carry out an investigation. It had been alerted by Steve Sargent, the financial director brought in in May 1989, at the insistence of the institutional investors. Sargent promptly blew the whistle on some of the grosser inadequacies of the accounting systems. 'I was appointed to help groom the company for its flotation on the USM,' he told *Retail Week*. 'I didn't expect to find the can of worms that came out.'

'We were reasonably well-received. They thought they'd see us off like everyone else,' recalls McKellar. But the more stones Cork Gully overturned, the worse the financial picture appeared. In reality, the company could only project losses for the following eighteen months. A forecast of £1 million profit was rapidly revised into a £1 million loss.

'Turnover was an interesting concept as far as Curtain Dream was concerned,' says McKellar. A posted turnover of £6.4 million was made up of £1.3 million in sales of franchises, £0.5 million tied up in properties, and regular trading income.

The management accounts showed net assets of £3,327,000. Cork Gully gradually whittled this down. £1.8 million of stock received a realistic valuation of £1 million; debtors of £2 million were reduced to £800,000; the value of fixed assets was knocked down by £500,000; profits turned out to have been wrongly included in the net asset figures; and there was a general understatement of creditors of about £500,000. Actual net assets were reduced to a mere £11,000.

'On a break-up basis, the company was worth nothing,' says McKellar. 'On a going-concern basis, they were just worth something.'

Curtain Dream went down with a net deficiency between assets and debts of £7 million – more than its reported turnover. Apart from the physical assets, such as sewing machines and some property, the only saleables were the franchise rights and moneys owed by franchisees. The remnants of the firm were acquired by Mostyns, a competitor based in the West Country, with a similar, but more viable chain of outlets of its own.

Lessons

Curtain Dream is a signal example of the entrepreneurial venture that grows too fast for its managers to handle. Among the critical problems:

● Its management neglected financial controls and internal controls of all sorts.

● Monitoring by the investors was slack.

● The company was dominated by one autocratic executive and an uncritical friend.

● Curtain Dream had to a large extent been promoted to investors on the back of its own public relations. Whitehead 'liked a high profile' says McKellar.

McKellar sums up the main lessons as: 'They grew a business that didn't have a proper infrastructure for controlled growth. They grew too fast, in too cavalier a fashion. Failure was inevitable.'

SEAMOUNT LIMITED

The waters around the Falkland Islands are some of the richest fishing grounds in the world. There was money to be made there, especially in the late Eighties after government initiatives limited fishing rights to preferred firms. Seamount was to have been one of those preferred firms. As a British–Falklands joint fishing venture, all it needed was a few trawlers and a bit of luck to make the most of the rich Falklands fishing resources.

The profit potential looked so good that a gold rush mentality took over. Unfortunately, this spirit of unbridled optimism took Seamount's would-be fish moguls well out of their depth.

A 1988 government enquiry into the affairs of Seamount uncovered a tangle of misunderstandings, miscalculations and personality clashes that led to the disastrous failure of a promising venture.

The Falkland Islanders have traditionally been farmers and had never developed a fishing industry to exploit the resources in their waters. Fishing by foreign fleets, however, led to concern in the mid-Eighties about a possible depletion of fish stocks. The United Kingdom and Falkland Islands governments responded with steps to manage and conserve the fisheries, the major part of which was the establishment, in October 1986, of an Interim Fishery Conservation and Management Zone of a radius of 150 miles from the islands.

From 1 December 1986 foreign fleets, which could previously fish without restriction up to the three-mile limit, required licences from the newly established Director of Fisheries. The licences were not especially expensive, but they were limited – and hence lucrative, given the then high fish prices and limited competition created by the new system.

The system was a sensible one, but it still did not turn the fishing resources to the benefit of the islanders. To answer this need, the Falkland Islands government launched a joint venture system, under which the Director of Fisheries gave preference in licence allocation first to Falkland Islands firms and secondly to joint ventures with a majority held by a Falkland Islands firm.

As there were as yet no local fishing companies, joint ventures became, effectively, the preferred set-up. The government, through the Falkland Islands Development Corporation (FIDC) launched a subsidiary, Stanley Fisheries Ltd, specifically for the purposes of entering into these joint ventures. During 1987 Stanley Fisheries arranged fourteen joint ventures with fishing operators from around the world.

The usual arrangement involved a 51 per cent ownership by Stanley Fisheries and 49 per cent by the foreign partner. However, for most of these ventures, Stanley Fisheries' 51 per cent amounted to waiving the licence fee, which, as a subsidiary of a government agency, it was able to to. It did not normally contribute capital. Nor did Stanley Fisheries actually do any fishing. Its role was strictly administrative, as it owned no fishing vessels, nor indeed had any off-shore fishing expertise among its staff. Thus, although the ventures were profitable for the islanders – to the tune of £3.4 million in 1987 alone – they did not afford them any first-hand experience in fishing.

The FIDC recognized that the islanders would benefit even more from an arrangement that gave the Falklanders a chance to acquire experience in managing a fishing company. Seamount was seen to be just that.

In October 1987, Stanley Fisheries' board members were in London for a series of meetings with a number of potential joint venture partners, including Seaboard Offshore Limited, a Scottish operation run by two brothers: Roderick and Kenneth MacKenzie. Minutes of the meeting describe Seaboard as 'probably the United Kingdom's largest owners of stern trawlers, with six vessels'. This was not, however, strictly true as none of the vessels were used for fishing. They had all been converted to offshore support vessels.

During the next few months Stanley Fisheries and Seaboard negotiated a joint venture, called Seamount Ltd, with equity from both parties and a low-interest loan from the Exports Credit and Guarantee Department (ECGD). The arrangement was unusual in that Stanley Fisheries was to commit its own capital for the first time.

The future looked rosy. With high fish prices, good yields around the Falklands and government financial support, little could go wrong. But it did. And badly. Seaboard never caught so much as a minnow, collapsing only a few months after incorporation under an unsupportable debt load. The failure was such an administrative and financial mess that the Falkland Islands government found it necessary to make a formal investigation into the firm's affairs.

The report, prepared in 1988 by Stewart Boyd QC, found the primary causes of Seamount's demise to be a weak financial base and mechanical problems with the vessels. There were, however, significant underlying problems as well – many of them pointing back to staffing problems at Stanley Fisheries.

Dr J. Beddington was a board member of Stanley Fisheries until December 1987, and was to have been a board member nominee on its joint venture subsidiaries. As Director of the Marine Resource Assessment Group (MRAG) at the Centre for Environmental Technology in London, Dr Beddington was the only director of Stanley

Fisheries with any significant experience of fisheries management, and played a leading role in the development of the joint-venture concept. He was asked to resign by the board in October 1987 on the grounds that his role as the government's Fisheries adviser was incompatible with his role as a director of Stanley Fisheries and the joint-venture companies. Unfortunately, his resignation left Stanley Fisheries with no board-level fisheries expertise during its negotiations with Seaboard.

Disagreements over Dr Beddington's resignation led, shortly afterwards, to the effective resignation of Stanley Fisheries general manager, Simon Armstrong. Although Armstrong nominally retained his position he took no further part in joint-venture negotiations – further weakening the team.

Brian Cummings was the chairman of Stanley Fisheries from June 1987 to June 1988. During October 1987, at a critical point in the negotiations, other board members expressed concern about a perceived conflict of interest between Cummings' governmental roles (as the Falkland Islands government chief executive and director of fisheries) and his commercial activities as chairman of Stanley Fisheries. 'In particular', says Boyd, 'the board was concerned about his long absences from the islands and concentration on fisheries at the expense of his governmental duties.' After he entered into joint-venture negotiations in Spain against the instructions of the Falkland Islands Governor (it was, at the time, an area of diplomatic sensitivity), Cummings was instructed by the Governor to withdraw from all Stanley Fisheries' commercial activities – pulling yet another important player from the negotiations.

After the resignations of Beddington, Armstrong and Cummings, most of the negotiations with Seaboard were left to the two remaining executive directors, assistant general manager Shane Wolsey and director Michael Gaiger. Neither of them, says Boyd, 'had the commercial or financial training or experience to handle a venture of this size or kind'.

In November 1987, Wolsey raised his concerns about Stanley Fisheries' staffing, reporting to the board that the structure was weak and that staff had too little time to deal with the joint ventures, to study proposals or do sufficient financial analysis. He felt that the operation badly needed a managing director and a secretary/accountant. The board agreed, but little was done to recruit the necessary personnel.

Stanley Fisheries staffing and structural weaknesses had a disastrous impact on the firm's financial records. Says Boyd: 'There were no accounting records or financial management systems for any of the joint-venture companies, even though it was Stanley's responsibilities to keep them. There were no ledgers of any kind. The management accounts for the year ended 31 December 1987 had to be prepared by the auditors themselves from such bank statements as there were, from supporting evidence in banking and correspondence files and from the recollections of management.'

Although Seamount itself, whose books were kept by Seaboard, did have proper records, Stanley Fisheries' administrative problems had a calamitous effect on the joint-venture financing. Says Boyd: 'When capital projects such as Seamount needed to be funded, it was virtually impossible to tell what funds were available from Stanley Fisheries' own resources and how much needed to be borrowed from elsewhere.' Despite Stanley Fisheries role as a commercial development subsidiary of the Falkland Islands Development Corporation, its capital projects were not subjected to the kind of financial analysis and appraisal which would be expected of such a company.

In October, Stanley Fisheries and Seaboard representatives agreed – orally – to buy and refit two hull steam trawlers at a cost of £6 million.

The proposal was never put in writing, but Dr Beddington did summarize it in a memo to his board. He wrote that he saw no major problems, but was expecting a revised cash budget from Seaboard with the proposed financing arrangements, and at that point: 'will revert if I foresee problems'. When the budget arrived it revealed that Stanley Fisheries was expected to provide £600,000 in capital, twice the £300,000 earlier understood, and that the venture would need more working capital, and sooner, than originally thought.

Beddington did not revert as promised in his memo – he did not have a chance as he had been asked to resign in the meantime. Gaiger was now alone on the negotiating team, with four days to finalize details and reach an agreement, with minimal information about agreements made so far.

Says Boyd: 'Mr Gaiger was a lawyer and not a businessman – and I am doubtful whether he fully understood what was being proposed. Gaiger, wisely, said he could not commit Stanley Fisheries to anything; that that could only happen after discussion with his chief executive, Mr Cummings.'

Cummings did arrive in London, but only to receive a letter from the Governor asking for *his* resignation. Fortunately for Gaiger, the assistant general manager, Shane Wolsey soon arrived in London to take over the next stage of the negotiations.

Unfortunately for Wolsey, however, the lack of communication preceding his arrival left him with the impression that the negotiations were far more advanced than they actually were. As he later told Boyd, he 'believed that his job was to put in place what had been already agreed in principle'. In fact, most of the financial aspects of the venture had yet to be analyzed.

The negotiations were, however, completed by November and Seamount Ltd was incorporated in Stanley. The shareholders' agreement had originally held that Stanley Fisheries was to be the majority shareholder with 51 per cent of the equity; and the remaining 49 per cent was to be held on a 60/40 basis by Seaboard and a British equity capital group Investors in Industry (3i).

However, by the time Seamount was incorporated (on 19 November 1987) 3i had dropped out and the agreement continued with 51 per cent stake held by Stanley Fisheries, and 49 per cent by Seaboard.

Perhaps 3i had sensed a bad omen. The months following the incorporation brought a series of misunderstandings and miscalculations that left Seamount with an extremely weak – and virtually terminal – financial structure.

First, the venture was to be financed with a £4.8 million ECGD loan, secured by the ship mortgages. Normally the ECGD expects a 30 per cent guarantee, but, says Boyd: 'It was assumed that no guarantee would be required from Stanley Fisheries or the FIDC on the grounds that the Falkland Islands government support would be sufficient.'

It was not. When the ECGD loan finally came through in February 1988, the terms stated that Stanley Fisheries was obliged to guarantee 30 per cent of it. Although according to the joint-venture agreement the two partners should have shared the obligation equally, the ECGD would not accept that arrangement and demanded the full guarantee from Stanley Fisheries.

Also, says Boyd: 'Stanley Fisheries assumed their investment for Seamount would be available in the form of dividends from other joint-venture companies. This proved not to be the case, and those funds also had to be borrowed.' This was no easy task. When the firm did try to borrow the £918,000 needed for its share of the investment, the bank refused the application. In hindsight, the bank's grounds proved sound; Seamount's cash flow forecasts made no provision for interest payments, and the income and profit projections were too sensitive to the volume of fish caught and the strength of the American dollar (though investments were made in pounds, the catch would be sold on world markets in dollars).

As the ECGD loan was some time in coming, Seamount had to secure a £2.8 million bridging loan. This was also guaranteed entirely by Stanley Fisheries, despite the terms of the management agreement.

Meanwhile, the cost of converting the ships was rising steadily and the bridging loan was insufficient to pay the shipyard. Seamount faced a vicious circle – without the boats, it could not fish, and without fishing income it could not continue.

At this point one might have expected help from Stanley Fisheries' parent – the Falkland Islands government. Perhaps, given the history of poor communication between the two, the government was not aware how serious the situation had become. The feeling at Stanley Fisheries, according to Boyd, was that the firm 'could make its own decisions so long as its total liabilities or commitments were covered by its assets. That presupposed Stanley Fisheries' management knew what the liabilities, commitments and assets amounted to. They did not. Nor was there any way of finding out.'

Building debt upon debt, even before starting operations, committed the firm to heavy financing costs from the start. Worse, management had not accounted for these costs when estimating the amount of working capital needed. As a result, Seaboard was completely dependant on fishing income to make the interest payments. 'Any delay in starting to fish would very rapidly leave the company with a cash crisis,' says Boyd. 'If fishing income fell below budget, they were doomed,' he says.

In the end, there was no fishing income at all. Seamount caught nothing. One ship, the *Mount Kent*, was out of commission due to technical problems after only a few days fishing. The other, the *Mount Challenger*, never even made it across the Atlantic – it was ordered back to Britain in late January when Stanley Fisheries failed to come up with the whole of the loan capital.

Even if the vessels had made it to the fishing grounds and Stanley Fisheries had found the financing, it is unlikely that the operation would have survived. Catches in 1988 were low, relative to previous years, and the dollar had declined in value against the pound. And, as the manager of the Standard Chartered Bank rightly pointed out, the cash flow forecasts were very sensitive to these two factors. The capital structure of Seamount was also excessively highly geared. 'Virtually the whole of the capital was borrowed and the working capital was at minimum. There was virtually no margin of error,' says Boyd.

The loss of fishing income led immediately to a cash crisis – and bankruptcy for Seamount. The failure involved such a tangle of errors that the Falkland Islands government found it necessary to conduct an inquiry into the firm's affairs.

Lessons

Seamount's troubles stemmed from management attitudes towards vision and controls. Says Boyd: 'The stakes were high. If all had gone according to forecast, large profits should have been made from the very first season. But something of a gold rush mentality affected everyone involved with Seamount. Ordinary business prudence was supplanted by limitless optimism.

The problems were, of course, severely aggravated by Stanley Fisheries' staffing weaknesses, and lack of board-level expertise. 'Mr Gaiger and Mr Wolsey were entirely without the financial skill necessary to carry out a commercial undertaking of this kind,' says Boyd.

The blame cannot lie entirely with Stanley Fisheries' management. 'Seaboard should have known that Stanley Fisheries would look to them for financial expertise, yet the cash flow forecasts they provided to their joint-venture partners were a wholly unsound basis for the venture. The fact that they accepted uncritically the optimistic forecasts of catches and selling rates endorsed by Stanley Fisheries may in part be attributed to their utter lack of experience in fishing, let alone South Atlantic fishing. It is clear from the limited cash flow forecasts they produced that no one on their side looked beyond the first two or three years,' says Boyd.

'The fact that the MacKenzie brothers, both of whom are accountants with considerable experience of business, should have been prepared to commit Seamount to such a venture on this basis is astonishing. It is difficult to believe that they did not themselves carry out more detailed analyses of the project,' he adds.

Overall, says Boyd: 'The most serious error was a failure to appreciate or to act on the need for independent advice on the financial and legal aspects of the venture, particularly as every one of the participants was at almost every stage completely out of his depth when evaluating, negotiating and establishing a capital project of this kind.'

HINARI

Knowing what will sell, how well it will sell and at what price, should have been a recipe for success in the highly-competitive consumer electronics market. But, as Scottish manufacturer Hinari learned the hard way, marketing talent is only as good as the financial muscle behind it.

Hinari was a rare British success story, reaching a turnover of £60 million in only three years with its British-designed, Asian-manufactured line of televisions, audio equipment and domestic appliances.

The firm's success, however, proved to be its Achilles heel. Unable to support the pace of growth, it fell victim to the hard winter of 1988–9 – the year interest rates knocked the bottom out of the consumer electronics market. After barely four years of trading, Hinari called in the administrators.

Brian Palmer, Hinari's founder and driving force had, as he says, 'served a long apprenticeship in the consumer electronics business'. A former marketing director at Philips, Palmer launched a wholesale operation of his own in 1978.

It was his entrepreneurial philosophy, as much as his previous success, that later led him to launch his own line: 'I'd always had a yearning to develop my own range and not have to accept other people's errors. I guess I want to be responsible for my own mistakes,' he says.

After four years of planning, including numerous trips to the Far East to negotiate with manufacturers, Palmer coined the Japanese-sounding name and imported the first Hinari television in 1985. Hinari's sales grew rapidly and soon outpaced the original wholesale business, absorbing its staff and operations. Yet despite its rapid expansion, Hinari remained very much a one-man show, with Palmer himself holding a 75 per cent share of the business.

The firm made rapid market inroads, soon averaging about 10 per cent of the 1.6 million unit 14″ colour TV market, 3–4 per cent of the 21″ market and a full 20–30 per cent of UK televideo sales.

The quick success was, according to Palmer, a matter of skilled marketing drawn from the management team's considerable experience in the consumer electronics market. 'We had been in the business a long time,' he says. 'We emerged out of the retail side and knew what would sell on the High Street, how well it would sell and at what price.'

The marketing strategy was a potent mix of quality design, good retail margins and sharp consumer price points. 'We took a lot of trouble about the look of the products so those at a given price point looked as good as their more expensive rivals. We supported the dealers with a sizeable advertising budget and gave them better margins than they were enjoying on similarly-priced retail products. Being new, operating in Scotland and having a relatively small infrastructure meant we were able to operate at tighter margins than our competitors,' says Palmer.

Frank Blin of Cork Gully, who eventually became Hinari's joint administrator, agrees that Brian Palmer had great marketing flair, but believes the sales volume may have come at too high a price: 'The design was well thought out and the goods were well priced, but making money was another matter.'

Although Hinari showed a good bottom line until its final year, Blin feels that management could have kept a closer eye on individual profit margins. 'You can't just buy turnover – you have got to know what the margins are on each product line and some lines weren't making as much money as they thought they were,' he says. 'With all that moving stock, Hinari needed a good computer system to know what was selling where, and how well, but it did not invest in that kind of back-up system.'

Palmer aimed to establish a European brand and in 1987, encouraged by success at home, opened operations in Spain and Germany – a decision he later came to regret.

'Opening new operations is costly, not only from a cash point of view but also in terms of management time,' he says. Hinari, like many other growing firms, underestimated the time and effort involved in a move into Europe. 'One of the major contributors to the lack of money in the business was the amount we used up in Europe by, for example, giving far too much credit to the dealer in Spain. Had we been managing with the benefit of hindsight we would have not have opened those new offices, but would have continued to sell through agents.'

Hinari was growing too fast. As Palmer later admitted, it was more than the existing management could cope with. 'We didn't stop and consolidate our existing business before we moved into Europe – that's the real tragedy of it,' he says.

By 1988, Hinari's growth was rapidly overtaking its financial backing. 'Hinari grew to be a large company but it did not have a very big capital base because most of its profits had been ploughed back into creating a brand,' says Palmer.

Palmer spent a good part of the year seeking capital to finance further growth, eventually raising £4 million from a group of five institutions, including merchant bankers, Hill Samuel and Brown Shipley. Together the five held a 14.4 per cent stake, entitling them to appoint two directors to the board.

This amount, however, proved to be insufficient. Says Palmer: 'I was probably too mean with the number of shares I gave out at the time as £4 million wasn't enough to turn on the type of borrowing we needed. Had we injected more capital then, we might have survived what turned out to be a very bad year.'

Used to running a one-man show, Palmer had some difficulties adjusting to the new partnership. 'It was a new experience having other people involved. I was, by mid-1988, spending too much time worrying about our outside investors, and perhaps not following my own instincts enough. Being answerable to others in a way I hadn't been before was not an enjoyable experience for me.'

Rapid growth on an insufficient capital base left Hinari vulnerable when hit with both a market downturn and a failed product launch in late 1988.

Christmas that year was disastrous for Hinari. All consumer goods manufacturers felt the effects of high interest rates, but the timing was particularly damaging for the highly seasonal consumer electronics industry.

'We deliver probably 50 per cent of our annual turnover between September and December, and that year we felt the effects of the Chancellor's measures on the market from about October,' says Palmer. Sales were down badly that year and for the first time Hinari finished the Christmas season with excess stock.

Among the leftover Christmas goods were several million pounds worth of 'Disk Decks' – the 1988 Christmas product launch that arrived from the manufacturer sometime after the 1989 January sales.

'We tried to launch a new product each year because it is the innovations, not the "me too" products, that put margin into the business,' explains Palmer. 'And of course there is always a risk in new product development – especially when the sales season is so short.'

The Disk Deck, a horizontal hi-fi system, could well have been a hit. 'We sold about 65,000 of them – £10 million worth – in advance but when the manufacturer failed to deliver in time for Christmas, we lost about £2.5 million on the launch,' says Palmer.

'It would have made so much difference to the bottom line in 1988 if we'd had it,' laments Palmer. 'Worse, it actually caught us twice because we couldn't deliver it pre-Christmas, and then we were stuck with it – at a time of high interest rates – right up to the day the business went into administration.'

'Development problems are one of the risks in this business. All you can really do is rely on the previous track record of the manufacturer and his had been quite good until then,' he says.

'We knew we had problems with the Disk Deck not arriving but we thought they were manageable. I don't think we were aware at the time that they were going to have such a tremendous impact on the future – or the non-future – of the business.'

By March 1989, however, it became apparent that Hinari's financial troubles had reached crisis point.

'By that time the investors wanted to sell the business and in retrospect that probably would have been the correct decision then,' says Palmer. 'But that wasn't what I wanted to do. I wanted to reposition, cut back where necessary, and introduce more capital so that we could carry on.'

To this end, Palmer spent most of Hinari's remaining months trying to raise more financing. 'I wanted to be able to buy out the existing investors or to reduce their stake, and to reduce my stake as well, in order to attract new money,' he says.

Palmer was unsuccessful, both in raising sufficient financing and in retaining the confidence of the existing investors. In August 1989 the board replaced him as chief executive on the grounds, according to the *Financial Times*, that the company needed a managing director more suited to a large, maturing company. It was a decision that Palmer understandably found distasteful.

'I'd always thought that to get rid of me in a difficult year was ill-conceived. I had bought the product and would have sold it, and probably could have realized more cash for it that way,' he claims.

John Robinson, a former managing director of Electrocomponents, replaced Palmer as chief executive and immediately set about consoling the creditors.

Explains Palmer: 'Robinson spent about eight weeks looking at the figures and forecasting results to the end of February 1990. Traditionally somebody, who hasn't been involved in a firm's existing problems, but realizes he'll be responsible for them, prefers to forecast a worst-case scenario and present it to the creditors on the basis that things can only improve.'

Robinson's worst-case scenario showed Hinari to be insolvent with debts of about £30 million. By law, Hinari could only continue to trade with the creditors' support. 'Unfortunately,' explains Palmer, 'Hinari had fourteen different banks and trying to get fourteen banks to agree was nearly impossible. Each was owed between £500,000 and £4 million pounds, so there was not one in it for more money than they could write off. If we had owed all the money to one or two banks, perhaps they could have been more interested in what we had to do to save the business.'

Without the banks' support, Robinson had no choice but to put the firm into administration. The procedure is one step short of receivership in that it allows the company to continue trading while holding the creditors at bay, in the hopes of salvaging the business.

Hinari was not, however, able to trade for long. Although the order book was substantial, (according to Palmer it contained as much as seven or eight million pounds worth of pre-Christmas orders) Hinari could not fulfil them.

Says administrator Frank Blin: 'The customers required assurance that the firm would be able to honour the warranty and supply spare parts. We couldn't guarantee that, nor did we have enough of a cash flow to continue trading. To make matters worse, the customers began to cancel orders as soon as the firm went into administration. I would have happily kept going, but it just wasn't possible.'

The Hinari name is, however, still alive and well on the High Street. The administrators negotiated a sale of the brand name and the stock to Alba plc, another British consumer electronics firm, which has, says Blin 'stood by the Hinari brand name and warranty'.

Lessons

Hinari's rapid growth was its downfall, as it had neither the management structure nor the financial backing for its size.

'There was no doubt that, in the push to grow, we had grown too quickly to a size that the existing management couldn't cope with,' says Palmer. 'It's a failing of most businesses that start from nothing to try to always promote from within. You don't plan the management for the size of business you'll create, you plan the management for the size of business you have at the moment. So you're always running about twelve months behind in the way you administer and manage the business.'

Finance was another major weakness among Hinari management, and Palmer himself recognizes that it was not his strength: 'You can't be an expert in everything. When I went to the City in 1988 looking to finance our growth, I was also looking for the financial expertise that venture capitalists could bring to a growing business. Unfortunately, the advice that I had at the time was not, in retrospect, the advice that was right for the business.'

Palmer says that he did later get the advice he needed from another merchant banker: 'He told me the form of investment I had was wrong. What I needed was a mixture of equity finance and mezzanine finance (a lower risk/lower return form of venture capital) of sufficient levels to have turned on borrowing from a major bank. Had I found, say, £4 million in venture capital and £8 million in mezzanine financing things might have been different.'

The capitalization that Hinari did achieve, was, according to Palmer, too focused on short-term rewards. 'In the UK everyone is interested in quick rewards. Venture capitalists are not prepared to wait it out until the company can make returns.'

Hinari's story is a classic case of marketing talent without financial muscle. As Frank Blin sums it up: 'Brian Palmer was an entrepreneur who built up business with a talent for finding the right market for an idea. But you can't just go for growth because it's available – you have to have the financial backing to make it possible. And at Hinari, they wanted to run before they could walk.'

Undaunted, Palmer is up and running again with another consumer electronics venture. The new firm, called Akura, will manufacture a full range of televisions, home audio and video equipment by exclusive arrangement with a Far Eastern concern in Cumbernauld as of mid-1990.

Palmer has learned from his Hinari experience. This time, he says, 'we will stay with what we are good at – focusing on our sales and marketing skills, but within a smaller infrastructure. We have also gone in with financial partners who will supply more money and more administrative and financial expertise than Hinari ever had.'

Palmer may well have found his success recipe – albeit the second time around.

PART VI
Appendix A

THE SURVEY QUESTIONNAIRE

• Although most failed businesses will have weaknesses in many areas, what do you find to be the most common underlying causes of business failure? (Circle as many as you feel are applicable.)

* Lack of financial control: poor financial information, lack of credit control.
* Poor financial structure: insufficient working capital, insufficient access to funds, too much debt financing, too much short-term debt, other.
* Faulty cost structure: insufficient margin, excessive overhead costs, other.
* Poor management: lack of commitment, divisions within management, inexperience, lack of control, poor employee relations, other.
* Strategic errors: lack of strategy, wrong choice of strategy, poor implementation of strategy, excessive risk-taking, insufficient risk-taking, other.
* Weak marketing: too wide or narrow a product line, poor understanding of the market, failure to adapt to new market circumstances, faulty pricing strategies (too high or low?), poor distribution, overdependence on a few customers, insufficient marketing effort, other.
* Production problems: obsolete or easily overtaken technology, too narrow technology, inadequate skills base, poor quality control, other.
* External factors: competitors' actions, change in demand, increase in materials costs, industrial disputes, skills shortages, legislation, creditors' or shareholders' actions, other.
* Others, please specify.

• Are these causes consistent across most failed firms, or do they vary in size, age and industry?

● Of the factors chosen, which are the most common causes of business failure? (Select up to three.)

● What do you look for as symptoms, or indications that a business will fail?

    * margins, sales trends, turnover, other financial indicators?
    * management abilities and attitudes?
    * demand forecasts, competitors activities?
    * other?

● In your experience, once a company is visibly in difficulties, how likely is it that a turnaround can be achieved with the same top management team?

    * 90% of the time?
    * 75–99% of the time
    * 50–74% of the time
    * 25–49% of the time
    * under 25% of the time?

Your additional comments:

● What are the primary reasons for changing the management team:

    * the need to instil a sense of urgency
    * as an example to others
    * the original team cannot adapt quickly enough
    * the original team is too close to the problem to take decisive action
    * other?

Your additional comments:

● In your experience, are chief executives of companies in trouble more likely to:

    * face up to the problems energetically?
    * largely ignore them and hope they will go away?

Your additional comments:

● What do you think would make managers ignore problems?

    * lack of confidence that the problems can be resolved?
    * refusal to admit the problem really exists?
    * fear of admitting failure?
    * other?

Your additional comments:

● When the crash comes, do these executives typically:

    * blame external forces (investors, competition, etc.)?
    * blame internal resources (staff, trade unions)?
    * blame anyone and everyone but themselves?
    * blame themselves?

Your additional comments:

● How many of these executives use the events as a learning experience to improve their managerial abilities?

    * two-thirds or more?
    * one-third or more?
    * less than one-third?

Your additional comments:

● Realistically, how willing are you/is your organization to invest in an executive who has been part of a team that failed?

    * it wouldn't figure in our decision at all
    * it would play a small or negligible part in our decision
    * it would play a substantial but not overriding part in our decision
    * it would be a major factor in our decision.

Your additional comments:

● From your observations, what typically happens within a troubled company as people begin to recognize that something is wrong?

    * internal politics and wrangles intensify
    * key people at a senior management level leave
    * key people at middle/junior management leave
    * employees at all levels become demotivated
    * customers/suppliers lose confidence
    * everyone mucks in to help overcome the problem
    * other.

Your additional comments:

No doubt you can illustrate many of your answers with specific examples. We would be very grateful for your recollections of some of these cases. A simple reference to, say, 'a small/large company in publishing/heavy engineering' will be an adequate identification if it is not possible to be more specific.

If you have a particularly good example you would be prepared to discuss in detail (again either with or without naming the company involved) we would be pleased to discuss in detail.

I would be happy to discuss specific cases. Yes.... No....

Appendix B

THE ENTREPRENEUR'S VIEW

In the main, this book has focused on the behaviour and attitudes of management. It seems only fair to include some comment, too, on the attitudes and behaviour of the investors. Initiatives by the Confederation of British Industry and others have pointed out the problems caused to businesses of all sizes by City attitudes. In particular, they have focused upon:

* short-termism – the constant pressure for profits now, which can undermine managers' efforts to develop long-term market and strategic advantage
* failure by investors to understand the businesses they invest in (the institutions would respond that their business is lending)
* a consequent impatience when organizations suffer setbacks
* an obsession with size, at the expense of innovation.

To what extent these attitudes influence the ability of companies to survive is difficult to assess. There is no doubt that some of the companies we examined were – on paper at least – still viable businesses or on the verge of success when the plug was pulled. Some of these decisions to foreclose were surely correct and avoided further huge losses; others appear to have killed the goose just as it was about to lay the golden egg.

One suggested means of distinguishing between these two sets of cases is by what happened subsequently. Was the receiver able to make the business pay? In practice, however, this test is more a measure of the companies' size and stage in the life-cycle. In deceased mature companies, the receivers or administrators are usually able to extract substantial value from the carcass. In the cases of start-ups, particularly in high technology, they were rarely able to recover much at all.

We have not been able to identify a practical means of testing whether the influence of investors upon survival is benign or malevolent in any specific case. However, we have encountered frequent comment from both the managers of troubled companies and the receivers that suggests it is disastrous for institutions to become directly involved in the executive direction of the business. Either they become too identified with the excitement of the business concept (as happened in a number of cases in computers and electronics) or they attempt to impose their own strategies, which often turn out not to be viable.

The managers' point of view is eloquently expressed by Data Magnetic's Denis Mahony, who provides eight basic lessons for the would-be entrepreneur who goes a-borrowing. Each lesson is based on a myth, as follows:

Myth 1: 'Time is on your side.' The institutions are used to negotiating over a long period. Mahony quit his job in anticipation of closing a deal, but it took a further six months to do so. He explains: 'As soon as you resign from the protection of full employment the real negotiations begin ... As an individual you get slowly hung out to dry and in the end I would have signed anything to get the money and start the business.'

Myth 2: 'It's your business; you own it.' Mahony points out that this is true only until you disagree with the institutions' non-executive directors on the board. Unless you hold a majority shareholding, or have the support of other shareholders, it isn't your business at all. Mahony clashed with the non-executive appointee of the Welsh Development Agency. 'Once Non-Executive Directors start taking orders from above,' he explains, 'and when the givers of those orders become politically remote, the slippery slope to demise becomes incredibly steeper.'

Myth 3: 'You are in it for the capital gain.' The entrepreneur is supposed to take a low salary, drive an inexpensive car and generally stint himself now for the potential gain later. Given the high risk factors, however, Mahony advises driving a bargain that provides a salary and benefits package at least equal to that available on the open market. (Apart from anything else, the executive who is worrying how he is going to pay the domestic bills may have his attention diverted from the demands of running the business.)

Myth 4: 'Our policy is one of long-termism.' If the institution means it (and accepting the statement at face value is rather like buying wrapped brown-paper parcels in a pub), its mechanism for staying in if things do not go as well as planned initially will normally be equity dilution.

The entrepreneur's efforts to hold the company together do not have a cash or equity value in renegotiations.

Myth 5: 'There's plenty of help we can tap into.' Yes, but usually at an enormous cost.

Myth 6: 'You need some good, independent advice.' The loyalty of accountants and solicitors is not necessarily with you as their client, says Mahony. Because so much of their work comes from institutions, there is sometimes a bias towards the hand that feeds them. Beware particularly any professional firm recommended by the institutions themselves.

Myth 7: 'The venture capitalist will get alongside your team.' Translated, this means that he will try to run your business for you, says Mahony. 'What they mean,' he explains, 'is that they are there to ensure that their goals are achieved, no matter what. The upside is that they will only read your information on the flight up to the board meeting, even though they have demanded so much that your accountant, secretary and most of your team have put in two weeks' work to get it done on time.'

Myth 8: 'Don't worry, we all want you to succeed.' True, as long as things go well. But in practice it is *their* business they want to succeed and the management team are replaceable instruments in making that happen.

Mahony admits his lessons incorporate a certain amount of bias, reflecting his own experience. However, he points out that anyone contemplating taking the risk of a start-up – and particularly a high-tech start-up – needs to recognize from the beginning both the extent of the risks he or she is taking, the relatively low chances of success and the plain, but often forgotten fact that nobody puts up cash because they like you.

Appendix C

AN AUDIT OF MANAGEMENT ATTITUDES

Score key: Up to four points per question as follows except where otherwise indicated according to how accurately they describe the organization – zero indicates the statement does not describe the organization at all; four describes it very closely.

Attitudes towards controls

Values
● Every top manager, especially the CEO, sees control information as either the top priority or joint top priority (with leadership and/or strategy) of his or her job.

● In general, speed of information is more important than detailed accuracy.

● In general, speed of action upon information is more important than lengthy consideration, as long as the risks are properly assessed.

● Executives feel comfortable with control information, i.e. they pull it out first from among the pile of papers on their desks.

● Gearing is held consistently below 30%.

● The management team regularly reviews all the risks the company may be exposed to – financial, technological, competitive, legislative, human resource – and establishes contingency plans against them.

Practice
● The company has a fast, accurate and efficient system to provide information on:

   * cashflow

* costs and margins
* overheads
* sales turnover
* market share and market growth
* receivables outstanding
* gearing levels
* staff turnover
* output per employee and throughput times
* cost of quality
* project management: documentation, planning and budgeting procedures
* customer satisfaction: gain or loss of customers and customer complaints.

(Score up to two points each, to maximum of twenty).

● The information is immediately used for discussion, with the aim of taking action, rather than put away for consideration.

● People in the organization
    * feel they have a useful input into this data (Score one point)
    * feel they have access to the data they need (Score one point)
    * feel the systems work for them rather than against them (Score two points).

● Responsibilities for generating the information are clear.

● Responsibilities for taking action on the basis of information are clear.

● Controls are appraised regularly.

● The information is presented in a useful and relevant format.

Attitudes towards the vision

Values
● The top team shares a clear vision of the future and how it will get there.

● The team is genuinely prepared to adapt the vision to the needs of the marketplace.

● The company encourages constructive criticism of the vision and how it should be achieved.

Practice
- The vision is backed up by articulate and well-researched short-term and medium-term plans.

- The plans are used as a working document, for regular measurement of progress.

- They are reviewed regularly (at least once every twelve months).

Attitudes towards the team

Values
- The top team recognizes the importance of a constructive balance among its members in terms of disciplines, backgrounds and personality types. In particular, it seeks a balance between visionaries and more down-to-earth, practical people.

- Managers at all levels feel it is an important part of their role to share information.

- Managers feel that constructive dissent is valued and encouraged.

- The top team is intolerant of consistently poor performers.

Practice
- The company is generally free from politics.

- There is a reasonable degree of stability among the top ranks.

- The company measures why people leave (and why they stay).

Attitudes towards customers and markets

Values
- All managers believe that creating opportunities for active, personal listening to customers is an important part of their job.

- The top team genuinely believes that customers *are* normally right.

- Everyone in the top team takes a strong interest in what is happening in the market and in trying to understand market behaviour.

Practice
- There is a comprehensive and effective system for obtaining, analysing

and using customer feedback (particularly complaints) as the basis for improvements.

- The majority of product or service enhancements is a result of customer feedback.

- The company is consistently introducing more innovations, more rapidly than most of its competitors.

Attitudes towards investors

Values
- The top team is able to put itself in the investors' shoes.

- It regards investors as an asset rather than a liability.

- It accepts the notion that there are numerous stakeholders in the business.

- It places a high value on good investor relations.

Practice
- The company provides rapid, accurate investor reports that anticipate needs for information.

- It initiates some or all meetings with investors, rather than wait for them to do so.

Attitudes towards learning

Values
- The members of the top team are committed to personal development (i.e. they value the opportunity to learn for themselves).

- They genuinely believe that mistakes are a useful source of experience and therefore to be valued (rather than something to be forgotten and buried as quickly as possible).

- They emphasise the importance of *listening* as part of their jobs.

Practice
- Mistakes and errors (both own and competitors') are analysed for lessons as a matter of course.

Attitudes towards winning and losing

Values
- This team is truly in business to win. Its members *hate* losing.

- It actively seeks to outdo target competitors (rather than to survive in its market).

Practice
- The company regularly researches its competitors' strengths, weaknesses and marketing strategy.

- 'Difficult' or unpalatable issues are typically tackled head on (rather than allowed to drift until they resolve themselves or can no longer be ignored).

These are not necessarily a prescription for dramatic success; rather a prescription for survival. Nonetheless, companies that do all these things will have a much firmer foundation on which to build success.

Values refer to perceptions about the roles of the organization and the managers in it. They are a major component of attitudes. Practice refers to what actually happens within the organization – and are thus an indirect measure of the strength of both values and attitudes.

How to assess your score
Add the scores together within sections.

For a new business (i.e. one with no track record) use only the values section or the experience of the top team in their previous companies. (Values absorbed in one company tend to remain with the manager as he changes organization. The longer the time with the previous organization, the more strongly absorbed those values will be.)

The values score indicates the likelihood of the firm's taking the right actions for survival. The practice score indicates the degree of risk resulting from not translating attitude into practical action. A strong values score may partially offset a weak practice score, because top management will eventually deal with this issue as it becomes important. A weak values score and a strong practice score indicates that the company is being held together by competent middle managers, while the top team needs close scrutiny.

The two scores can be added together to give a picture of how much at risk the company is. In our estimation, any company with an even spread of scores over 140 is at a low risk; below sixty, at a high risk.

Bibliography

Books and Booklets

Altman, E. I., *Corporate Financial Distress*, Wiley, New York, 1983
Argenti, John, *Corporate Collapse: The Causes and Symptoms*, McGraw-Hill, Maidenhead, 1976
Aris, Stephen, *Going Bust – Inside the Bankruptcy Business*, André Deutsch, London, 1985
Boyd, Stewart, 'An Inquiry into the Affairs of Seamount Limited', HMSO, December 1989
Clutterbuck, David and Nelson, Rebecca, *Turnaround*, W. H. Allen, London, 1988
Clutterbuck, David and Crainer, Stuart, *The Decline and Rise of British Industry*, W. H. Allen, London, 1988
Clutterbuck, David and Goldsmith, Walter, *The Winning Streak*, Weidenfeld & Nicolson, London, 1984
Homan, Mark, 'A banker's Guide to Survival', Price Waterhouse, undated collection of articles
Kharbanda, O. P. and Stallworthy, E. A. *Corporate failure – Prediction, Panacea and Prevention*, McGraw-Hill, Maidenhead, 1989
Kharbanda, O. P. and Stallworthy, E. A. *Management Disasters and How to Prevent Them*, Gower, Aldershot, 1986
Slatter, Stuart, *Corporate Recovery – Successful Turnaround Strategies and their Implementation*, Penguin, London, 1984

Articles and Papers

Anon, 'Insolvency Sea Changes Wash Up More Work', *The Accountant*, 20 January 1987
Anon, 'Company Directors Disqualification Act', *Natwest Small Business Digest*, April 1988
Anon, 'Cork on Cork', *The Economist*, January 1989
Anon, 'Doom and Gloom', *Machinery*, August 1987.
Boyle, Denis, 'Reversing the Cycle of Decline', *Strategic Direction*, April 1986

Bush, Janet, 'The Collapse of the Hunt Family Empire', *Financial Times*, 24 August 1988

Buxton, James, 'Refinanced Rodime Resurfaces', *Financial Times*, 23 June 1989

Clutterbuck, David, 'How the Japanese Rebuilt Fort Dunlop', *The Director*, September 1988

Fennell, Edward, 'Experts Who Go for Broke', *The Times*, 20 June 1989

Finegan, Jay, 'Turning Point', *Inc*, April 1989

Hamilton, Alan, 'Riding Out a Rough Patch', *The Times*, 14 March 1986

Hoffman, Richard C., 'Strategies for Corporate Turnarounds: What Do We Know About Them?', *Journal of General Management*, vol. 14, No. 3, Spring 1989

Houlder, Vanessa, 'Do Company Doctors Kill or Cure?', *Investors Chronicle*, 22 May 1987

Houlder, Vanessa, 'Doctor Morrow's Casebook', *Investors Chronicle*, 8 January 1988

Huxley, John, 'Down and Out Down Under', *Sunday Times*, 26 November 1989

Inman, Bill, 'When Mergers Fail', *Business*, June 1986

Mitroff, I., and McWhinney W., 'Disaster by Design and How To Avoid It', *Training*, August 1987

Oates, David, 'How Gerry Took One Byte Too Many', *Your Business*, July 1984

Powlet, Roger, 'How Businesses Bust Themselves', *Management Today*, July 1986

Richardson, Robin, 'Insolvency – Permission to Practise', *The Accountant's Magazine*, July 1986

Scoular, Caroline, 'Spilt Beer, Lightning and Other Problems', *IBM System User*, August 1988

Smith, Arthur, 'Back-peddling on a Loss-maker', *Financial Times*, 23 January 1987

Smith, Colin, 'Priorities for the Turnaround CEO', *Strategic Direction*, December 1986

Waters, Richard, 'Corporate Collapse Claims Many Victims', *Financial Times*, 6 September 1989

Whatley, Garrod, 'Trapped on the Debt Mountain', *Chief Executive*, September 1987

Wiles, Q. T., 'Company Doctor', *Inc*, February 1988

Williams, C. M., 'When the Mighty Stumble', *Harvard Business Review*, July/August 1984

Index